GOD BLESS CAMBODIA

GOD BLESS CAMBODIA

RANDY ROSS

The Permanent Press
Sag Harbor, NY 11963

For information, address:
   The Permanent Press
   4170 Noyac Road
   Sag Harbor, NY 11963
   www.thepermanentpress.com

Library of Congress Cataloging-in-Publication Data

Ross, Randy, author.
   God bless Cambodia / Randy Ross.
   Sag Harbor, NY : The Permanent Press, 2017.
   ISBN 978-1-57962-490-3
        1. Man-woman relationships—Fiction. 2. Voyages and travels—Fiction. 3. Depression in men—Fiction. 4. Love stories.

PS3618.O84678 G63 2017
813'.6—dc23   2016053019

Printed in the United States of America

In loving memory of my grandparents:
Tulla and Max Rosenhirsch and Miriam and Maurice Ross

"What people forget is a journey to nowhere starts with a single step, too."

—CHUCK PALAHNIUK, *novelist*

"As a dog returns to his vomit, so a fool returns to his folly."

—PROVERBS 26:11

"Remember, we're all in this alone."

—LILY TOMLIN

CHAPTER ONE: **BOSTON**

The morning sun streams through my bay window and illuminates a cheap print of Crane Beach and a row of golden vials in my double-wide medicine cabinet. I stand there pondering this week's big question: Vicodin, Ambien, or Heineken—what *do* unemployed people have for breakfast?

Lately, making even the smallest decision has become an ordeal. Cash or charge? Draft or bottle? Girl-on-girl or teens-with-toys? I wash down a Vicodin with a beer and crawl back into bed.

The phone wakes me at noon. I lift my sleep blindfold to check caller ID. It's Abe. He's been my closest friend for ten years, but in recent months I seem to have slid off his priority list.

Whenever I call him, I get voice mail and maybe three days later an e-mail. If I e-mail, it takes a week for a response. I know he's alive and ambulatory because I see the posts from Amy, his wife of one year, about their trips to Vermont, weekends in Newburyport, and drinks in Boston's South End with people I don't recognize.

When he does call to get together, it's always at the last minute: "Hey, Burns, the wife's busy tonight. How about drinks at the Minuteman?"

The phone rings again and again and finally goes to voice mail. I take a sip from the lukewarm beer on my nightstand. Through a Vicodin fog, I consider the twenty-five-dollar print of Crane Beach, which I picked up three years ago at Costco. Every time Abe sees it, he says the same thing: "Burns, you got fleeced."

Abe is an abrasive guy. I'm drawn to abrasive, angry people. My therapist, Dr. Moody, says I'm attracted to people and things that make me uncomfortable. Maybe so.

• I'm shy, but drawn to women with rabid, foaming, over-the-top personalities.

• I'm terrified of cancer, but crave Marlboro Lights and cheeseburger clubs.

• I'm afraid to be alone, but find most people dull and annoying. Except for the abrasive, angry ones.

This doesn't make much sense. Therapy hasn't made much sense and neither has paying $125 an hour to a shrink named Dr. Moody. I stick with it because I like Moody. He's kind of a dick. Like Abe.

The phone starts ringing again. I imagine Abe cursing on the other end because he knows I'm home and not answering. Fuck you, Abe.

Moody says that I take people's actions too personally and that relationships naturally ebb and flow. He may have a point.

Over the last year, all my close friendships seem to be ebbing. Maybe it's because we're all in our late forties and pre-occupied with the developmental milestones of our age group:

• Finding a reliable sleeping pill.

• Acquiring a long-term care policy.

• Securing a relationship with that special someone who will pick us up after a colonoscopy.

When Abe had a colonoscopy two years ago, I found the time to pick him up. But now that Amy manages his calendar, can I count on him to reciprocate? I decide to take his call.

"What's up, Abe?"

"Burns, you wouldn't believe the fucked-up thing that happened to me last week."

This is how we begin all our conversations. It's our standard greeting, our secret handshake. Generally, the ensuing monologue covers his job and today is no different:

"In the weeds . . ."

"Goose eggs in sales . . ."

"Zeroes in accounting . . ."

I half listen. His voice soothes me like the satin lining of my sleep blindfold.

Abe pauses to tell someone that he's on an important call. Maybe I should cut him some slack.

"Sorry about that," Abe says to me. "Some fag from human resources. Anyway, this is your first Monday without a job, how are you holding up?"

"I'm holding up." I take a sip from the warm beer on my night table.

"I knew you would. Ask Amy, if you don't believe me. So, how's the miserable game?"

The "miserable game" is online dating. Years ago we met women at parties. Now no one gives parties because no one wants to subject their throw pillows and tufted rugs to the spilling crowds. Including me. Especially me.

I take another sip. "Match.com is a horror show. Shiksa-Mingle, a freak show. Last week, I signed up for a new one called Fish in a Barrel. It's like casting into a wading pool filled with old Band-Aids and dirty diapers."

"Sounds appealing."

"So you wouldn't believe the fucked-up thing that happened to *me* yesterday. Ricki e-mailed."

"Holy crap! Not her again. She's bonkers. Burns, please tell me you ignored her. You need to meet some new people. Why don't you hit the Museum of Science?"

I put the blindfold back on. "I'm not up for culture."

"Who said anything about culture? Where do you think divorced babes take their kids during the day?"

"You're kidding me, right?"

"Burns, I know you don't like kids, but you can't be so picky anymore. Not every chick with kids has a blown-out body. And you're no prize. You're forty-eight. You got no job. Your car is an embarrassment. Amy's no hard-body plus she's two years older than me. But she makes me feel normal. I'm not that sour guy eating alone at the bar every night. I have a date on New Year's. Burns, everyone settles. Or dies alone."

I stifle a yawn. Abe continues.

"You say you want a relationship, but look at all the women you've had that went nowhere. And now you're in a drought and it's all Boston's fault: Everyone's too young, they hate middle-aged white guys, there's nowhere to meet people over forty. You think that's going to get better? My brother just turned fifty and the only women on Match who write him are in their sixties. He's moving to New York. Are you ready to move? You're out of work. How you going to afford it?"

I lift the blindfold and take another sip.

"So you'll stay put like you always do. You'll be the hero, the man of steel who won't settle. You'll keep waiting for an outlier, a babe who's thin as a wand and kooky and skis and likes noir and porn and the Red Sox. An introvert like you. She'll have the magic, the x-factor, the secret sauce. Burns, wake up: There is no outlier. Your dream woman doesn't exist. All that head-over-heels stuff is Hollywood crapola."

Maybe I deserve this. I've been dating for almost thirty years and have nothing to show for it. I had always accepted the boom and bust of dating as predictable, inevitable, what we all did. Then Abe decided to get married and I began whining to him about being alone, as if it were somehow his fault.

I put the beer back on my night table.

"Burns, are you drinking?"

I don't bother answering.

"Burns, look, you can't get back with Miss Borderline Personality and you can't spend your life in the Dark Place. How are you fixed for meds? Amy just got a root canal, so we've got inventory."

I check the Vicodin vial on my nightstand: It's half full. "I'm good for now, Abe, but thanks for the offer. I should let you get back to work."

Two hours later, the phone wakes me again. It's Rachel. I run a mental search for recent offenses and can't find anything except she's got a new boyfriend, Arturo. It's only a matter of time before she'll back-burner me too. I answer the phone: "Hey, Rachel."

"How are you doing? I heard Ricki e-mailed."

"Good news travels fast."

"Do you think maybe she's worth another shot? What else have you got going?"

There are two things Rachel does that annoy me: She offers advice in the form of a question, and now that she's hooked up, she worries about me, which should be nice but feels patronizing at times. Like now.

"I hear the tenth time is the charm," I say.

"Relationships take effort, right? I read that romantic love lasts for maybe two years. I love Arturo, but we've got our issues. We work on them every day and we've only been dating for six months."

I want to say that this doesn't sound like much fun or that maybe Arturo isn't right for her or that I just got laid off and I've had it with work for a while.

But she means well.

Abe means well.

So what if they both settled?

I take a swig. Backwash.

"Abe said you're spiraling down. Have you tried the Cambridge Whole Foods? That's where I met Arturo. Just a thought."

I met Rachel and Abe ten years ago at the bar of the Minuteman, a health club a few blocks from my apartment in downtown Boston.

The three of us liked the same things: Ronald Reagan, Bill Clinton, *The Three Stooges*, and a weekly cigarette. We also hated the same things: everyone under twenty-five and uptight Massachusetts liberals.

After Rachel hangs up, I reach over to shake the snow globe on my nightstand. Little white flakes dance around a photo of me and my childhood dog, Harold the basset hound. In the picture, I'm looking into the camera and Harold is looking up at me.

I think of Harold and my childhood in New York. Relationships were simpler then: People loved you or they didn't, no gray areas and no confusion.

Maybe I need a dog.

Maybe I need to relocate.

Maybe I just need to get laid.

Definitely I need to get laid.

I've never liked crowds, sightseeing, or public spectacles, but the next morning I fork out twenty dollars for the Museum of Science. Inside, women whiz by with tricked-out, all-terrain strollers. Most have short hair and no makeup. I picture them in housecoats.

When Abe was single, he would have referred to this crowd as a bunch of blown-out bust-ups. Now, it's pay dirt for guys ready to settle. I try to picture myself in a housecoat.

I finger the twenty-dollar ticket stub in my pocket. I've only been here for ten minutes, that's $120 an hour, about what Moody charges. I can't leave yet.

A three-wheeled jogging stroller with full suspension, knobby tires, and a rain canopy dodges me. The operator has long hair and lipstick. She pulls up at a nearby exhibit. She's wearing a Red Sox hat and a ski vest. An outlier. Her little boy is wearing a Red Sox hat and a ski vest. I observe for a few minutes, and then idle a few feet from them. I grip the exhibit railing. It's sticky.

I make a cast. "Having fun?"

She smiles half a smile.

"This is some rally," I say.

She offers the other half a smile.

Her little boy licks a lollipop and then licks the railing. I open my sticky palms and think about saliva and strep throat and rabies. I try a new line: "Can I borrow your Purell?"

She loads the kid and peels out.

That night, Cambridge Whole Foods is sponsoring a poetry reading and wine tasting. The evening's theme: Writers of color celebrate diversity.

I don't care for poetry or wine, and as far as· I'm concerned, diversity means everyone except middle-aged white men. Like me. But the event is free, so I go in.

The reading is at the back of the store. The crowd is mostly fussy-looking guys and women in logging boots. The MC is a women's-studies professor from Harvard. She's big.

Her boots are big. I set the timer on my watch for five minutes and stand near the exit.

First a black poet reads, then a Hispanic poet, then a Samoan. All their poems are about "the man":

"The man got me down."

"The man got my check."

"The man got my babies."

The poets seem to be looking in my direction when they read. I scan the crowd. I'm the only middle-aged white guy here.

I imagine grabbing the microphone to deliver my own tirade, which Moody refers to as my "Great White Whine." It goes like this:

I'm a middle-aged white guy, the worst thing you can be in this country. In sitcoms, we're portrayed as buffoons with wives and cute kids who are always putting something over on us. In commercials, we're wimps with enlarged prostates and erectile dysfunction—guys with dicks that don't work.

We have no feelings and no right to complain because our forefathers are to blame for the last 200 years of suffering of women, minorities, and snail darters.

Women no longer want equality, they want to get even. They'll take our flowers, little boxes, and fancy dinners, but they don't really want us. They can support themselves, have babies on their own, and marry each other. They refuse to put up with any crap, including the kind of crap we put up with from them. Look at all the fat, happy lesbians. They act like they're on a permanent vacation because they don't need to diet or exercise to please a guy.

At the end of this monologue, Moody always gives me a round of applause and says, "Bravo, bravo. A *tour de force*. How can any woman resist you?"

At home, I consider myself in front of the double-wide: bald head, graying eyebrows, parentheses of lines around my nose and mouth. Forty-eight, never married, and the way things are going, I'll be hitchhiking back from my next colonoscopy.

When some people get depressed about dating, they consult friends, relatives, or an astrologer. Me? I consult a dating spreadsheet that lists women I've dated over the last twenty years, how we met, and how long we lasted. Analyzing past trends reminds me that I've survived droughts before and by projecting the data forward, I've even been able to predict when I'd next meet someone. But when I open DATES.XLS this time, the forecast isn't good. It's late spring and historically summer is my slow season. Worse still, there's no data for how I'll fare without a fancy job title—I am literally and figuratively in uncharted territory.

A lesser person in this situation might languish in the Dark Place, but I'm a man of action or, as Moody says, reaction. Take "Nickie" listed in Cell A30. I dated her on and off for three years in my thirties until she finally gave me the heave-ho for offenses too numerous to recount. For weeks, I moped around the house. Then I moped around a Barnes & Noble where I spotted a book on how to grow marijuana in a closet. I figured if growing the plants didn't help me forget Nickie, smoking the crop certainly would.

I stocked up on organic potting soil and high-potency fertilizer, and then scored a fluorescent light large enough for a two-car garage. After lining the walls with aluminum foil to reflect the light, my four-by-eight-foot closet replicated the climate of a Jamaican ganja farm.

Within four months, I had five bushy plants and a new girlfriend (Alex, Cell A31). True, the relationship didn't last long, and I'll never know if she wanted me just for my Maui Wowie, but at least the pot project kept me out of the Dark Place.

Now, it's 2007, I'm out of a job and fifteen years older. I need something big, an all-consuming distraction, a project to get me out of the house and away from online dating. I head to Barnes & Noble.

In the Self Help section, I see some familiar titles:

How to Get a Woman to Split the Check
I bought this for Abe who regifted it to me after he got married. "Good luck with this one," he said.

How to Please a Woman
Ricki bought this for me, but there was no pleasing her.

If We're So in Love, Why Do I Hate You?
Nickie bought this for me. Her note on the inside cover began: "Dear John."

I browse the Home and Garden section:

How to Grow Marijuana in an Armoire
Been there.

Bathtub Brewing for Fun and Profit
Extracts, boiling, fermenting: Too messy.

Kitchen Meth-Labs: A DIY Guide
Hmmm . . .

I drift into the adjoining section, which used to be Money and is now Travel. The book covers are a blaze of jungle greens, banana yellows, and sunset reds. My head fills with the imaginary sounds of screeching macaws and bellowing howler monkeys. I swear I smell coconut suntan oil.

I skim a *Lonely Planet* and then a *Rough Guide*. And then another and another. Central America. North Africa. Southeast Asia. Elephants and Buddhas. Islands and beaches. Temples and statues. Directories and indices and glossaries and rating systems and lists and maps and more lists and more maps.

After an hour, I'm parched, disoriented, and can't turn another page. Outside it's getting dark. Then I spot a small book, *Solo Salvation: Travel the World on Your Own*. It has a mango orange cover and inside, a simple itinerary, and a titillating passage on "vaginal thrush."

The author's bio includes a color photo of a guy with graying eyebrows, a bald head, and parentheses of lines around his mouth. He has his arm around a young Asian woman with golden skin. He's a fat slob. She's a wand. They're wearing tie-dyed pajama pants, tie-dyed bandanas, and wedding bands. He's looking into the camera. She's looking up at him. This has to be self-published.

I turn to the copyright page: "Random House."

I worked in publishing for fifteen years. I know how hard it is to get a book deal with Random House.

I flip back to the author bio:

"In 2001, Wallace Pittman was a divorced, unemployed architect, who at age fifty was forced to move back with his parents. Then, he embarked on the journey of a lifetime and has never looked back. Today, he runs the All-American Language School in Ho Chi Minh City, previously known as Saigon."

Some douche named Wally pulled this off?

I jump to the Author's Preface:

"Traveling the world on your own is easy, deciding to go is hard. Are you ready to go eyeball-to-eyeball with life? Some numbers to consider:

• 95 percent: The number of people who will read this book and not take the trip. (I'm OK with that—I get paid either way.) You 5-percenters have an open invitation to visit me in Saigon. I will make it worth your while.

• 70 percent: In travel as in life, experts are right about 70 percent of the time. The other 30 percent of travel and life is a crapshoot. It's what's known as magic, experience, and destiny.

I check the price of the book: 50 percent off. Destiny.

At home, I Google "Wallace Pittman" and find a glowing review of his book in the *New York Times*. The reviewer refers to Pittman as "an original." On his website, there are quotes from athletes, writers, and celebrities: Tom Brady, Paul Theroux, and Bruce Willis.

But who has time for a life-changing trip? I consult my Day Planner: Nothing in May. Nothing in June. Or July, or August. No meetings. No interviews. No dates. The only item on my to-do list is to apply for Social Security in twenty years.

If I left in September, I could go for four months, hit the five continents listed in the itinerary, and return in time for the holidays. I feel better already.

But there's one glitch: I'm neither an adventurous person nor an experienced traveler. I once went to France. For five days. And I couldn't wait to get home to my own six-inch, pillow-top mattress.

I call Abe and for once he answers on the first ring. Good omen?

"Abe, you wouldn't believe the fucked-up thing that happened to me in the bookstore today."

"What?"

"I found this book on vaginal thrush and I'm thinking of taking a trip around the world. It would be cheaper than moving to New York."

"Are you fucking kidding me? When you travel the only thing you enjoy more than complaining is coming home."

"You're taking that out of context."

"Is that one of those books that promises world travel will change your life? You'll come back cultured, experienced, the world's most interesting man? Eyeball-to-eyeball with life and crap like that?"

The phrase "eyeball-to-eyeball" sounds familiar. Did Abe read Pittman's book and chicken out? I say nothing.

"My uncle took a trip like that," Abe says. "It changed his life all right. He drank some bad water in Africa and got this three-foot parasite, a guinea worm. It traveled around under his skin for a year, then popped its head out of a blister on his foot. The cure? Some witch doctor had to grab the worm by the head, wrap it around a stick, and spend nine hours pulling it out, inch by inch. He's never been the same."

"So what's your point?"

I try Rachel.

"I'm thinking of going abroad for a few months. A little adventure might do me good."

"What's it going to cost?" she asks.

"The guidebook says I can do it for ten grand. I have my severance, and I'll go to less-developed countries where things are cheaper. I can stay in some hostels to cut costs. And when I get back, I'll hang on to the Honda Civic for another ten years."

"That's a lot of money. Today's *Journal* said the economy is in a tailspin. Did you know Josh just got laid off? When was the last time you looked for a job?"

"Late nineties. But the trip will look good on my résumé: international experience, familiarity with other cultures, and ethnic diversity. We all know how important diversity is. And I'll stick out from other job hunters: Eighty percent of Americans don't even have a passport. None of you guys have one."

"You know we're behind you no matter what you do. By the way, what did Ricki want?"

"Blood. Money. More blood. She read my blog post about getting canned and sent me a sympathy note. In other words, she wanted to rub it in my face."

"That's weird. Why is she suddenly reading your blog? Does she miss you after two years?"

"I doubt it. You want to know the really fucked-up thing? I was actually happy to hear from her. Don't tell Abe."

After hanging up, I run a quick tally: Abe "no" and Rachel "yes—sort of." I need a tiebreaker: Lenny.

I met Lenny a few months after Abe and Rachel ten years ago at the same Minuteman bar. Abe, Rachel, and I were having dinner. Lenny was sitting a couple of stools away and hard to miss: He was wearing white gabardine trousers, drinking Green Chartreuse, and ranting to the bartender.

He ranted about Boston women: "If you see a woman in a bar wearing a blazer, she's hiding fifteen pounds. For a black blazer, it's twenty."

He ranted about marriage: "I'll tell you why married people go to bed early: All the arguing, all the stretch marks you have to ignore, all that effort to make it work, it just wears you out."

He ordered another Chartreuse, looked at his watch, and then down the bar at us. "It's after ten, you guys must be single. Can I join you?"

Soon after, the four of us started the "The Chronic Single's Club" and began throwing monthly parties at the Minuteman. Our first event had fifteen people; the second had forty; our third more than a hundred. We later added Josh, a friend of Lenny's, to our inner circle. We had some good times.

A few years later, Josh met a woman and they stopped coming. Last year, Abe met Amy. Without Abe, attendance dropped back to fifteen, the same fifteen who had come to every event including the first one. We put the club on hiatus.

Since Rachel met Arturo two months ago, Lenny and I have been living in unspoken terror that one of us will hook up and the other will be left behind to field last-minute drink invites from the married people.

Lenny recently joined a dating service that charges $5,000 a year. "It's kind of like a prostitution ring, but at least I have a date Saturday nights with a different, smoking-hot girl."

I thought of joining. But spending twice that on a world trip now seems less desperate.

Lenny picks up on the second ring.

"Hey, Lenny, I'm thinking about, maybe, traveling a little. Maybe overseas. Maybe for a few months."

I hear him sigh.

"Let me ask you something," he says. "Don't you always joke about putting two layers of paper on public toilet seats?"

"You joke about using three."

"But I'm not going to spend months crapping in squat toilets that have *no* toilet paper, much less seats. Are you prepared to wipe your ass on the ground like a dog? What about the guinea worms? You're going to miss all the fall parties. Who will be my wing man?"

"I'm going to places known for partying: South America, Southeast Asia, South Africa, Europe, Australia. I checked the CDC site. Those places don't have guinea worms."

"Who said there's partying?"

"This guidebook I just bought."

"Isn't South Africa Ground Zero for AIDS?"

After we hang up, I go outside, trade a homeless guy a dollar for a cigarette, and head to the Public Garden to smoke and fume.

I thought friends were supposed to encourage you to take risks and bust out of your comfort zone. I should've known better. Abe's last big adventure was a trip to Boca Raton. For Rachel, it's dating a guy named Arturo. And Lenny? It's joining a prostitution ring for $5K.

Back home in front of the double-wide, I realize all three of them have points. I also realize that it's happy hour and reach for some Klonopin.

The next week has its ups and downs.

Monday

After four rejections on Match, I consult my cousin Joey who met his wife while skiing in France.

"Bring a load of rubbers," he says.

OK, I'm in.

Tuesday

Receive an offer for a seventy-five-dollar-an-hour editing job. Send e-mails to three women on Fish in a Barrel. Create a list of things I hate about traveling.

• I don't like sightseeing.
• I don't like foreign accents.
• I don't like spending money.
• I don't like loud noises or weird smells.
• I don't like crowds, strangers, or people who sweat.

The trip is off.

Wednesday

Learn that the job is in Cleveland. At the gym, the personal trainer with the sparkly navel asks what I'm doing now that I'm unemployed. I imagine telling her, "I'm taking a trip around the world," instead of, "I'm collecting."

Bring on the thrush.

Thursday

The current issue of the *Morbidity and Mortality Weekly Report* discusses hemorrhagic dengue fever outbreaks in South America and Southeast Asia. Hemorrhagic dengue is like the flu only it turns your insides to strawberry yogurt and causes bleeding through the mouth, eyes, and other orifices.

Off again.

Friday

I receive two rejections on Fish in a Barrel. I haven't heard from my friends since Wednesday. In my experience, people are usually there the first few days of a crisis. Then they return to their lives and you return to the double-wide.

A quick tally shows that three days out of five this week, the trip was on.

Everyone can kiss my ass: I'm out of here.

Saturday

I'm haunted by images of bleeding orifices. On. Off. Stay. Go. I'm making myself crazy. Time to apply my foolproof method for making big decisions: Take the advice of the next person who calls.

Sunday

The phone rings. It's a local number I don't recognize. Probably a telemarketer.

The phone rings again.

I need to be open to all possibilities and all sources of input. "Hello?"

"Yes, is Mr. Burns there?" The speaker has a Russian accent.

"This is him."

"Mr. Burns, this is the Robert Mapplethorpe Institute and we have an opening we're looking to fill." The speaker now has a Spanish accent. He coughs. Something about him sounds familiar.

"I'm very flattered," I say, "but I just accepted a rear-entry position with the Moulin Pink Ballet."

My Caller ID flashes.

"Hey, Abe, let me call you back. My mother is on the other line."

In my family, we like our space: We're spread around the continent and communication is usually limited to quarterly updates of no more than 140 characters. So, when one of us calls, we answer.

"Hi, Mom."

"Hi, Randall. Your father saw your post about the layoffs. How are you doing?"

Something rings on her end. "This is probably your father at the door with my new printer. Excuse me for a second, dear."

Since retiring five years ago, my mother and stepfather have been keeping busy. She's writing a cozy holocaust mystery and bartending at The Blue Hare. He has 50,000 Twitter followers.

"I'm back," she says. "How's your social life? Ever hear from the morose one?"

My social life is my dating life. The morose one is Ricki.

Something dings on her end. "Hold that thought," she says.

She's probably in the kitchen. Mother in the kitchen, father doing the heavy lifting. I'm a middle-class cliché: Divorced mother, a biological father I never see, a stepfather I can't talk to, and an evil stepsister named Harriet. Moody insists my childhood was "atypical and worth exploring." My cousin Joey says most guys would be jealous. I'm not sure what to think.

"I'm back," my mother says. "So what's new, dear?"

"I'm thinking about taking a vacation," I say.

"Sounds nice."

Swipe, swipe, click. She's fiddling with some kind of touch-screen device. I open a beer.

"A long vacation, Mom."

"Be sure to post."

"Actually, I'm considering a four-month, solo trip around the world—you know, third world countries, squalor, hemor-rhagic fevers, human trafficking."

"Will you be back in time for Chanukah?"

Chanukah is the one time of year we all get together: me, my parents, Harriet, her daughter, and a husband when she has one. Every December, we have a reasonably nice time together, and then disperse for another twelve months.

A washing machine churns in the background. Then something else dings.

"I'm so sorry. One second, sweetheart."

I catch myself getting angry. So she's a little distracted. So she's a little oblivious. She's better off than most of her relatives. After forty, her side of the family, the Pascals, hits a hereditary wall. Brain chemicals flow in the wrong direction. The Dark Place comes for an extended stay. At forty-nine, she had a six-month affair and my stepfather took her back. Other Pascals weren't so lucky. Some did time in prison, rehab, mental hos-pitals, or homeless shelters. Two others offed themselves. Ever since I turned forty, I've been looking over my shoulder, dodg-ing cracks in the sidewalk, picking up lucky pennies.

My mother returns. "So, where were we? Have you spoken to Harriet?"

"Not lately, I've been a little preoccupied."

"Oh, right. Are you asking my opinion about this trip, sweetheart?"

"Mom, I'm a grown man."

"Now, honey, you've been in Boston for, what, twenty-some-odd years?"

"Some very odd years."

"You'll be fine."

This has always been her stock line for skinned knees, broken hearts, and lost jobs. I toss the empty beer can into the trash. Fuck the five cents.

Monday

Arrange emergency session with Dr. Moody.

"So, you're considering a four-month, solo trip around the world?" Moody asks.

"You always say I'm too passive. This might be a good kick in the pants for me."

"Let's parse this out. You worked for the same company for fifteen years and just lost your job. Your friends are settling into relationships and you're feeling alone, abandoned, and angry. Whenever you get depressed, you become passive and then, to avoid sinking into the Dark Place, you explode with a flurry of misguided activity."

"What's your point?"

"You need to be aware of your process, a process that may not be working for you. You may want to consider sitting with uncomfortable feelings before making impulsive decisions."

"So, I shouldn't take the trip."

"I thought we agreed that you were going to start making your own decisions—good or bad—without looking outside yourself for answers and advice."

"I'm not really asking for advice. I'm just a little confused."

"Confusion masks the obvious."

"What does that mean?"

"You'll have to answer that yourself."

"So, I shouldn't go?"

"I can't tell you what to do. But it might be good for you to learn how to have fun, go with the flow, worry less about outcomes, women, and dying alone."

"So, I *should* go?"

"Perhaps, but there is no pressure to do it now when you're depressed, vulnerable, and confused."

"But fall is the cheapest time to travel. I either go now or wait a year and burn through my severance."

Moody and I engage in one of our ritual staring contests.

I break the silence: "I'm feeling angry because I'm imagining that you're toying with me, holding out on me. And I'm paying you a lot of money."

"I understand you're feeling angry. You *are* paying me a lot of money and you feel like I'm toying with you. I am not toying with you."

"How do I know that? Just because you're the shrink doesn't mean you're not a rotten, sadistic person."

Moody scribbles on his yellow pad of paper. I always try to read his comments but never can.

"Getting out of Boston never hurt anyone," he finally says.

"What are you saying?"

"Maybe it's time for you to see the world, how other men your age are getting along. There may be other ways of living that you're not aware of. Find some guys who aren't 'settling.' You also may learn about yourself if you travel alone. You may learn to sit with loneliness, make peace with the Dark Place. You've been in a horrible drought with women. You may even get laid."

Another staring contest.

I break the silence: "I heard from Ricki."

He holds his stare and asks: "How are you set for medications? There's another sleeping pill you may want to try instead of Ambien."

His phone rings. "My next patient is here. Don't make any hasty decisions. Bon voyage."

What a dick.

Using the instructions in the *Solo Salvation* guidebook, I spend five days filling my Day Planner with action items. For the first time in weeks, I sleep without chemical assistance. The following week, I embrace my destiny.

Monday: Buy Gear

The book recommends saving money by traveling like a backpacker. I decide to skip the bandanas and tie-dyed pajama pants, and go for the backpack. As fate would have it, the sales clerk at a local camping store has just backpacked through Southeast Asia. He's wearing a Bob Marley T-shirt. I wait for him to finish dripping Visine into his eyes.

Me: "I'm traveling around the world and need a sixty-liter pack and a waterproof cover."

Clerk: "No problem, dude. Check out this men's large. Hey, don't know if you're hitting Bangkok, but if you are, I recommend Tug's for the Asian massage."

Me: "I'll certainly add Tug's to my itinerary. Do you have a long-sleeved, SPF 50 shirt with a hidden security pocket?"

Clerk: "Got you covered, bro. In Phuket, Shooters offers an epic all-night back rub."

Me: "Another must-see. Do you have 30-percent DEET insect repellent?"

Clerk: "No worries, my friend. And in Koh Samui, definitely check out The Curious Finger Body Spa."

In the end, I spend $500 with the knowledgeable salesman and avoid shaking his hand.

Tuesday: Book Accommodations and Activities

Since I recently learned to windsurf and can now sail from point A to point B without help from the Coast Guard, I reserve two weeks with the recommended outfit on Venezuela's Mojito Island, and then e-mail another top-rated company on the Greek island of Cyclonos.

Me: "Can I walk from the hotel to the windsurfing area?"

Response in fractured English: "the hotel ist 3,5 – 4 km faraway from beach. If need per walking time 45 minute."

After another six e-mails, it's time to buy.

Me: "Let's do this."

Response: "Please to pre payment 50%."

Me: "Can I pay by credit card?"

Response: "we have no creditcard maschine or can use a creditcard-No. If notpossible to make payment transfer?"

Translation: I'm supposed to wire $500 to someone I've never met, who speaks second-grade English, and lives in a country I've never visited. This doesn't strike me as a particularly smart investment. I wire the money.

That night, I have trouble sleeping and treat myself to an Ambien.

Wednesday: Visit Travel Clinic

A nurse wearing a black hoodie under a starched lab coat hustles me into her office. Her skin is paler than a snake's belly. Her computer sports a bumper sticker: "I stop for entrails."

"Where you headed?" she says, tracking something outside her window.

"Venezuela, Greece, South Africa, Thailand, Vietnam, and Australia," I say, watching her watch what is probably a squirrel.

"Sounds like fun."

After clicking at her keyboard a little too long, she looks directly at me for the first time. "You're going to need seven shots and we'll need some blood."

My hands grip the armrests. I feel myself rocking in my chair. A breath is stuck in my lungs.

"A newbie, eh? You'll be fine," she says, handing me pamphlets on malaria and chikungunya fever. Then she starts doling out prescriptions. "If you get the runs in Venezuela, take Ciprofloxacin. In Thailand, take Azithromycin. In Vietnam, take Pepto-Bismol daily—it can turn your tongue black, but some women like that look."

By the time she finishes with me, I'm afraid to leave my apartment, never mind the country.

That night, I pretreat with two Ambien and get five hours of splintered sleep.

Thursday: Finalize Flights

My travel agent calls. "We're all set! Just come down, pick up your tickets, and the journey of a lifetime can begin."

"What's the final price?"

"It's a little more than we quoted, but still a deal at $6,180."

"Can I get an e-ticket?"

"This itinerary is too complicated. I've got a stack of fourteen paper tickets—it's about half an inch thick, Very impressive."

"How many red-eyes?"

"One, two, three . . . five, but that's how we kept the price down. One thing: For trips like this, we recommend travel insurance. You know how it can go, life being what it is."

"How much?"

"About $700, but it includes the works: trip cancellation, lost baggage, medical expenses, repatriation of remains, and loss of a hand, a foot, or an orifice—just kidding about the orifice."

I pop open a beer. "Oops. That's my other line, let me call you back."

As I hang up, I hear him shout, "Remember: this is more than a vacation, it's a life-changing experience."

The tab has now topped $12,000.

I have a bad night, complete with full-body twitching, staring contests with the alarm clock, and rapid eye movements so violent I worry that my eyeballs will be pitched from their sockets. Treatment: three Ambien with a Heineken chaser.

Friday: Counteroffers

Haven't heard from Abe in a week. Finally he calls. His cousin Denise, the hard-partying yoga instructor, is single and up for a date. At Abe's wedding, I noticed Denise and was taken with her. But at the time, she was also taken—by her fiancé.

Maybe I'm not meant to go anywhere; maybe I'm meant to be with Denise.

Later, Rachel calls. A friend of hers is starting a website and needs a contract editor. He's got an office on Newbury Street. "He used to read your magazine column and already got a good reference from your ex-boss. Just send a résumé by Monday."

Upshot: I could blow $12,000 and end up as a bag of remains or earn $30,000 and spend three months in a cushy office in downtown Boston. A woman and a job. I can always take the trip next year or, better yet, never. Hell with my deposits.

That night I get nine hours of deep, chemical-free sleep.

Saturday: The Phone Call

"Hi, Denise. It's Randy Burns, Abe's friend. We met at his wedding. What's going on?"

"The usual, I'm doing sun salutations in my french maid's outfit." She laughs. I laugh. Then I hear a puffing sound followed by a breathy exhale. I picture smoke slipping out from between her lips.

"Are you really six two?" she asks.

"I'm five eleven, why?"

"Abe said you were six two. No biggie. How are things at *Business Week?*"

I reach for a beer. "I was at *Personal Computer Computing Week.*"

"Abe said you were the editor at a national business magazine. So, I just assumed."

"Actually, I was a senior editor with the emphasis on *was.*"

"Don't worry about it. I'm no great shakes, either. I've put on some weight since Abe's wedding."

I pop open the beer. "Ooops, that's my other line. Can I call you back?"

Fucking Abe. Why would he lie like that? Maybe this is a ploy by him and Rachel to get me to stay. Are they jealous? Trying to save me from myself?

That night, no sleep.

Sunday: The E-mail

While updating my résumé, I get an e-mail from Ricki.

Hey Burns:

Read your post about planning a trip around the world. What a laugh! We just got back from Southeast Asia. You won't last a minute! If you go, can I borrow your HTML book? And if you don't come back, can I have your mountain bike? Ha ha.

P.S. If you reach Asia in one piece, avoid Cambodia. The State Department just issued warnings about typhoid, Japanese encephalitis, and street gangs throwing battery acid. We skipped it.

—RRRRRR

We? Who the hell is "we"?

After three months of planning, it's finally August 27, the night before I leave for Venezuela, my first stop. Abe has organized a *bon voyage* dinner at the Minuteman. I arrive on time at eight, and the gang is already sitting at a corner table, a prime spot to watch the Red Sox and Yankees game on the big screen.

Abe's "I beat anorexia" T-shirt is stretched across his 250-pound frame and he's yelling at the TV. I come up behind him and apply a man-hug. "Where's the little missus?" I ask.

"Probably home watching tranny wrestling."

I grab an open seat between Abe and Lenny. Abe pats my smooth-shaved head. "My little pet, did you call Denise?"

"Not much point. I'm going away for four months. I'll give her a holler when I get back." I don't mention her weight gain.

"So you're really going through with this?" he asks.

"All locked and loaded."

Lenny offers a high five without looking away from the TV. "My man, my man, my brave little man."

I tug the lapel on his seersucker suit and point to his white loafers. "You look like the little old pedophile from Pasadena."

"A single guy has to be ready for action in any way, shape, or form." Lenny always says he'll never settle. He always says he'll never stay in a hotel that doesn't offer fresh wheat grass juice. Lenny always says a lot of things.

Rachel is sitting across from me and leans over to kiss me on the cheek. "We're all so proud of you."

She's OK, they're OK, I'm OK.

"I thought Josh was coming," I say.

"Either the Scientologists got him or he's still with that girlfriend all the time," Abe says.

I stifle a comment about friends who disappear once they're hooked up.

Lenny leans toward me, still looking at the TV. "Josh's girl is packing on the pounds. Poor guy."

Abe cuts in. "You two aren't happy unless the woman is wasting away on an IV drip."

"Ricki wasn't that thin," I say.

"And neither was Karen Carpenter," Abe says. "And Karen Carpenter was probably saner. I mean that in a good way."

He pats my head again, turns to the waitress, and orders a Guinness for me.

Lenny quickly changes the subject. "Get all your shots?"

"Got poked more times than a Saigon bar girl," I say.

"Smart," Lenny says. "I just read that the State Department issued another dengue warning for South America. They said it's carried by mosquitos."

"I don't think there's a vaccine for dengue," Rachel says.

"I'm bringing clothes impregnated with bug repellent," I say. "Plus 30-percent DEET spray for exposed skin." My hands grip the armrests. "The guidebook says dengue shouldn't be an issue."

Abe asks: "Now that you've blogged about leaving the country for four months, want us to clean up your condo each time you get robbed?"

"No worries. My Uncle Heshie is going to house-sit."

"Uh, oh," Abe says.

"Who?" Rachel asks.

"My uncle," I say. "He's a successful shoulder surgeon, owns a nice place in Manhattan. I let him use my place, he may let me use his."

"Isn't he the sixty-year-old who dates twenty-somethings?" Lenny asks. "The guy with a Hooters gold card?"

"It was my mother's idea." I feel myself rocking in my chair. I take a deep, full breath and let it out to the count of fifteen.

Later, after the Sox lose, Lenny and Rachel stand and say they're going to the bathroom. They're probably going to pay the bill. Abe turns to me. "Burns, you're going to have a rotten time. Why are you doing this?"

I look into my beer as if there might be an answer inscribed in the foam. I turn the drink coaster over and read the Guinness advertising copy. Finally, I just come out with it: "I don't know."

Lenny and Rachel return with a slice of deep-fried cheesecake with a candle. "Brother, you have to come back in one piece," Lenny says. "Otherwise, who's going to wash my pooper when I'm old and alone?"

Rachel says, "Burns, come back with a wife."

"Or at least the thrush," Abe says.

I blow out the candle.

We share the cake four ways, put our forks down, look at each other, and smile.

"Should I bum some cigarettes off the bartender for old time's sake, the end-of-night, Chronic Single's Club smoke?" I ask.

Rachel looks at her watch. "I'll have to pass. Arturo doesn't like it when I smell like smoke."

Abe looks at the TV. "Amy says I'm too fat to be smoking."

Lenny watches a woman in tennis shorts bend to tie her shoes. "Not tonight, my brother. My throat's a little scratchy and tomorrow I have a date with a babe from the prostitution ring. Got to be on my game."

I check my watch: ten o'clock. I don't repeat Lenny's line about miserable married people who go to bed early. I watch the three of them shuffle out the door. Then I turn to the TV and watch the defeated Red Sox players shuffle off the field. The bartender offers me a cigarette.

I'm about to blow twelve grand. I better come back with something that doesn't require antibiotics: a job, a woman, or at least some fodder for my Match profile.

CHAPTER TWO: VENEZUELA

The true adventurer sees his glass as half full,
even when there are things swimming in it.
— WALLACE PITTMAN,
Solo Salvation: Travel the World on Your Own

On August 28 at 6:20 A.M., I depart for Venezuela with one piece of luggage—my new $200 backpack crammed with overpriced travel clothes, medications, water-purifying tablets, earplugs, nose plugs, dust masks, safety pins, bobby pins, duct tape, Scotch tape, surgical tape, Allen wrenches, and other gear recommended by Pittman's guidebook.

As the flight attendant discusses water landings, sweat collects beneath the money belt strapped under my pants. I glance at my seatmates, two elderly women sucking on hard candies and chatting in Spanish. They don't seem worried.

The plane engines hum, my seat hums. I imagine a whirlpool without water, a massage that won't require a tip. I tighten my seat belt low and tight across my lap and close my eyes.

Last year I went to France and came back in one piece. But Venezuela is a little more dangerous than France. OK, it's a lot more dangerous than France. OK, it has one of the highest murder rates in the world. And at the Caracas airport a driver is picking me up at the international terminal *just* to take me the hundred yards to the domestic terminal because it's not safe to walk around outside unescorted.

But if some greaseball draws a weapon, I'll just fork over the decoy travel wallet around my neck containing twenty dollars and an expired Macy's charge card. Pittman knows all the tricks.

As I'm adjusting the decoy wallet, I hear a loud crack and clutch my seat cushion, which I've heard can double as a floatation device. A cloud of cinnamon stings inside my nostrils. The old Spanish lady next to me is chomping a Fireball. I sneeze into the sleeve of my moisture-wicking oxford and resume my personal inventory. A hidden security pocket in the shirt contains photocopies of my passport and credit cards, plus United States consulate phone numbers for the seven countries I'm visiting. My money belt holds my wad of plane tickets, $500 in cash, and a list of Western-trained doctors on each continent. I e-mailed myself scanned images of my tickets, passport, and immunization card. I've taken every precaution recommended by the guidebook and the State Department. The rest is up to fate.

Cr-a-ck!

Damn foreigners can never eat quietly.

The flight attendant announces something in Spanish. Around me, passengers cackle in Spanish. This is what it's going to be like for the next four months—surrounded by foreigners, which I guess makes me the foreigner. This better be worth it.

My biggest concern: What to do if I descend to the Dark Place? I can't just call Abe. Or Lenny. Or Rachel. Or Moody. That would mean admitting defeat and a costly international call. Hopefully I'll make new friends in Venezuela. Beautiful, surgically enhanced friends. Then I'll call Boston. Collect.

There's a tap on my arm. I instinctively cover my money belt with my hand. The old woman next to me smiles and hands me a Jawbreaker.

"*Gracias*." I smile and slip the wrapped candy into another security pocket. Once we're airborne, I look out the window at a puffy summer sky, a divine pillow top, a pasture of meringue, deep and untracked.

Cr-a-ck!

My seatmates laugh, an elbow brushes mine. I relinquish the armrest and stare at the ceiling. The seat belt sign goes off. The drink cart is free to move about the cabin.

I wash down two Ambien with a beer and don my sleep blindfold.

Nine hours later, the plane touches down in Caracas. Except for the Spanish signage, the terminal looks like any other: Day-Glo carpets in psychedelic patterns, kiosks advertising Chivas Regal, and steel, stone, and glass objets d'art dangling from the ceiling. I'm not sure if I'm relieved or disappointed.

There is one thing unique about this place—most people milling around the terminal are dark-skinned like the Latinos who work at my health club. But these people aren't wearing Minuteman uniforms and sneakers; they're wearing suits and pointy shoes. Mercenaries. Banana republicans. Friends of Hugo Chávez.

I follow the other passengers to the exit and spot a blonde at the end of a long line. She's pulling a paisley wheelie and wearing a navy blazer with black flats. White, preppy, about my age, probably unarmed.

"Excuse me," I say. "Is this the customs line?"

"Yes, it is. Are you American?"

She has white skin and a delicate Spanish accent. An outlier?

"I'm from Boston," I say.

She smiles. "I was just on Nantucket visiting friends."

Her hand brushes mine. I flinch and automatically cover my money belt. We both look at my hand on my crotch. I feel my face redden.

"I've read some bad things about crime down here," I say.

She glances at my backpack and SPF 50 bouldering pants, and then gives me a playful squeeze on the arm. "Don't believe everything you read. And in case you're wondering, I've never worn a leaf blower and there are no live chickens running around my living room."

She laughs and introduces herself as Bennie. As the line inches forward, we chat about her life in Venezuela, her family's Mercedes-Benz dealerships, and the local economy. She doesn't mention Hugo Chávez and I don't ask. My arm still tingles from her touch.

I whisper, "Where can I get the best exchange rate for my American dollars?"

"Try a hotel or local store," she says casually, as if I were asking about postcards or Pepto-Bismol.

I squeeze *her* arm, lean in, and whisper, "Isn't that illegal? Is there a chance I'll get arrested?" *And subjected to a little South American-style justice?*

Bennie smiles and answers in her outdoor voice. "Just don't change money in front of a policeman, unless you want to give him a cut." She hooks her little finger around mine and pulls me toward her. Her breath smells of wintergreen. "I promise you'll be fine, pinky, pinky."

She grabs a pen from her purse. As she writes, I look at her more closely: tapered cheek bones, petite chin, tapered and petite all around. In Venezuela, home to this year's Miss

Universe, Bennie probably doesn't get a second look. But in a Cambridge Whole Foods, she'd collect the grand tiara.

"Here, call me if you get into trouble." She squeezes my arm again and walks off. I glance down at my watch: One hour, one phone number. Not bad.

I look up in time to see her exit the terminal and disappear into the arms of some guy in a suit.

Maybe she's just being friendly to me. Or to him. Or maybe after thirty years of dating, I still don't understand why women do what they do.

I scan the terminal and spot a white guy holding a card with my name on it, "Mr. Randall Burns." I pop the old lady's Jawbreaker into my mouth and stride over.

After a thirty-minute flight from Caracas across the southern Caribbean, we land on Mojito Island, Venezuela's Cape Cod, my home for the next two weeks.

Outside the small airport, I approach a cab driver standing by his car and recite from the guidebook: "*Cuanto cuesta a el hotel* Bonzi?"

The book says the ride should be 25,000 bolivars, or about twelve dollars.

The driver says, "*Treinta*."

I don't know what '*treinta*' means, but it sounds a little high, so I say, "Ten dollars US."

He mumbles something that sounds like "ka-brone" and opens the car door.

Twenty minutes later, at dusk, we pull into Playa El Playa, a world-renowned windsurfing town. One-story shops pop up on the ocean side of the road. On the other side, huge signs promote vacation real estate, and beyond, a vacant field is strewn with trash. The air is hot, humid, and redolent of rotting fish heads. A few dark-skinned guys in board shorts lean against a rusty fence and wave to the driver. Several loose dogs chase our cab for twenty feet and then duck into the brush.

The Bonzi hotel is two stories of peach-colored stucco engulfed by ferns, fronds, and palms. An al fresco bar, an open-air roof deck, an empty hammock shading an empty margarita glass. I imagine sputtering blenders, sloppy happy hours, and arm-squeezing beauty queens without husbands.

The manager takes my backpack and gestures to the staircase. A dog passes us on our way up. I try to look away but can't. It has six swaying a-cups, a nursing mutt, the first breasts I've seen in months.

"That is my dog, *señor*," the manager says. I'm not sure if he's simply stating a fact or letting me know the animal is spoken for.

He shows me to a room with rattan furniture, a Caribbean view, and a queen-sized bed with a mosquito net.

"Will I need that net?" I ask.

"No, *señor*. We have no mosquitoes this time of year."

No mosquitoes, no dengue fever. After the manager leaves, I secure my money belt and medications in the room's wall safe, drop my bag, and pass out on the bed.

The next morning, I hit the Bonzi's free breakfast buffet just before it closes. The spread covers three card tables in the open-air, roof-top restaurant. The offerings: tropical fruit, cereal, yogurt, cold cuts, fresh juices, and a yellow beverage flecked with black things that are either seeds or microorganisms. *In Venezuela, take Ciprofloxacin.*

Below, in the pool area, an elderly man suns himself, black moles the size of raisins hanging from his skin. No babes. They must already be at the beach.

The dining area is empty except for a thirty-something couple seated in the middle. The woman looks up and returns to her meal, but the guy waves, smiles, and gestures for me to join them. I guess once you leave Boston, everyone is friendly.

Aurek is stocky, balding, and resembles a muscular elf. His girlfriend, Zofia, scowls at me from behind skinny, severe glasses. Her shoulders are lightly freckled and her toned triceps are shaped like little horseshoes. Aurek has done well for himself.

He speaks perfect English and says they're from Poland and have stayed at the Bonzi several times. Zofia says nothing and proceeds to cut her food into tiny pieces. Maybe she's shy.

"How's the food?" I glance at Zofia while she eviscerates a cantaloupe. Her biceps flex with every cut. She doesn't look up.

Aurek smiles. "It's good in the hotel, but you should check out a place on the beach called Manrico's."

"How about the water?"

"Warm," Aurek says. "We're just north of the equator."

"But is it true that you're only supposed to drink bottled water, brush your teeth with bottled water, and keep your mouth closed in the shower?"

Aurek looks at me curiously.

Even Zofia looks up.

"Is this your first time out of the US?" he asks.

Zofia shakes her head and returns to cutting her food.

I wasn't always so concerned about dirt, germs, and life in general. As a kid, I had the usual fascinations with bodily functions and all things gooey. I collected green and yellow boogers in a shoebox hidden under my bed. Later I graduated to slimy pets such as frogs that ate worms, turtles that ate goldfish, and snakes that ate mice. I never thought twice about kissing Harold the basset hound on the mouth or nipping him on the ear if he nipped me on mine.

In my teens, I worked in a kennel cleaning cages. When I ate lunch, I might have a drippy Reuben sandwich in one hand and a steaming dustpan of beagle crap in the other.

But once I hit forty, something changed. I worried that every cold was TB, that every pimple was malignant, and that every annual checkup would be my last. And now I'm about to spend four months traveling through countries with hygiene practices that would horrify Jane Goodall.

Aurek looks at me, possibly with pity. I chug my glass of juice flecked with swimmy things.

At the Playa El Playa beach, the sand is warm, powdery, and interrupted only by clusters of palms and beach umbrellas. The water is greener than a key lime daiquiri. Small hotels, restaurants, and tiki bars line the shore. Unlike the real Cape Cod, the Venezuelan version is not crowded.

I catch a whiff of coconut suntan oil and margarita mix. A few people in skimpy bathing suits are drinking and jabbering in Spanish. Loose children run around throwing sand at loose dogs.

The guidebook warned about thieves working the El Playa beach. I perform a quick security check: My money belt, credit cards, and plane tickets are locked in the hotel-room wall safe. Ten dollars in cash, the room key, and a photocopy of my passport are sealed in a watertight bag zipped into a hidden pocket in my hat.

I proceed to the windsurfing center where the staff greets me by name, "*Hola, Señor* Burns. Welcome to World Boardsailing."

The good news: The center isn't crowded. The better news: The center is offering a free group lesson and today I'm the group. I recall the guidebook saying that partying typically runs late. Everyone must be sleeping off hangovers in their rooms.

My instructor, Edmundo, is about my age and bare-chested. He sports a near-black tan that would qualify him for the cover of *Melanoma Weekly*. He isn't wearing sunglasses. With mine still on, I look up at the equatorial sun: The last time I saw anything this bright, it was followed by a mush-room cloud.

I half listen to his opening remarks thinking: Isn't he wor-ried about cataracts? Or skin cancer? If he's a forty-something windsurfing instructor, how is he going to retire? How do people who don't own Mercedes-Benz dealerships retire in this country?

Edmundo stops talking and looks me up and down. I look me up and down: long-sleeved windsurfing shirt, match-ing sun-blocking tights, sailing gloves, rubber booties, and a sunhat the size of a garbage can top. The SPF-50 sunscreen on my face is so thick it probably looks as if it had been applied with a spackling knife.

"Hey, ka-brone. Nice pants," he says. "What you want to work on?"

Ka-brone? Where have I heard that before?

"Beach starts," I say.

"Let's see what you got."

A beach start is a move in which you stand in the water on one foot, put the other on the windsurfer, and let the wind pull you up into a sailing position. This is an alternative to the uphaul start, in which you bend over, grab a rope attached to the mast, and pull until a disc pops in your back.

I attempt three beach starts and fall each time. Edmundo shakes his head. I feel my face redden under the sunscreen.

There are two types of windsurfing instructors in the world. The "nursery school teacher" is warm and effusive, and talks to students as if they were frightened hamsters. The "dick" is cool and condescending, and spends most of the class trying to sell students pricey, private lessons.

Edmundo is a dick. He snatches my board, enters the water, and starts tossing around terms like "broad reach," "windward," and "clew." He might as well be speaking Spanish. After he demonstrates, I follow his example and actually get up on the board.

Edmundo is a good instructor.

I agree to three future lessons for $120, perform a shaky beach start, and head offshore. Zipping around, I rake the sail back to turn or pull it in to speed up. The wind feels good. The nose of the board rises out of the water. Soon I'm going so fast the board is skipping across the water like a flat stone. This is a maneuver called "planing," something I've never done before.

Two other windsurfers pull out in front of me and wave: Aurek, closely followed by Zofia. I detect a smile on her face, probably her first in ten years. Her calves are toned and slick with sea water.

There are two types of women who travel. The "twat" is attractive, condescending, and usually has a boyfriend. I've heard there is another type, but I've never met one.

I pull in my sail to catch them.

Windsurfing experts say that the faster you go, the more stable your board becomes—unless you're riding a wobbly, oversized beginner board like the one I'm on. Aurek and Zofia are riding small, sleek expert boards. The nose of my board shudders.

At a certain speed, water changes temperament from soft and forgiving to hard as ice. If you fall at that speed, you will need evacuation insurance and a doctor who speaks English. Your remains may need to be repatriated. I'm not sure what that speed is because I don't normally windsurf this fast, but by the sound of the water thudding against my board, I must be pretty close.

I'm gaining on Zofia, who is no longer smiling. My board shudders again.

I imagine wiping out and cartwheeling across the water. Two years ago, I was skiing too fast, hit a snow mound the wrong way, and went cartwheeling across the Vermont ice. When I came to a stop, my foot, ribs, and wrist were all fractured and I was laid up for months.

As I rocket across the sea, I think: Am I going to replay that accident every time a little adrenaline kicks in, every time I'm looking down a steep chute or into one of life's barrels?

Damn straight.

I let the sail out to slow down and head back to shore as Aurek and Zofia head out to where the water changes from iguana green to marlin blue.

Manrico's tiki bar has a hempy roof overhanging a row of cane stools. One stool is occupied by a white guy with thinning hair who is nursing a shot of black liquor. Next to him, a dark-skinned beauty queen traces the leafy patterns on his yellow aloha shirt. The other stools are vacant. Beyond them, ten tables with cabana umbrellas sit unoccupied in the sand.

The guidebook has a photo of Manrico's at full throttle: DJs with face paint, palm trees with tinsel, and wet girls sprinkled with confetti. None of that tonight, but maybe that's because it's a Monday.

I hop a stool at one end of the long wooden bar. The bartenders are both female and half my age. One wears a flimsy outfit that barely covers what has to be an upgraded torso. She ignores me. The other bartender, the plump one, smiles and takes my order: a beer and the seafood dinner special.

A flat-screen TV is tuned to the Yankees and Red Sox season finale. I imagine Lenny, Abe, and Rachel watching at the Minuteman.

The El Playa beach is dark and empty except for a torch that illuminates two bony cats fighting over a dead finch that will barely feed one of them.

A wiry stranger takes an open stool near me. The attractive bartender chats with him in Spanish. Passers-by greet him.

He's probably about my age and wearing flip-flops and a large, expensive-looking watch. He glances at my Keen water shoes and flame-retardant shorts. He points to the Yankee player at bat. "Bobby Abreu is Venezuelan," he says in a slight accent that could be French or German or Russian. I'm not good with accents.

"We don't like him in Boston," I say. "He's too good."

He lights a filter-less cigarette from a pack of Gitanes sitting on the bar.

My beer arrives. It's in an eight-ounce bottle, half the size of the pints I drink back home. I finish it in three gulps and consider the tiny bottle. A nip for beer drinkers.

"The small bottles stay cold longer," the stranger says. "Welcome to the tropics."

He returns to the bartenders and speaks to them in Spanish.

I return to my seafood special: pasta with rubbery strands that could be squid, octopus, or old windshield wipers. I want to ask where everyone is, but my head aches, probably from too much sun, so after eating, I leave a tip and head for the Bonzi.

The next morning, I join Aurek and Zofia again for breakfast. He is very chatty. She is very tan. I notice that she's armed with a steak knife.

"How long have you been riding?" Aurek says.

"About a year."

"You're not bad for a beginner. Maybe you should try a smaller board. They're faster."

Zofia smirks into her plate.

I gesture at the room. "Where is everyone? I've seen a few couples around town—and no offense—but I was expecting it to be a little more lively."

"Oh, didn't you know it is slow season?" Aurek asks.

My stomach spasms: empty beach, empty bars, a nonrefundable flight, twelve more days in El Playa. Did I overlook something or did Pittman?

Zofia smirks again. I haven't lost my touch. Women still love to see me suffer.

"Cheer up," Aurek says. "You probably saved a lot of money traveling off-season. And they love dollars down here."

"Have you changed any money yet?"

"Yesterday. The bodega in town pays 3,800 bolivars per dollar."

"Wow!" I say.

The legal exchange rate is 2,100 bolivars. So 3,800 is a good deal. Maybe too good a deal. I want to ask about the risk of arrest, but that would likely yield another smirk from Zofia.

I change the subject. "How's your Spanish?" I ask Aurek.

"*Bon,*" he says in French.

"OK, wise guy, what's the polite response when someone addresses you as 'ka-brone'?"

"Kick them in the balls," he says. "Or you could punch them in the face. Either will do. *C-a-b-r-ó-n* means a man with no *cajones*, a major asshole, and other flattering things. Isn't that right, honey?"

Zofia looks up, pinches her mouth shut, and goes back to disemboweling her papaya. Her steak knife scratches the porcelain plate. *What's the feminine for* cabrón?

From the outside, the bodega is small, dark, and seedy-looking. From the inside, it is small, dark, and seedy-looking. The walls are dotted with shelves of American delicacies: Mars bars, Cheez Doodles, Almond Joys. A few couples are shopping for wine or balsamic vinegar or lube or whatever it is that couples shop for.

A big guy with long, dark hair mops the floor. Another big guy eyes me and mumbles something to the mopper. I examine a *Cat in the Hat* Pez dispenser, and then glance up at the two guys, and then back to the Pez.

Thug One and Thug Two
don't like me one bit.
They glare and they glare
as if I were shit.

I pretend to read the Spanish Pez packaging and have second thoughts about this whole caper. The State Department warned against illegal money changing: Apparently, Chávez and his boys consider it theft. Bank theft. El Playa is a small town; there would be no place to hide.

Still the guidebook includes money changing on its list of "Things to do in El Playa." Aurek does it. Zofia does it. Even blonde Bennie who visits Nantucket does it.

The young woman behind the counter notices me fidgeting. "Change money?" she asks. I look around. The thugs are gone. I'm the only one in the store.

"*Sí,*" I whisper.

"How much, *cabrón?*" She speaks in a normal voice. I decide to let the insult drift by.

"One hundred dollars, US," I whisper.

She pecks some numbers into her calculator and shows it to me: 3,800.

I nod, "OK."

I'm going to walk out with 380,000 bolivars. For $300, I could be a Venezuelan millionaire.

She rummages around in the change drawer, retrieves a stack of pastel-colored bills, and counts out seven orange notes and some smaller bills. I fork over the $100 bill and throw the bolivars into my daypack. I exit the store slowly and, once outside, I run for my hotel like a kid who has just committed his first Halloween prank.

Saving money has always been a preoccupation. For me, money is a source of security, a defense against scarcity, my protection against ending up on the street when I'm old and alone. I'm a hoarder, not a spender.

After college, my first full-time job paid minimum wage. My apartment was a second-floor walk-up with a sad, little space heater that I couldn't afford to turn on until November, when I could see my breath indoors. For meals, I'd buy a family-sized box of Corn Flakes and a pound of hamburger, which I split into gum-ball-sized portions that had to last a week. Eventually I turned to a life of crime.

My favorite target was the corner store, Kitty's Kwick Stop. I started out swiping bags of Beer Nuts, which I'd hide in one of my mittens. Soon I graduated to pricier things, like bars of cheddar cheese. I even began to save money and went out for an occasional beer. One day, as I was paying for a carrot, the manager said, "What about the block of cheese in your mitten?"

People in line peered over my shoulder. A guy on his way out of the store stopped to look back.

I couldn't speak or breathe.

"The clerk refilling the beer case saw you," the manager said. "Take out the cheese, get the fuck out of my store, and don't come back."

"But I'll pay for everything, I'm really sorry."

"Get out before I call the cops."

From then on, I imagined my photo hanging by the Kitty's cash register. On the way home from work, I'd cross the street so the store employees wouldn't see me. I had learned my lesson about shoplifting, but I was more convinced than ever that poverty wasn't for me.

Next I worked as a waiter, which paid mostly cash. Instead of schlepping to the bank every week, I stashed the money in the dirty socks in my laundry bag. White gym socks were crammed with singles. Dark socks with larger bills. When I ran out of socks, I started stuffing the inside pockets of the coats in my closet. Being surrounded by all that cash made me feel safe and warm, as if I were floating in some kind of amniotic fluid.

Six months later, I landed my first full-time magazine job. Six months after that, the publisher was fired. Then the editor-in-chief was fired. The remaining editor decided to boost morale with team-building exercises, such as happy hours featuring Twinkies, Devil Dogs, Hostess Cup Cakes, and Schlitz. After four months, the magazine moved to New York and we were all fired.

I swore I'd one day accumulate enough money so I'd never again worry about unemployment checks or Twinkie hangovers.

Eventually I snagged a senior editor job at *Personal Computer Computing Week* and was able to save 10 percent of my paycheck. After fifteen years, I was starting to feel financially secure. Until five months ago, when I got laid off again.

But looking into my bag filled with 380,000 bolivars, a familiar sensation returns: I'm safe, warm, and ready for a beer.

Blog Entry: August 30
Playa El Playa, Venezuela

Dear Friends and Family:

Made it to South America in one piece, having a great time. The natives are quite friendly. The highlights:

• Two flirty Latin women on the plane who plied me with local delicacies.

• A Venezuelan beauty queen at the airport terminal who gave me her phone number.

• An attractive Polish surgeon in the hotel's four-star dining room who invited me to join her and her boyfriend for breakfast two days in a row. Is there an accent over the "a" in ménage à trois? (Just kidding, Mom.)

The second night, I went to the local tiki bar: good food, great crowd, dueling DJs, fire show, fog machines, confetti cannons, mosh pit, go-go girls in suspended cages pouring margaritas on the crowd. At dawn the police sent us all home. Slept till noon. Am I getting too old for this? Will find out tonight when I go back.

Also have been picking up a little Spanish.

Cocos *(breasts)*

Melónes *(breasts)*

Tetas *(breasts)*

Culo *(ass)*

And an insult that you would love, Abe: Chinga tu madre, cabrón. *(Go have sex with your mother you cuckold with no testicles.) Sorry, Mom.*

Ciao for now,

—Burns

Two nights later, I put on a clean Red Sox T-shirt and give Manrico's another shot. Same empty cabana tables, same barren bar scene. The guy who wore a yellow aloha shirt the other night is now wearing a red one. Instead of a local beauty queen, tonight he's drinking with a man with a thick Sasquatch beard. I take a cane stool next to the wiry stranger with the big watch from the other night. Everyone is drinking little beers.

As I try to assemble a Spanish conversation starter without the words "tits," "asshole," or "motherfucker," the stranger lights a filter-less cigarette. I watch a loop of smoke leak from his mouth. I think of Abe's cousin Denise before she gained weight. I think of the ritual Chronic Single's smoke.

The stranger slides his pack of Gitanes and lighter along the bar to me.

"Help yourself," he says. "You traveling alone?"

Before I can answer, Edmundo, the windsurfing instructor, walks in from the dark beach, his arms wrapped around a clinking, unlabeled box. He puts it on the bar and ignores me.

"Manrico." Edmundo gestures with his chin to the wiry stranger I'm talking to.

This must be *The* Manrico.

Edmundo opens a box flap just enough to peer inside. Manrico counts the contents, nods approvingly, and extracts a bottle. Edmundo leaves.

The bottle is filled with dark liquid. Manrico pours four shots and puts one in front of each of us at the bar. "Chin chin," he says to me.

Another item on the guidebook's list of "Things to do in El Playa" is to sample the local black moonshine.

He downs his shot. I down mine.

The black hooch has a smooth licorice flavor like sambuca.

"Nice," I say. "So where are you from originally?"

"Rome," says Manrico.

He tells me he's owned this bar for five years. "Once owned a bar in Key West. Had to sell it," he says. "Owned a bar in San Tropez. Had to sell that one too. And then there was the bar in Bali. Hated to sell that one."

On the dark beach, I hear sandy footsteps, whispering voices, and then a sputtering motorboat.

"How's the crime here?" I ask.

"Not too bad. Last year at high season, some punk snatched the watch off my wrist. I lost the little prick out on the beach." He smiles exposing a black space where a molar used to be. "I bought mountain bikes for the El Playa police to make it easier for them to patrol the beach. They're regulars here. You traveling alone?"

He keeps asking if I'm alone. As I decide how to answer, the attractive bartender saunters over. Her outfit is as transparent as a mosquito net. She sits on his lap and acknowledges me with a shy smile. Her hands are cupped, as if she's holding something, a secret, a magic wish for the right guy. Right now, I'd like to be that guy, Manrico with the big watch.

She peeks into her cupped hands and opens them, revealing a huge, gorgeous moth. She strokes its furry little head. Manrico asks for a closer look, and then gives the bug a nasty flick. It hits the ground. A bony cat sitting nearby pounces on it.

The girl tightens her smile and returns to work.

Manrico pours us each another drink. "So, Mr. Red Sox, what do you do in Boston?"

"I'm in publishing and taking some time off to travel."

"You're a publisher."

I'm about to correct him and say that I was just a senior editor. But I'm 2,000 miles from home. I can be anyone I want, the world's most interesting man. "I was publisher of a business magazine," I say.

"*Businessweek?*" he asks.

"Something like that."

I stub out my cigarette and he offers me another one. "Some local business owners are getting together tomorrow night to party," he says. "You should join us."

An invite to the inner circle. I imagine a crazy Latin party filled with surgically enhanced beauty queens. Who cares about Manrico's disappearing businesses, his missing tooth, and that poor moth? I'm in.

"Meet me here at five thirty tomorrow night," Manrico says. "We'll take my car. Where you staying?"

"The Bonzi."

"Oh." He stands, yawns, and stretches. "Don't let the bed bugs bite."

Manrico and his girl head onto the unlit beach. I try to picture him chasing divorcées around a science museum. Not a chance.

The chubby bartender comes over. "More drink?"

I look at her plump face and arms. Part of me wishes she were sitting on my lap and wearing only a mosquito net. But what I really want is Manrico's girl.

I try to picture a life in Boston with a girl like Manrico's. I'd learn Spanish. She'd learn English and how to ski, and she'd get a college degree and a white-collar job. Not too good a job, but enough so that I wouldn't have to pay for her all the time.

Friday nights she'd don a gauzy outfit and we'd go for steamers at the Minuteman. Lenny would stop by our table to flirt with her. Abe would stop by to say, "Burns, you were right not to settle."

She and I would sit side-by-side, my hand on her thigh. She'd take a clam by the neck, peel off the scabby foreskin, and dip it in broth and butter. She'd jiggle it in front of my face, flick the clam belly several times with her tongue, and deep-throat it. Butter would drip down her cheek. She'd lean over for a kiss. Our lips would meet and she'd slip the buttery bolus into my mouth.

For someone like her, I'd do the whole deal: six-figure wedding, six-figure honeymoon, new furniture, heated leather seats, kids, more kids, family portraits, time-outs, private school, reform school, his and hers housecoats, silent treatments, infidelity, couples' therapy, divorce, debt, bankruptcy, and Thanksgivings at her five-bedroom Victorian with our kids and her new husband. I swear, I'd do it.

On the way back to the Bonzi, I spot Aurek and Zofia at a pizza joint. He's glad to see me and waves me over. She's now blacker than a seal. Her usual smirk has been replaced by a scowl.

"Where's the action?" I ask.

"Right here." Aurek raises his black after-dinner drink. Zofia stares into her bowl of vanilla ice cream.

"If it wasn't for you two crazy kids, this place would be dead," I say. "Where's all the drunken, Latin, nakedness?"

"Did you try Manrico's again?" Aurek says.

"It was pretty empty again. Just a few regulars. But I met Manrico and he invited me to a party tomorrow night."

"Be careful, my friend." Aurek raises his hand to the waiter and taps his glass. "We're leaving you tomorrow morning. Tonight we party."

A shot of dark liquor appears before me. We toast.

"*Cabrón*," I say.

"*Cabrón*," he says.

The booze has a familiar licorice flavor, the black hooch of El Playa.

"What's in this stuff?" I ask, finishing it off.

"Nobody knows, but it's supposed to stir the passions."

He looks at Zofia. I look at Zofia. She stabs her ice cream several times with a spoon, and then looks at us like we might be next.

I'll take a surly woman over no woman anytime.

Maxie: Cell A40
First encounter: Online dating, September '01

I met Maxie on Match.com. After weeks of e-mailing back and forth, we agreed to meet at a bar downtown. I waited forty-five minutes. No Maxie.

Back at home, I checked my answering machine.

"Message one: 'Where the fuck are you? You better not have stood me up. Christ, this always happens to me. Bartender. Bartender!'"

"Message two: 'I just drove by your house and the lights are off. You better call with a good fucking excuse.'"

Maybe I should have been put off by Maxie's outbursts. But her e-mails had always been a little testy and, when it comes to women, I've always had a problem telling passion from pathology. Moreover, I was suffering through a drought and hadn't touched a woman in months. Against my better judgment, I called.

"Guess who?" I asked.

"Where the hell are you?"

"I'm home. What happened to you?"

"I was at the Meridien for thirty fucking minutes."

Our date had been arranged online and we'd never spoken before. I found her language both titillating and terrifying. I considered hanging up, but worried that I might find a dead cat nailed to my door. Then I remembered her online photo: auburn hair, black running tights. I pressed on.

"Weren't we supposed to meet at the Tavern on the Charles?" I asked.

Maxie sniffled.

"Are you OK?" I asked, feeling guilty for something I couldn't identify.

"I'm sorry," she said. "It's been a bad week. Do you want to come by for a beer?"

Maxie opened her apartment door wearing an oversized man's T-shirt that hung from an exposed collarbone to midthigh. She swirled a huge glass of red wine and directed me to the couch. I watched her walk to the kitchen. Everything about her was long and toned as advertised.

She returned with a beer. As I sipped, she spoke about her ex-husband and her demeanor softened. He had died a year ago, and she was now raising two kids and working full-time. She advanced across the cushions, asked why I wasn't married, and brandished a tin of Altoids.

When I hesitated, she asked in a little-girl voice, "Don't you like me?"

"Umm, yeah, you seem like a nice person," I said, retreating to the far corner of the sofa. She advanced some more and leaned in for a kiss. Against my better judgment, I puckered up.

Then she bit me on the lip. As I felt the sting of her teeth, the image of a hooked marlin flashed through my head. A moment later, I had her pinned against the armrest.

"What are you going to do now, homo?" she said.

"Where'd you get that mouth? Are you from New Jersey?"

I looked down at her breasts as they rustled in her T-shirt. Droplets of sweat circled her navel. I thought about marlins. I thought about dead cats. Then marlins again.

She rubbed me through my pants and flicked my zipper. "Looks like maybe you do like girls. Let's go to my room."

She shooed two beagles off her bed, relocated an armful of stuffed animals, and pulled back the duvet. We grappled for several minutes and jettisoned each other's clothes until we were down to our underwear.

"Wait a minute," she said.

Maxie rooted around under her pillow and handed me a humming, black oval. I hummed around her slick belly and over her hips. I traced my name across the crotch of her panties. I whispered her name into her panties. Her stomach clenched and relaxed and clenched again. I tugged the elastic to the side and rested my face on her smooth-shaven skin. She smelled like lavender. Her breath deepened, she started to groan, and I heard the clitter-clatter of beagle feet as the dogs scurried from the room.

Over the next four weeks, Maxie and I established a pattern of engagement. She'd call me at the last minute and say, "Come over now and fuck me until I'm numb." I'd cancel my plans and race over. At some point during the evening, we'd get into an argument and she'd say: "You turn my stomach," "You're spineless," or "I need to find a rich radiologist to support me." I always shrugged and said, "Fine." A few days later, she'd call again and I'd run over.

One night as I was leaving, she said, "This isn't working for me." And then, "I just met an oral surgeon."

I was upset for a while, but Maxie had ended my drought. And I met her in September. And now it's almost September again. My high season for meeting women, surly or otherwise.

I catch the waiter's eye, tap my glass, and two more shots appear.

The next morning, the boardsailing center is empty except for Edmundo who is contemplating an open closet filled with plastic buckets, pots, and copper tubing. He ignores me. Next door, Manrico's bar is empty except for Manrico who gestures for me to join him. He probably wants to remind me about the party with the local crowd.

"*Qué pasa?*" I say.

"*Clausurado,*" he says. "The Venezuelan IRS just visited El Playa. They say we have 'irregularities.' The town is being shut down for twenty-four hours." He seems more annoyed than worried. He lights a cigarette without offering me one.

I'm annoyed and worried. I don't recall a *clausurado* section in the guidebook or on the State Department website. I don't ask if buying black hooch out of an unlabeled box is considered an irregularity.

"Catch you later," Manrico says. I've been excused.

In town, white crime-scene tape has been strung across the front of every store except one.

Inside the bodega, Thug One mans the cash register while Thug Two mops. Edmundo emerges from a backroom carrying a glass beaker, tongs, and a thermometer. He leaves without acknowledging me.

A regular from Manrico's bar is on the checkout line with a six-pack under his arm. It's the guy with the aloha shirts. He looks fiftyish and wears a big watch. I grab a six-pack and get on line behind him.

"Looks like a good day to drink beer," I say.

"Every day is a good day to drink beer." He sounds Russian. He turns away to chat in Spanish with a young Latina dragging a child by the hand. She nods and leaves with the kid.

He turns back to me. "The little woman."

I file this away: average middle-aged guy, beautiful exotic wife, gets to drink beer in the middle of the day.

He introduces himself as Becker from Germany. He owns a local hotel and says he's lived in South America for more than thirty years. "I came here in my twenties to study psychotropics. I forget what I concluded."

I could learn from this guy.

I pay for my six-pack, and then follow Becker across the street where another regular, the one with the Sasquatch beard, is standing in the shade. The guy not only has a six-pack, he has a bottle of black hooch at his feet.

Becker says to him, "Morgan from Seattle, this is Randy from Boston. Onward."

Manrico's bar is now sealed with crime-scene tape and he's sitting with a middle-aged woman at a table on the beach. Becker and Morgan take seats next to the woman. Manrico gestures to an open chair. I sit down. The beach is empty: no dogs, no kids, no parents. No one here but us regulars.

The middle-aged woman has blonde hair, blue eyes, and a weathered face that resembles an old hunting boot. No babe, but she probably knows some.

Morgan's beard collects foam as he slugs down his beer. "I hear Boston has a good baseball team." He shakes my shoulder a few times. "How's Manny behaving?"

"Two weeks ago, he left a big game with a mysterious knee ache," I say.

"Those Dominicans are even lazier than the Brazilians," Morgan says.

"But nobody is lazier than the Italians." Becker gestures to Manrico.

Manrico's only response is to open a bottle of hooch and pass out glasses.

We all do a shot.

I feel relaxed for the first time in months. It's like I'm back at the Minuteman with Abe, Lenny, and Rachel during the good times.

"How did you guys end up down here?" I ask the group.

Becker says he was a chiropractor in Munich. No further details.

Morgan says he was a lawyer in Tacoma. No further details. The woman says she had a husband in Sydney. No further details.

I say I was in publishing and leave it at that, hoping no one mentions *Businessweek*.

Manrico refills our glasses and raises his. "To *clausurado*," he says.

Apparently *clausurado* is a regular event. Every few months, the feds come to town, check a few accounting ledgers, and shut every business except one.

"How come the bodega didn't get *clausurado-ed*," I ask.

Morgan says: "That's Edmundo's store." No further details.

Manrico refills my glass and offers me a cigarette. "Edmundo and his sons hate Americans. They think you're all sons of Bushes. Just keep buying windsurfing lessons from him and you'll be fine."

Extortion: Venezuelan for retirement plan.

I look into my empty shot glass. "Does this stuff do anything?"

"I put it in my motorbike when I can't find petrol," the Aussie woman says.

"It's good for taking hair off your tongue," Morgan says.

"It adds two inches to your *schwanz*," Becker says.

"Ask Manrico, it doubled the size of his," Morgan says.

"Laddies, this is where I leave you." The Aussie woman stands and walks off.

Manrico refills our glasses, and then leaves to talk to someone wearing a big watch seated at a nearby table. Manrico's girlfriend walks by and waves to us.

I turn to Morgan. "Lot of good-looking women down here."

"All it takes is money," he says. "You rent a house for the girl's family and give her a job. You could get one like her for four grand a year. You should move down here and start a business."

Four grand, that's cheaper than joining Lenny's prostitution ring.

Becker, Morgan, and I toast: "To money."

At two P.M., we get up to leave, siesta time. As I pass by Manrico's table, he tells me that the party has been postponed till tomorrow night. "Meet me here at five thirty," he says. "The bar should be open by then."

I stroll the dusty path through town and back to the Bonzi. Pink, green, and brown lizards shimmer on the ground like rhinestone jewelry. In the middle of the trail, a green creature five inches long, about the size of a muscle-bound bratwurst. A giant grasshopper. I tap it with my shoe to see if it will move along. Nothing. I throw a stick to see if it will fetch. Nothing. I give it wide berth.

El Playa is wacky, irregular. Prehistoric grasshoppers, black-market money, black-market booze, and *clausurado*—the floating, random, unscheduled federal holiday. This is a home for middle-aged guys who still want to kick some ass, play chicken with the Venezuelan government, party with beauty queens. Guys who aren't settling.

I could start a writing business here, teach English, and hire hot local girls. Or I could work for Manrico or Becker, or someone I meet at tomorrow night's party. All I need is $4,000 a year. There's nothing keeping me in Boston.

At 5:20 the next afternoon, I stop by Manrico's bar.

"How's the windsurfing?" he says.

"Great, you should come out."

"Nah."

"Is the party still on?"

"Nah." He smiles a molar-less smile. Edmundo appears and the two of them ignore me and confer over an unlabeled box.

No party. No dancing bartenders. No El Playa inner circle. Jilted by friends at home and now ditched by strangers. Haven't slept with a woman in months. This is just a stretch of bad luck; I'm overdue for a break.

I take the dusty path back to the Bonzi. Same rhinestone lizards, same giant grasshopper. A few more feet, another obstacle, a black, moth-eaten pile of fur. A dog covered with scabs and sighing. I think of my little Harold, his last days, his red eyes and droopy face. I hum a few bars of "Eleanor Rigby" and head to my hotel room.

Seven days down, seven more to go, and no choice in the matter. I slip into a routine.

Friday
Awake groggy.

Get to beach, forget wallet.

Lunch at Manrico's: Attractive bartender ignores me. Chubby bartender teaches me Spanish for "chicken," "beer," and "check please." I tip generously. She is the only person I talk to the entire day.

Later, check e-mail

One from Lenny:

Dear All,

Abe and I are inviting folks to watch the Sox at the Minuteman on Wednesday. We need more guys. RSVP.

—L

I RSVP.

Dearest Leonard,

Appreciate the invite. However, am in Venezuela this week and then Greece, South Africa, Southeast Asia, and Australia. Remember that dinner send-off two weeks ago?

—Burns

At bedtime, count eleven mosquitoes in room. Kill three and trap one in bathroom; others remain at large. Sleep under mosquito net, which is like sleeping inside a giant dry-cleaning bag.

Meds: one Ambien, one *cerveza*.

Saturday

Get to beach, forget water bottle and windsurfing gloves.

Holiday weekend, El Playa packed with families and couples. Bring windsurfing board to water's edge. Wave at bobbing kids to get out of way. They come closer. Wave at adults to get out of way. They wave back. Jump on board, dodge surgically enhanced grandma, and fall off. A beauty queen on beach laughs, points, and calls out in Spanish. I attempt clever repartee. "*No hablas Español. Solamente 'pollo,' 'cerveza,' 'la cuenta por favor.'*" No phone number. No response. Check please.

Lunch at Manrico's: Overweight bartender off for weekend. Eat alone and have disturbing thoughts. Five months ago, I managed projects and people. Now I manage minutiae.

Today's to-do list:
• Clip toenails.
• Talk to strangers.
• Tape holes in mosquito net.

Meds: two Ambien, one *cerveza*.

Sunday

On way to beach, see mangy black pile of dog. He looks like I feel. Offer my lunch. Dog gulps it down. Arrive at beach having forgotten nothing. Dog gets my lunch from now on.

No conversations. No incidents. Sun, surf, more nothing. Later, check e-mail.

One from Ricki:

Hey Burns,

Must be some typos in your blog. No way you're having a good time. With all those hot Latin guys, women not going to give a whiney Jew like you the time of day. You don't even speak Spanish. You may want to find a cheap hooker. Also the blog is boring, writing is lame. No wonder you're out of work.

—RRRRRR

The next night I substitute Lunesta for Ambien and have two nightmares I haven't had since childhood. In the first, I'm an infant in my bassinet. The room is dark except for a spotlight shining on my face. I'm warm, dry, and comfortable, but I want someone to hold me. I want to cry out, but I'm afraid to. What if no one comes? I lie in the darkness without making a sound.

In the second nightmare, I'm ten and the family has moved to a house with a noisy central air-conditioning that generates a pounding, metallic noise, the footsteps of a giant space monster. I tiptoe to my parents' bedroom but the door is closed. I go back to my room and spend the night hiding under my bed.

I imagine Dr. Moody's analysis of these dreams. "Randall, you've acted passive and helpless for forty-eight years. How is this behavior working for you?" Have I mentioned that Moody is a dick?

I awake to buzzing sounds outside the mosquito net: Three mosquitos intent on infecting me. I imagine oozing orifices, US consulates, and think of the scabby dog being mauled by insects all night. Poor Harold.

Under my net, I practice some self-soothing:

- In two days, I leave for Greece.
- In 108 days, I will be back in Boston.

After five minutes, I'm soaked in sweat.

Later, in front of the bodega, I find the dog heaped in a pile and wonder if he's done for. I hand over my chorizo and cheese on toast, his favorite. He springs back to life.

"Poor thing." It's a young woman's voice. Hopefully she's referring to the dog. I look up and see a brunette holding hands with a guy sporting a full head of hair. Nearby a young couple is on a bench playing kissy face. On another bench, another couple. And another. And another. One woman has dangly feather and metal earrings that resemble trout spinners. They also resemble the earrings I bought for someone I might have married seventeen years ago. I know where this is heading, but can't stop myself.

Dani, Cell A26
First encounter: *Framingham Tribune News*, October 1990

Dani was long, angular, and wore modest, earth-toned clothes and thick Buddy Holly-style glasses. She was one of those attractive women who never attracted attention. She worked across the hall. I was a part-time copy editor. She was a full-time reporter.

One day she popped into my cube and invited me for a drink. At the end of the evening, she said, "So, when are we going out again?" From then on, we were an item—no fussing, cursing, or biting.

There were other problems. For one, she had a master's in journalism from Columbia. She could look at a map, absorb it through some kind of osmosis, and in seconds determine where we needed to go. Math calculations down to two decimal points? She could beat most scientific calculators. Define words with more than four syllables? She was a walking SAT answer key. I couldn't figure out why she was interested in a guy who only had a bachelor's degree from U. Mass Boston. Worse still, Dani was ready to get married and have kids, and I still considered myself a kid.

The biggest problem, though, was that she didn't have a moody, sarcastic cell in her body. We rarely argued. She tolerated my sense of humor, but didn't enhance it. It began to drive me crazy. She was a smooth surface and I needed some friction to rub against to generate a spark.

The only time she got angry was when I suggested we take some time apart. She responded with a suggestion of her own: I could go to hell. She even drew me a map.

On my last day in El Playa, the wind is mild and steady. I decide to take Aurek's advice and try a smaller, faster board. Soon I'm zipping around pretty well.

But while trying to make a turn, I slip and smash my pinky toe against the mast. I keep sailing and assume the pain will go away. It doesn't. I'm done. Edmundo meets me at the shore and takes my gear. "*Adios*, Burns." A small improvement: I've graduated from *cabrón*.

I hobble back to my room, ice, and take three ibuprofen. A few hours later, the toe looks like it has a black eye. Probably broken.

Using the guidebook's instructions, I create a splint using surgical tape, an Allen wrench, and a flip-flop. If I don't aggravate it, the toe is supposed to feel better in a week.

I limp over to Manrico's bar hoping for a sentimental good-bye meal. Edmundo's son, Thug One, is behind the bar.

"How's the chicken curry?" I ask.

"Sorry, the kitchen is closed, *Señor Cabrón*."

"I know what *cabrón* means."

"*Sí, Señor Culo.*

At a nearby table, Manrico is conversing with a group of local guys. I notice that they all have big watches. His girlfriend is on his lap. Neither of them looks up. I'm now officially invisible.

Hot, cold, on, off: What's with the people down here?

I shuffle on to the pizza joint. The brunette I talked to in front of the bodega the other day is sitting at a table. She waves. A different guy is holding her nonwaving hand.

I sit alone across the room, order a black hooch, and consider the female situation on El Playa: It's been a disaster. I met a knife-wielding Pole with a boyfriend, a chubby local girl who barely speaks English, a beach heckler, and assorted women half my age with boyfriends. Some guidebook, some life-changing adventure.

My toe starts to throb and my worry turns to relief. If I broke a bone, this is my million-dollar wound, a legitimate reason for heading home—a catastrophic injury.

After dinner, I hop to the web café to check on flights home and download a travel-accident claim form.

My e-mail inbox has a note from Ricki.

Burns,

Haven't seen any blog entries in a while. You must be pretty anxious and depressed by now. How are all your little sleep rituals and cocktails? Ha! You're whacko, you know that?

I bet you're following every recommendation from some stupid guidebook and carrying it around like a bible.

How's the social life? Probably bad. You've got some strange ideas about love and women. You like the idea of having a relationship more than you like being part of one. A relationship is more than a sex date on Saturday or having a cute girl to parade around to your friends to convince them you're normal. You probably don't even know what I'm talking about.

—RRRRRR

I hit delete, check the weather in Greece, and after logging off, I buy a sandwich for the dog, and head back to the
Bonzi.

CHAPTER THREE: GREECE

On the road, all things are possible, whether you are
as mighty as the oak or as meek as the potato aphid.
—WALLACE PITTMAN

After a nine-hour red-eye flight, I exit a Greek subway at three P.M. in a part of Athens known as Omonia. It's like stepping back in time. Not exactly an ancient world. Or the birthplace of Western civilization. More like Times Square circa 1985: little porn shops, fast-food joints, and minimarts advertising rolling papers and baklava.

Two guys in skull caps walk by me pushing a shopping cart filled with kittens. I pat the decoy wallet around my neck. Pittman warns that Greece can get a little hairy, but it can't be anything like Venezuela. Greece is Europe. Greece is culture. Greece is the land of mythology, destiny, and Irene Skliva, Miss World 1996.

Three blocks from the subway, I spot a blue neon sign that may have been stolen from an all-night diner. The Kalamata Suites, my hotel.

The man sitting behind the check-in desk has a burning cigarette in one hand and a strand of worry beads in the other. He appears to be asleep.

The guidebook recommends using a word or two of the local language whenever possible. "*Signomi*," I say.

The worry beads start to move as the man's eyes creak open. He rests the cigarette in an overflowing ashtray and gestures for my passport.

Tacked to the wall behind him, there's a large blue and white flag covered with photos of celebrities: Alex Karras, Telly Savalas, Olympia Dukakis, Greg Louganis, George Michael, Tommy Lee, Jennifer Aniston.

"You like Jennifer Aniston?" he asks.

According to the guidebook, *neh* means "yes" and *ohkee* means "no." Or maybe it's the other way around. I play it safe and say: "Jennifer Aniston. *Sí, Neh, Ohkee.*"

"She Greek," the deskman says. "Tommy Lee? Greek. They all Greek. Many famous Greek peoples in United States. Democracy? Is Greek, but we let you use it."

He puffs on his cigarette, looks down at my Keen sandals, up at my backpack, and says, "Who greatest tennis player in the world?"

He flicks his worry beads. I feel sweat collecting under my money belt. Europe is supposed to be even more liberal than Massachusetts, so I try to think of someone politically correct.

"Serena Williams?"

Flick, flick, flick.

"No. She black. Pete Sampras, Greek."

He makes no move to sign me in or give me a room key. I look at the flag and photos again. "I always liked George Michael."

"He *poosty*, but Greek. Greg Louganis. *Poosty.* Greek."

He removes the cigarette from his mouth and rests it on the edge of the counter. Still no sign-in card or room key. My injured toe starts to throb.

"I believe I have a reservation. My name is Burns. Randall Burns."

He takes a puff from his cigarette and through a cloud of smoke asks: "What is healthiest food in the world?"

Flick, flick, flick.

I recall the guidebook's advice about displaying frustration in foreign countries: Don't. Ever.

I force a smile. "Mediterranean?"

"Mediterranean diet is Greek diet."

He opens my passport.

"United States. Bush is best president since Spiro Agnew. Bill Clinton? *Malaka.*" He makes a masturbating gesture with his fist, and then flips through the passport.

"You Boston?"

"*Si. Neh. Ohkee.*"

"Boston. Michael Dukakis, Paul Tsongas. Fred Smerlas."

"That's right. Fred Smerlas, All-Pro defensive lineman. Boston sportscaster. Great moustache."

He hands me a room card to fill out. The price is fifty euros, about sixty-five dollars, almost ten dollars cheaper than advertised.

"Does that include the breakfast buffet?"

Another cloud of smoke. "Problem with America? Too many Turkish people, too many Chinese people, too many Mexican people."

Better not ask about the buffet again or he'll add Jews to the list.

He looks at the completed room card.

"Only one night? Where you go? Turkey?"

Flick, flick, flick.

I'm not sure of the right answer, so I tell the truth. "*Si, Neh, Ohkee.* Whatever. No, I'm not going to Turkey."

"I teach you Greek: Turkey is *skata.* Turkey prime minister is *malaka.*" Again with the hand gesture.

"I was considering the island of Cyclonos."

He puts down his cigarette, leans in, and looks me in the eyes. "Owner of Buffalo Bills, his family from Cyclonos. Greek. Cyclonos is good, lot of pretty girls. You must learn to relax, my friend. Enjoy your stay."

OK, maybe the guy was just breaking my *arhithia*. And at least he didn't call me *malaka, poosty,* or *cabrón.*

My room is serviceable: a double bed, a blue and white flag above the headboard, a veneer armoire housing a picture-tube TV, and a showerless bathroom featuring a tub with a long-hosed spray handle that may have been stolen from a kennel or commercial kitchen.

I dump my backpack and decide to take the guidebook's "Quick and Dirty Walking Tour of Athens." The first stop is the Temple of the Olympian Zeus, which is a mile from the hotel. The temple's fifteen marble columns are fifty-six feet high. The book says the structure took 650 years to build. Maybe it's the ugly American in me. Maybe it's jet lag or an Ambien hangover. Or maybe it's just getting dark. Regardless, the Zeus reminds me of an unfinished parking garage.

Next I wander the narrow alleyways of the Monastiraki shopping district. In one boutique, a tourist couple is trying on hats and leather sandals. The woman giggles too much and her dangly earrings remind me of Dani. I leave without trying on anything.

More ruins. More marble columns. Moth-eaten dogs sleeping on ancient slabs. Poor Harold. I drift by outdoor tavernas trying not to notice the couples gazing into each other's eyes over warm candle light.

Sightseeing has never been my thing. As a kid, I didn't like to *just* look at pretty stuff. I drew on it, jumped on it, and threw it to see if it would survive a crash landing on a tile floor.

Sightseeing is now one of those activities, along with furniture shopping and apple picking, which I do only with a girlfriend, and even then, only as foreplay.

Dani once dragged me to a Vermont country fair. While she gazed upon the distant mountains, I contemplated her tanned thighs. While she marveled at the works of local artisans, I thought about her extensive bra collection: lace, push-up, plunge, backless, racerback.

Dying dogs, gazing couples, memories of Dani's fabulous rack. I haven't gotten laid, in what, six months? My mood is starting to spiral. Time for a gym.

Back at the Kalamata, there's a new desk clerk, an attractive thirty-something reading a magazine. She's pregnant and puffing on a cigarette. Same overflowing ashtray.

"*Signomi*," I say. "This may not be your area of expertise, but is there a health club nearby that's open tonight?"

Through a plume of smoke, she answers in a heavy accent: "Who greatest football player of all time?"

My toe starts to throb. I feel my jaw tighten. This Hellenic Who's Who is getting old.

I reexamine the photos on the wall behind her. "Let's see. It's not Alex Karras. Not Fred Smerlas. Must be Olympia Dukakis."

"Good one," she says in perfect English. "I couldn't resist. I heard my father busting on you last night. Here's a free pass to Stefanos Gym two blocks away, open till ten. Try to relax, *koukla mou*. Remember, you're in Greece."

Blog Entry, September 10
Omonia Square, Athens
The people, the sights, the culture—I could go on and on, but these Internet cafés charge by the hour.

The highlights:
People
• *As advertised: More warm and welcoming than the Mediterranean sunshine. (Lenny: The women are all smoking hot.)*
• *Big on relaxation and fun. Only thing that puts them in a bad mood: A no-smoking sign.*
Sights
• *How to describe the awesomeness of the Acropolis or the majesty of the Temple of the Olympian Zeus? Impossible, so let's move on.*
Culture
Went to Monastiraki, the party district last night. Ended up in a taverna: ouzo, bouzouki music, belly dancers, plate throwing, waiters setting fire to the floor. Danced around the flames and shards. Greeks yelled "opa." I yelled "huppa." Somehow I ended up back at my hotel before lunch.

Got to run. Catching an eighteen-hour, overnight ferry to the Greek island of Cyclonos for a week of windsurfing and plate Frisbee.

Antío sas,
—*Burns*

At three A.M., eight hours into the ferry ride, I am standing on the rear deck of the *Patsas Express*, wide awake. The deck seats are empty except for one in the far corner occupied by a tall blonde in low-slung jeans. She's gabbing on her cell phone in a language I don't recognize.

I look away and pretend to take in the Mediterranean. Engines hum, water whooshes and swirls behind the boat in an endless wake. The moon reveals passing islands that vanish into shadows. I glance back. Her belly-button ring twinkles in the moonlight.

I move to a seat at the opposite end of her row. White lights strung above us illuminate the now familiar blue and white flag.

She finishes her conversation, snaps the phone shut, and waves me over.

I start to move. Then reconsider.

What the hell am I doing? She must have a boyfriend. She's too young, too hot, too out of my league.

But why is she up here alone? More importantly, am I as mighty as an oak or as meek as a potato aphid?

I take the seat next to her and give her my only pickup line: "Having fun?" I ask.

"I am Nadine. From Russia."

"You speak English?"

"Speak the Russia and the Germany."

It turns out she *does* speak some English, including a few phrases this insomniac longs to hear:

"Me divorce."

"Whisky-whisky."

"You look like Bruce Willis."

She finishes her cigarette and throws the butt overboard. She lights another and hurls the lighter into the water.

Good arm.

She says she's going to Crete, a few stops before Cyclonos. We've got six hours together.

"Whisky-whisky?" she asks.

Before I can answer, she bolts inside, and soon emerges with two Cokes and two cups filled with ice. From her handbag, she extracts two nip-sized bottles of Johnny Walker Black.

Maybe Pittman is right, "On the road, all things *are* possible."

As she's preparing to throw an empty bottle overboard, I put my hand out to stop her. "Your velocity is good," I say. "You just need a little motion on that fastball."

Her eyes narrow. "What is this? What is this?"

Did I just blow it? What do I do now?

I caress her throwing hand. Her fingers are long, her nails are lacquered, and her skin smells like a fresh sliced apricot. I spread her fingers into a little peace sign around the bottle.

"Split fastball," I say.

She smiles and whips the bottle into the Mediterranean.

I hand her another empty. "Nadine, if you mix in some off-speed stuff, you'll be unhittable." I move her fingers into another grip and show her how to impart topspin. "Curveball," I say.

Splash.

She opens her purse and starts grabbing things: a tube of eyeliner, a plastic comb, a portable mirror, more tubes, more combs, a tampon.

As she throws, I yell out pitches. "Change-up, four-seam fastball, forkball, fuckball, spitball, snotball, red-eared slider."

She reaches for her wallet.

"No, no. Wait. Not that." I try to distract her. "How about a whisky-whisky?"

She nods.

As I'm fixing her a drink, I hear a splash. "Fuck the money," she yells to no one in particular.

I snap my head in her direction. She's smiling and holding her wallet. The cushion from the seat next to her is gone.

"Messing with you," she says.

I mix another round.

As we drink, she talks nonstop in what I'm guessing is Russian with some German thrown in. At one point, she flashes her middle fingers overboard and yells: "*Scheisse!*"

Then she waxes lyrical: "*Scheisse, scheisse,* meissa, mouse-a, moose-a."

I join in: "*Scheisse, scheisse,* fo-feissuh, banana fana fo feiss-uh."

"Bruce Willis, you funny man."

The engines rumble and the ferry begins a wide turn, then it backs up to a concrete pier. Nadine points beyond the pier to an illuminated switchback of roads leading to the top of a thousand-foot cliff.

"Santorini!" She jumps up and starts to dance.

I yell "Santorini!" and jump up to join her.

She brushes against me. She brushes against me again.

Then we're in a full-body embrace. My lips are inches from her right earlobe. It looks like a tiny grape. I take a nibble. Nadine groans and pushes me away. She shakes the ice in her empty cup. "Excuse," she says and heads inside.

Good idea, Nadine, this party could use a little more whisky-whisky.

I stand at the railing and wait.

And wait.

There's a commotion on the gangplank below. A uniformed man is gesturing to a young woman. Nadine. "Lady, lady, your ticket for Crete, *Kriti.*"

Nadine shouts: "Santorini! Santorini! Fuck the money. *Scheisse!* Banana fannah fo feishuh."

She stumbles onto the pier, a little purse in one hand and a seat cushion in the other. She smiles up at me and waves. "*Auf Wiedersehen,* Bruce Willis."

I watch her zigzag into the night.

The engines start to hum. Water begins to swirl behind the boat in an endless wake. The moon reveals a drifting still life of the night: a soda can, a crumpled cigarette pack, a fish gone belly up. I head inside for a whisky-whisky.

The ferry reaches the craggy Cyclonos coastline twelve hours later at five thirty P.M. Tambonia, the main town, is

ringed by low-rise, alabaster-white hotels and boulder jet-
ties. Moored fishing dories bob in the water. Taxies idle on a
stone quay. A scene straight from Pittman's guidebook. I exit
the ferry, hung over, and spot a stocky, middle-aged woman
standing in front of a black Volkswagen Beetle. She's holding
a sign that says "Club Monsoon Welcomes Rudolf Burns."

Must be a typo. I let it go and offer a smile as warm and
welcoming as the Mediterranean sunshine.

"I'm Randy Burns," I say, raising my sunglasses to be
polite.

The woman does not smile or raise her sunglasses. "I am
Charlotte. Welcome to Club Monsoon." She has a gravelly
accent that I'm guessing is German. Or Russian. Or Israeli.

"Was that you I e-mailed last month to make my reservation?" I ask in my friendliest tone.

"Ya. Now come."

Charlotte weaves her Beetle through the quiet streets of
Tambonia. Outside of town, rolling brown mountains rise like
the shoulders of the Minotaur. We pass boulders, hills dotted
with shrubs, small trees bent at forty-five degree angles, a flock
of shaggy goats, more boulders, more goats, fewer shrubs and
trees. A lone donkey on the hillside. After a night of Scotch
nips, my mouth feels as parched as the landscape.

Club Monsoon consists of a rustic main building and taverna, windsurfing facilities, and a dozen blue-trimmed, white
bungalows. The guidebook says the Monsoon offers a Club
Med experience at half the price.

"I will show you to your room," Charlotte says. "Come."

I follow obediently along a dirt path to a bungalow sporting an oversized wooden door. Inside there's a queen bed
facing a Mediterranean view: setting sun, rocky cliffs, miles
of azure sea between us and the nearest landmass. I imagine

sharing this scene with a Bennie or a Nadine or an Irene Skliva.

The next morning, I am in the Monsoon's taverna for a late breakfast. A blackboard on one wall describes the day's windsurfing conditions as "Beaufort 5," whatever that means.

The spread resembles the one at the Bonzi: cereal, cold cuts, bread, and fruit.

"*Guten morgen*, Mr. Burns." So Charlotte is definitely German.

Her skinny, severe glasses are like Zofia's. I'm not sure if this is a good omen or bad. She directs me to a table for two overlooking the beach. Glass salt and pepper shakers, a flower vase, and an unlit candle form a perfect arc above the silverware. A woman would love this.

I scan the room for available women. There's only one, seated alone by the window, an extra place setting and a steaming coffee cup opposite her. She looks to be in her thirties and is wearing a black T-shirt for the band Scorpions and not much else. Her thighs are coppery, her lips are glossed, and her earrings are hooped. She notices me noticing her and looks away.

Charlotte fills my juice glass and confiscates the extra setting.

"*Danke*," I say. Other than the lone woman, the other diners all appear to be in their sixties and speaking German. "Is everyone here German?" I ask.

Charlotte scowls. "I am Austrian." She points to the buffet.

Two older women look on from a nearby table. They probably feel sorry for me eating alone. One of the women is wearing a jean jacket over her bathing suit. She's wearing punchy red lipstick. Her gray hair is long and plaited. She was probably a beauty in her day. Maybe she has a daughter. I smile. She smiles and toasts me with her juice glass.

At the buffet table, I start piling on the food.

Next to me, a blond guy about my height and age is filling two plates. "*Guten morgen,*" he says.

"Good morning," I say.

He introduces himself as Karl. We appraise each other. He's wearing the same Scorpions T-shirt as the coppery girl. Bummer. I am in full windsurfing regalia: sunproof shirt, swim tights, rubber booties.

"Wind is not so very much strong today," Karl says. "Beaufort 5. A day for 7.2."

I still don't know what a Beaufort is, but I do know that a 7.2-meter sail is larger than anything I've ever used. Karl has just established which one of us is the hotshot windsurfer.

"Good idea," I say. "How far is the windsurfing center from here?"

Karl points down the beach. "Not so much far. See you on water."

"See you on water."

He sits down with the girl, reaches over to rub her thigh, and kisses her on the mouth. I turn away and watch a paper bag on the beach spiral up and out of sight.

The view on the way to the windsurfing center is disquieting: swaying trees, spraying white caps, several sixty-year-olds on small boards zipping around.

"I'm Randy Burns," I say to the guy behind the counter. "Or maybe Rudolf Burns."

He checks a clipboard. "Not on list."

He looks at my outfit. "You know the water start?"

The key difference between a beach start, which I can do thanks to Edmundo, and a water start, which I can't do, is that you perform the former in two feet of water while standing on a sandy bottom. The latter you typically perform offshore in water over your head.

"I've seen it performed on TV," I say.

He doesn't laugh.

"You know the jibe?" he asks.

A jibe is a maneuver in which you change direction at top speed. Edmundo, Aurek, and Zofia can jibe. I say nothing.

After a few moments of silence, he points to a small cove a hundred yards away. "Tadpole Beach," he says.

At the Tadpole windsurfing center, two teenage guys run out to greet me. They know my name. They are expecting me. They tell me I am going to be the only tadpole this week. I feel a spasm in my nearly healed toe: Empty windsurfing center, remote island, cranky women in severe glasses. I'm being punished for something.

I ask about the weekly barbecue, the one with the beer and bikinis featured on the company website.

"Only for summer," the taller guy says.

I point to the sun. "What do you call this?"

"Autumn," the shorter guy says.

A gust of wind kicks up some sand that ricochets off my sunglasses and stings my cheek.

I point to the whitecaps and spraying sea. "I'm a low-intermediate," I say. "Can I windsurf in this?"

"We give you small, slow sail. If very too much wind, you blow to other side of cove. Water shallow there, you paddle back."

A hundred yards across the cove there's another windsurfing center, Viva Windsurf, Pittman's top pick for partying. Even at a distance, I can see that the place is hopping—guys waving beer bottles and girls in stringy bathing suits.

Originally, I tried to sign up with Viva, but like Club Monsoon, it's a German-speaking company and their e-mail English wasn't very good. Being a good consumer, I had questions.

- How far are you from the ferry?
- Do you stock light beer?
- What did your grandparents do in World War II?

After a few days, they stopped responding to my e-mails, so I went with Club Monsoon, the guidebook's backup recommendation.

I am set up with a windsurfing rig that includes a 3.7-meter sail, which is about the size of a king-sized sheet. I point to a sail about the size of a wedding tent.

"How big is that one?"

"It is 7.2 meter. No good for you," says the tall guy. *Karl's sail.*

The wind must be pushing twenty-five miles per hour, stronger and gustier than anything at Mojito. The water is also choppier with waves about three feet high. I decide to make the best of the Beaufort 5 situation, manage a wobbly beach start, and start whipping across the cove.

Through my rubber booties, the water is noticeably colder than the water in Mojito.

My sail has a transparent panel for seeing obstacles on the other side. I look for buoys, oversized waves, or oncoming windsurfers but notice, in the distance, only a beach full of wasted girls and chest-bumping guys. Why isn't anyone from Viva windsurfing today? Novices.

I pull in the sail to pick up speed. The nose of my board shudders.

I am approaching the Viva end of the cove, which means I have to turn around, a maneuver called a tack that I've never been good at. I shudder.

I slide the sail toward the back of my board to tack. The trick in tacking is knowing when to hop to the other side of the board, slide the sail forward to catch the wind, and begin sailing in the other direction. Tacking is as confusing as it sounds. If the process does not go smoothly, you stall out, oversized waves knock you off the board, the wind blows the sail onto your head, and you find yourself in the situation I'm in now.

As the sail presses my face under water, salty water burns in my nostrils. A breath would be good about now. The sail pushes me farther underwater until my feet touch bottom. I push off and swim out from under the sail.

A crowd at Viva has gathered to watch. I pretend to ignore them and climb back on the board, which is now drifting out of the cove toward Turkey, which I hear is full of *skata* and *malakas*.

At this point, a novice windsurfer might give up and paddle his board to the nearest beach. But I am not a novice.

I attempt to lift the sail, but the wind blows it out of my hands. A four-foot wave tosses me back into the water. I rinse and repeat several times. Each time, I drift farther toward Ankara. In the distance, I notice a guy from the Tadpole windsurfing center who has stopped what he's doing to watch.

For the low-intermediate windsurfer, there is only one thing more humiliating then being unable to reboard your board, and that's having the beach staff rescue you with a powerboat, while a beach full of drunken douchebags watches.

I scramble back onto the board, stand, and grab the uphaul rope. A second Tadpole guy joins the first to watch.

I lift the sail a foot out of the water and rest for a second. A disc twinges in my back. My arms are getting tired. One of the Tadpole guys wades into the water toward the powerboat.

I yank the sail out of the water and pull it forward. The wind catches and I start moving. I give a thumbs-up. The Viva crowd disperses.

The next gust of wind blows me back in the drink. Submerged, shivering, and sneezing salt water out of my nose, I paddle my rig back to the beach.

"So much fun?" the Tadpole guys asks.

"Not so much."

A gust sends sand ricocheting off my sunglasses.

During the ensuing week, the punishment continues.

Day *Eins*

I am the only American at Monsoon. It's like being in a foreign film with bad subtitles.

Act 1, Breakfast

Me: I read that you rent mountain bikes for five euros a day.

Charlotte: Bike insurance?

Me: For what?

Charlotte: If someone take bike or bike break.

Me: Is there a lot of crime on the island?

Charlotte: Additional five euro for week.

Me: Can I take that as a "yes"?

Charlotte: With bike lock, seven euro more, plus deposit. More juice?

Day *Zwei*

Awake with vague feelings of isolation.

Act 1, Take 2: Breakfast

Though I sit in the same seat every meal, my table is always set for two. Today, Charlotte grumbles as she removes the extra setting. I am an inconvenience, an untouchable, because I have no dining partner and everyone else does.

Act 2: Lunch

Karl and his coppery girlfriend are now wearing matching Lynyrd Skynyrd T-shirts. She feeds him cold cuts while he massages her thigh. I try not to think of oxytocin, the feel-good hormone that is released when we're fed or touched. Oxytocin—no relation to OxyContin—is what bonds mothers to babies, lovers to each other, and humans to all things warm and fuzzy. Oxytocin is the "*ox*" when someone signs a letter "*oxoxox*." I am suffering from a severe *ox* deficiency.

Act 3: Rest of the Day

Wind hits Beaufort 6, about thirty miles per hour. Following a powerboat rescue, I'm given a 2.5-meter sail, a little larger than a baby blanket, and still spend the rest of the day submerged. At dinner, Karl offers to teach me to water start. He is wearing white Capri pants and clogs. I decline his generous offer.

Day *Drei*

Windsurf alone, eat alone, sleep alone.

Experience loneliness that would have broken Papillon.

Day *Vier*

Weather sunny, mood overcast. Mojito and Cyclonos: resort islands, off-season, no available women. I've bet my severance on a guidebook riddled with factual errors. I look for a mangy dog to feed, but don't find one.

Day *Fünf*

More of the same. Starting to feel as if I'm shrinking, fading, becoming lighter, hollow. I need to connect to someone, find an anchor or I'm just going to drift away like a broken kite or a lost balloon.

Consult the guidebook's "Things to Do on Cyclonos," which recommends Viva's Weekly Dance Party.

Call Viva to ask if I can attend.

"*Nein.*"

Go anyway.

German crowd, American hip-hop. Ouzo and lager. Guys without body hair, dancing girls on the bar. Ouzo and pilsner. Three casts, no bites, a too-friendly guy in a proboscis-style Speedo. Ouzo and ouzo. Fifty euros later, hate party, hate life, hate ouzo.

Day *Sechs*

No gym on island. Create a calendar. Hang on bathroom door. Cross off today. Only two days more to go on Cyclonos. Otherwise, ditto.

E-mail Pittman with a list of inaccuracies in his book. Receive an immediate response:

Dear Mr. Randolf,

Thank you for submitting "Fifteen Factual Errors in Your Piece-of-Shit Guidebook." We appreciate the opportunity to consider your work for publication.

Next Year in Saigon!

—W. Pittman

That night Charlotte says, "In Greece, it is not proper to eat dinner alone." She seats me with the two older women from breakfast.

The women are Swiss and probably in their sixties. We eat *mezethes*, Greek appetizers: sardines, squid, and octopus. We drink ouzo. We eat more unappetizing appetizers: frog legs and snails. One of the women excuses herself.

The remaining woman, the one who was probably a beauty in her day, moves her seat closer. She tells me I'm fit. She tells me about her three divorces and says I'm smart for

not getting married. She says the magic words: "Don't settle."
I move my seat closer.

She feeds me lamb sweetbreads, something I swore I'd
never eat. Her elbow glances my chest. Is she hitting on me?
I give her the once-over: Distressed skin stretched over a skull
face. Bummer.

More ouzo, more weird food.

She says the Swiss are a very sexual people and don't enter
menopause until their late sixties. Once again, I give her the
once-over: withering legs streaked spidery blue. Why couldn't
she be young, like Nadine?

She tells me she can yodel and is leaving the next morning. She invites me back to her room.

I awake the next morning with a *mezethes* hangover. I
recall the older woman's room, the couch, the knuckles of her
neck, reaching under her blouse, a sick octopus in each hand,
a hairy herring, me saying: "I really have to go, seafood aller-
gies." Her saying, "No worries." Cool lady.

At breakfast, Charlotte seems unhappy with me. I'm
unhappy with me: I just blew a chance to get laid. But Nadine
was young and beautiful and made the first move. I've still got
it. I'm not ready to settle.

Blog Entry, September 19
Somewhere on Cyclonos

Here in Greece, the partying never stops. Met a Russian
blonde on the ferry. Dancing. Champagne. Making wishes and
tossing pennies into the Mediterranean. Too bad she got off on
Santorini or I might be married now.

Learned to water start like a pro.

Should have come for a month instead of a week.

Auf Wiedersehen,

—Burns

Today is Yom Kippur, a day for reflection. I reflect on the cruelty of the fates and my stunted spiritual development.

When I was eight, I developed a ritual designed to assure my future status as a Hall-of-Fame athlete:

1) Got into bed and swallowed three times to open private line to God.

2) Repeated the following prayer three times:

"Please make me the greatest baseball player who ever lived with the most RBIs, home runs, and highest batting average. Also the greatest football player who ever lived. I want to be a running back or a wide receiver, either way, most yards would be great, and if we can avoid any knee surgeries that would be good too. And the greatest basketball player who ever lived, overall points would be fine. You can give the most rebounds to someone else; I don't want to be a *chazzer*. While you're at it, can you please make sure my parents buy me that chameleon I want, you know the one that looks like a little monkey and has a tongue that can shoot out of its mouth to snag a cricket a foot away?"

3) Disconnected by swallowing three times.

My parents bought me the chameleon. But after three months, it went the way of all flesh. I then decided waiting twenty years to be inducted into the Hall of Fame was too daunting and abandoned the ritual to focus on other childhood projects, such as learning to smoke a cigar.

At thirty-five, I attempted to reconnect with my spirituality by donating time and money to a local temple. I volunteered ten hours a month and donated 5 percent of my salary, excluding stock market gains, real estate appreciation, 401k matching, and employee stock options. Three years of volunteering didn't produce a single date. Faith has its limits.

Since then, there's been little volunteering, praying, or temple-going, but I have developed an appreciation for the universe and the unseen mysteries of life: Wi-Fi and compound interest, intuition and compulsion, the calming effects of a sleep blindfold, a Karen Carpenter song on a rainy Monday, the smell of greasy french fries coming from the Monsoon taverna.

Charlotte greets me with a worried look as I enter the dining room, perhaps because I skipped breakfast and lunch. I don't mention Yom Kippur or that I'm supposed to be fasting. She puts her hand on my shoulder and guides me to my seat. My shoulder tingles from her touch. At this point, I'll take my oxytocin any place I can get it.

The table has only one setting. I assume it's because she's being thoughtful and not because she thinks I'm hopeless.

I notice Karl and his girlfriend sitting in silence, hands in their respective laps. No massaging of thighs or kissy-face over the sauerbraten. She's wearing glasses, no makeup, and a ripped T-shirt for the heavy-metal band Rammstein, Germany's answer to Black Sabbath. He's wearing a linen suit. Something must be up.

As I'm finishing my linzertorte, Karl comes over.

"Are you feeling much well?" he asks.

"Yes, *danke*."

"Join us for a wine?"

I don't like this guy. Every morning at the buffet, he asks what size sail I'll be using. Then he spends the rest of the meal massaging his girlfriend's snatch under my nose. Does he get off on humiliating me?

As I'm wishing I could say in German, "Hey *malaka*, leave me the fuck alone," Charlotte carries a chair and a wine glass to the couple's table. She removes their untouched meals. I am seated opposite the girlfriend, Sabine, who fills my wine glass.

"In Greece, it is not normal to eat alone," Sabine says.

So I've heard.

Sabine's English is accented but pretty good. It's disconcerting that my lack of company has attracted so much attention.

"Actually I'm a travel writer on assignment." I show her Pittman's book. "The job involves a lot of solo travel, but I've gotten used to it. I'm heading to South Africa next and then Southeast Asia."

Sabine smiles in approval and leans in closer to me: "Charlotte says you are from Boston. You like Aerosmith?"

We exchange the names of our favorite songs.

Sabine removes her glasses and strokes her ponytail. Karl picks at the wine label.

It turns out that Sabine once worked for Siemens in Boston. We talk about the Cars, the J. Geils Band, and other Boston groups.

She takes out a cigarette and offers me one. As we smoke, Karl waves at the smoke wafting in his face and mocks a cough. She smiles and fingers her ponytail.

"How is your windsurfing?" she asks.

"Ever heard of the song, 'The Wreck of the Edmund Fitzgerald'?" I ask.

"No."

"How about the movie, *The Perfect Storm*?"

It takes a second to register, and then she laughs. Even without makeup, her skin is smooth, not a line on her face.

She touches my wrist and I feel a jolt of oxytocin. "I hate windsurfing," Sabine says. She is stroking her ponytail again. I find myself stroking the back of my head and trying not to look at her perfect, caramel-colored thighs.

She's flirting with me and Karl is glaring at both of us. Is he pissed off with me? Or her? Whose idea was this little party?

Was this another of Charlotte's attempts to improve my social life? Maybe Karl wants to break the tension between them by introducing Sabine to the one person at this resort who's worse off than she is. Or there's the long-shot option: Sabine agreed to go windsurfing if Karl would watch her bang another guy. I'm not in Boston anymore and all things are possible.

Karl pulls out a new iPhone. He swipes the screen a few times, and tilts the screen in my direction. "Tomorrow, the Beaufort 7."

Sabine taps my arm again. "You like James Taylor?" she asks.

OK, I get it. They're both using me. I'm nothing more than a prop in their little drama.

I turn to Karl. "I was thinking of getting an iPhone. How do you like it?" I worked for a computer magazine. I know how to bond with guys over gadgets.

He shows me the onscreen keyboard, the GPS, and the camera. Out of the corner of my eye, Sabine is picking at the wine label.

"How about if I take a picture of you two?" I ask. She's not happy but obliges.

Then she excuses herself.

Karl and I agree to meet on the beach tomorrow. Us middle-aged *malakas* got to stick together.

At breakfast the next morning, the extra table setting is back. Wood slats in the taverna roof rustle ominously. I glance at Sabine and Karl: She's massaging *his* thigh. They don't acknowledge me.

A teenager comes over, removes my extra table setting with a flourish, and offers me juice.

"Where's Charlotte?" I ask.

"She is feeling not so much well."

The teenager closes the window near me. "Beaufort 7," he says. "A great day, no?"

"A great day for a small-craft warning."

I look out at the boulders, cliffs, and scree. No wonder this place is so desolate: Anything green was probably blown into the sea centuries ago.

I wander into the lobby to check my e-mail.

One from my mother:

Hi Sweetheart,

Your father and I are so glad you're having a nice time. We just knew you would. Nothing new here. Don't hurry home. Same old. Same old.

Love,

—Mom & Dad

One from Uncle Heshie:

Randall,

Love your crib.

One question: When does the maid come?

—HM

I don't have a maid. Distressful imaginings: Uncle Heshie hosting wild parties. Merlot on the throw pillows, pesto on the tufted rugs, footprints on the ceiling.

One from Rachel:

Dearest All,

Arturo and I are having an open house . . . at our gorgeous, new apartment. That's right we're moving in together! Our new 50-inch flat panel will be hooked up so we can all watch the last game of the season and celebrate the Sox clinching the division.

Please RSVP so we know how much deep-fried cheesecake to order.

—A&R

I consider a snarky RSVP, but then think better of it. And finally, one from Ricki:

Hey Burns,

Another bullshit blog from the world's biggest sissy. Glad you had fun with the Russian blonde. Clearly, you're still obsessed with other people's hair because you don't have any.

But instead of writing all that baloney, you might want to read up on the country you're visiting. Some recent State Department headlines for Greece: "Avian flu outbreak," "Strikes, Riots, and Grenade-Firing Terrorists," "Arsonists Set 100 Fires in One Day."

Didn't your little travel bible mention any of this?

Also, wanted to share a funny story. I started talking to a BRUNETTE named Nickie at a party. She was describing the cheapest guy she ever dated. The guy put heel taps on all his shoes, even his flip-flops. He drove a '91 Honda Civic with a tiny engine that sounded like an electric pencil sharpener. I said: Was his name Burns? We couldn't stop laughing. Did you really keep a spreadsheet of all your girlfriends? Good luck finding someone to put up with all your crap.

Also, just saw your itinerary—next stop is South Africa, the world's biggest shit show. You're fucked my friend.

Best,

—RRRRRR

I stare at the screen until a bouncing bratwurst appears. Outside the window, windsurfers are being blown off their boards and others are quitting for the day. The sky is overcast. I feel a Beaufort 9 headache coming on.

Venezuela sucked. Greece sucks. And South Africa will probably suck more. Pittman is full of shit and I'm out $12K. Heshie is trashing my apartment. Ricki's still Ricki, only nastier. Rachel's paired off, no one else is writing me, and once

Lenny hooks up, I'll be the only member of the Chronic Single's Club.

The Dark Place is beckoning.

I swallow three times, put my hands on the keyboard, and pray for guidance. The bratwurst disappears, the computer screen illuminates, and I'm bathed in a white glow. A blank Word document appears before me. I stare at the perfect emptiness.

A college writing instructor once advised me: "Write the book you'd want to buy."

I begin to type: *Finding Someone to put up with Your Crap*

I read it back. Then I delete it and type: *The Loneliest Planet.*

Not quite. I type: *The Chronic Single's Handbook*

I roll the title around in my mouth: a little bitter, but it works.

The Chronic Single's Handbook
Chapter One
Finding Your Match: The Five Romantic Personalities
1) Martyrs

- *Feel everything intensely, especially love, rejection, and Red Sox playoff losses.*
- *Claim to know exactly what they want in a mate; say smug things like "I will never settle."*
- *Spend most Saturday nights alone.*
- *Cry at crapola love stories like* The Bridges of Madison County.
- *Capable of great happiness when involved and great bitterness when single.*
- *Examples: Jackson Browne, Vincent van Gogh, Billie Joe McAllister.*
- *Favorite quote: "My heart is your piñata."*

2) Settlers

- Martyrs who marry suddenly because of an external event like a scary health problem, a milestone birthday, or an aging parent who wants to see them hooked up.
- Husbands who settle are often happy with this arrangement.
- Their wives often seek divorce after children leave for college.
- Examples: Too many to list.
- Favorite quote: "I'll have the baked chicken, no skin, butter, salt, oil, or bread crumbs. And a glass of water with no ice."

3) Mercenaries

- Approach love as if it were just another transaction, to-do item, or mission.
- Emotionally detached with flat, even moods.
- Tend to be content instead of happy.
- Examples: Ted Bundy, Dirty Harry, Angelina Jolie.
- Favorite quote: "Kill them all and let God sort them out."

4) Bonders

- Born with good brain chemistry.
- Can connect with most anyone and be happy in most situations.
- Are good as friends, but boring as lovers.
- Examples: Anyone who manages to stay married more than two years.
- Favorite quote: "Let a smile be your umbrella on a rainy day."

5) Barnacles

- Don't have the stomach for dating.
- Always in a relationship—for better or worse.

- *A bad choice for spouseless vacations; without a partner they glom on to you.*
- *Examples: Zsa Zsa Gabor, Elizabeth Taylor, Mickey Rooney, and other people married at least eight times.*
- *Favorite quote: "Needy people are the luckiest people in the world."*

I save the file to my thumb drive and slip it into my pocket. My headache is gone. Next stop, Cape Town.

CHAPTER FOUR: SOUTH AFRICA

Channel the spirit of the wind and
champion the heart of the nomad.
—W. PITTMAN

Boarding the flight to South Africa, I scan the plane for seat 36C and don't like what I see: baby, baby, baby, fat person eating something greasy, pimply teenager groping his girlfriend, unshaven guy with a bad cough, people blowing their noses and rubbing their eyes. The air is filled with a sour smell that is either sweat or a burning toupee.

Greece didn't deliver, but at least it wasn't dangerous. Now Pittman has me heading to another country like Venezuela, where murder and mayhem are national pastimes.

OK, the State Department says most people who visit South Africa get out alive. And my well-traveled cousin Joey said that South Africa is full of hostels, backpacker chicks, and blonde NGO PhDs in cargo shorts. I'll have three weeks to prove him and Pittman wrong. By then, if I'm still miserable, I can say I survived the world's biggest shit show and go home.

A slender torso is leaning into 36C. I pause and clear my throat.

"Sorry." By the accent, I guess she's Irish.

She glances at my Boston Celtics T-shirt and sherpa-lined yoga pants.

"American?" she asks.

"Lucky guess."

"Anyone ever tell you that you look like Bruce Willis?"

When she leans back to draw the seat buckle low and tight across her waist, her breasts stir in her black sweater.

"I'm Randy," I say, holding out my hand.

"Ha! I bet you are. I'm Jeanette."

Her hand is warm and scented.

It turns out Jeanette and I have a lot in common. She likes to jog. I like to jog. She's an executive at a computer company. I used to work for a computer magazine.

She applies lip gloss. We talk. I tell the truth. Mostly.

"You were a senior editor at *Personal Computer Computing Week*?" Jeanette asks. "I subscribe to that magazine. Must have been fun."

"It was a nice gig," I say. "We got to play with the latest tech toys. I had a little hat with a propeller on it. We had a good group of writers and editors."

Actually, the day after I was laid off, I traded the hat to a homeless guy for a cigarette. In the five months since, only one coworker has e-mailed to see how I'm doing. Time to change the subject. "Where you headed?" I ask Jeanette.

"I'm going home to Joburg to see family."

She runs a finger across her lips. I find myself running a finger across my lips.

As she talks about her company's new mobile computing products and her cats, I am lulled by her voice and my thoughts drift.

Great mouth. Great hair. Great figure. No wedding band.

Flirty, age-appropriate, flying alone.

What's wrong with her?

When we reach cruising altitude, a flight attendant asks for my cocktail order. I request a beer and turn to Jeanette. "Since you're a loyal reader, your first five drinks are on me."

"Clever lad. Sorry, I'm going to nod off in a few minutes," she says.

"Oh, come on. You're not going to stay up and party?" I ask. "The pilots said you were a lot of fun."

"Ha, ha. I'm an old bird. Got to have a sleep. I'm meeting up with my husband's parents tomorrow."

I reach for my Ambien and order a second beer. Jeanette is out in minutes. I wash down a double dose of sleeping pills with beer number one. After dozing for half an hour, I wake up, wired. The cabin lights have been dimmed. Jeanette is asleep and her body is four inches from mine. It's like we're in bed together.

I trace her glossy mouth with an imaginary finger. I nibble her chin with imaginary lips, and then stop before I'm hand-cuffed by a real-life sky marshal.

After beer number two, I glance at Jeanette in her snug sweater, cram the empty into the seat pocket, and fall into a deep oblivion that lasts the rest of the flight.

At noon the next day, I exit the Cape Town terminal. A graying black man holds a sign that says "Randy Burns."

"Welcome to Cape Town, my friend," he says. "I'm Sam."

I shake his hand and out of habit say, "I'm Randy."

"I know, I wrote the sign." He laughs and motions to a nearby minivan.

As we drive down a tree-lined highway called N2, Sam chats away in a soothing, singsongy African accent. "You're going to have a great time. Everyone loves the Frisky Bonobo hostel. Even folks your age. Anyone ever say you look like Bruce Willis?"

Cinder block shacks appear on the side of the road. There's a woman wearing a Rolling Stones T-shirt with a dirty sari around her waist. A group of children play with a stick, bare feet kicking up clouds of dust. Several men roll a tire toward the highway. One guy is carrying a red metal container with a long gray spout, a gas can. I recall warnings about necklacing, tire fires, and impromptu roadblocks.

The minivan speeds up.

The guidebook offers succinct advice about visiting these townships: Don't. Ever.

Soon the shacks are replaced by office towers, restaurants, and parking lots flanked by a high, flat mountain. I begin to relax.

"Table Mountain," Sam says. "A good hike. The waterfront here is also nice. Lots of beautiful ladies, Mr. Randy Randy."

He raises his palm toward me and I return the high five.

We pull up in front of the Frisky Bonobo on Long Street, the main drag in the backpacker part of Cape Town. Hidden away from the office towers, the area is crammed with Western-style bars and African-themed restaurants: Mama Afrika, Five Flies, Bushman. Like many buildings in the area, the Bonobo has a large balcony that would be perfect for throwing Mardi Gras beads. But now the streets are empty except for a few black teenagers milling around in soiled yellow smocks that say, "Security." It's two in the afternoon.

Sam and I sit in silence for a minute, and then he gestures toward my door. I get out of the cab, grab my bag, and pull out some loose cash from my pocket.

"Put that away!" Sam is no longer singy or songy.

I duck, freeze, and get back in the car. I reach for the cash.

"For fok sake, man. Keep your hands down!" He snaps. "Don't be flashing money around here."

"But it's the middle of the day on a main street."

"Just listen to me, boy."

I hold the cash below the dashboard and count out 200 South African rand, about thirty dollars. Sam whips it into his pocket.

A gaunt, black man with rheumy eyes and a red skull cap calls out to us from an alley: "You want some crazy, good fun?" A kid in a soiled yellow security smock walks by ignoring the rheumy man and us.

Finally Sam points to my door. "OK, my man, time to go." Then he says in a softer tone: "Don't worry, friend. It's safer here now than it's been in years."

That night at the Bonobo, I head to the living-room bar and order the house specialty, Carling Black Label. At the bar, girls in halter tops. On the couch, girls in short-shorts. On the balcony, girls in ripped T-shirts. Average age: twenty-two, even with me in the room.

I glance at my watch and notice what is either a large freckle or a liver spot on my wrist. I stash the hand in my pocket. In planning this trip, I knew I was going to be traveling with people young enough to be my kids. To prepare, I had my back and chest waxed, and every day, I shave my head to hide the gray. But I'm not fooling anyone. Bruce Willis is in his fifties.

I start to feel annoyed, isolated, unwelcome, like I'm back home among the twenty-something kids who've overrun my neighborhood, who mock people my age, give us an ironic face slap by embracing all the worst crap from our generation: Ron Jeremy, the Green Hornet, Mountain Dew, beer in a can, Pabst in anything, clothes with holes, tie-dye, Hush Puppies, headphones worn outdoors, ski hats worn indoors, hoodies on people who aren't defendants or gym teachers.

These kids reject our best stuff: chest hair on guys, skirts on girls, money, shoelaces, size thirty-two waists, size two dresses, caring about your career, caring about your job, caring about anything.

Recently the twenty-something baristas at Starbucks, cashiers at CVS, and bouncers at the Clink Lounge have started addressing me as "sir," as if I've been retired by society, yanked by life's hook, like I'm one of those guys who can't get a hard-on without a prescription.

Lenny says to accept it; the kids have taken over, like we did in our day. *Not helpful, Lenny.* The young guys get the attention of women their age, of women our age, of Madison Avenue. Forty-something men are invisible. I glance at two girls on the couch wearing Minnie Mouse T-shirts and pink shorts. Their belly buttons sparkle and wink. I wink back.

In the Bonobo living room, I spot one other middle-aged bald guy standing by the foosball table, hands in his pockets. His eyes are tired. His face is unshaven and flecked with gray. His unripped T-shirt says "Ozzie Softwear."

He sidles up to me, hands over some cash, and says, "Hey, mate. Order us a couple coldies. This one's on me."

He introduces himself as Steve from Sydney. He tells me he just sold his T-shirt shop on Bondi Beach and is traveling around South Africa for a few months. "Thirty-eight and semiretired," he says.

"I just got a severance check and I'm traveling for a few months myself," I say. We high-five.

Turns out we're both taking the same bus tour up the coast in two days.

I point out two girls with corporate haircuts and black leggings.

"Dutch birds. Untouchable," he says. "Late twenties, I'd say. They'll be on the tour too, but won't give a guy the time of day."

"And them," Steve nods toward two girls and a guy wearing beige ski hats, "I wouldn't even bother with them." The guy has a T-shirt with an American flag in the shape of a snarling pit bull. The girls are giggling and spitting beer on each other.

"America's finest," Steve says. "The guy's name is Matt. A dipshit. The girls, Tara and Ivy, aren't so fit as you can see. They're on the bus tour too. Aren't we lucky?"

I consider canceling, but recall the refund policy: "Don't even think about it."

Steve suggests a change of scenery, an Irish bar across the street called Kimba O'Reilly's.

We pass the Bonobo's front desk where I notice a sign on the wall: "After dark, we recommend hiring a taxi instead of walking." Steve ignores the sign. I follow.

The scene at O'Reilly's resembles the scene at the hostel: same crowd of annoying kids, same old tired music. The only difference is there are now more guys.

When Van Morrison's "Moondance" starts to play, Matt, the American kid with the snarling T-shirt, starts crooning into a beer bottle and moves onto the dance floor. Even though his Teva sandals are held together with safety pins, he made good time getting here. Periodically he bops over to the two untouchable Dutch girls and thrusts his bottle in their faces to get them to join in. They ignore him. The guy is a douche but he's got balls. The back of my head starts to itch. I scratch and detect some stubble.

Steve and I are nursing our beers at a high-top table when two attractive black women approach. "I am Naledi," one says. She is tall and slender.

"And I am Ola," the other says. She is shorter with round cheeks and straightened chin-length hair.

I wait for Steve to make a move. He moves on Naledi, gives me wink, and leads her onto the dance floor.

Ola is twenty-one years old and has a singsongy African accent like Sam's. Her skin is at least 80 percent cocoa.

"Having fun?" I ask.

"Always," Ola says, dancing in place.

"You like Van Morrison?"

"Who?"

She drains her beer, grabs my hand, and leads me onto the parquet floor. She shimmies. I shimmy. She musses her hair. I muss my stubble.

Ola is wearing a low-cut T-shirt. An exposed bra strap looks like a ribbon, a gift for the right guy. She brushes against me and the oxytocin starts to flow.

Some might say Ola is voluptuous. I would say she is about five four, 135 pounds with a Body Mass Index of twenty-three, the upper range of normal. But her *melónes grandes* are the kind you don't find on a slender woman. True, I usually go for super-skinny types, but tonight I am open to all options.

Ola smiles and leans into me. I feel her breasts upon me, intent and urgent.

In recent years, I've developed mixed feelings about large breasts. On young women, a full rack was a taunt, a tease, a reminder of my expired youth, something I was never going to see, touch, or kiss. On women my age, I didn't want to see, touch, or kiss them. They were best supported, secured, and clothed. In the bedroom, I preferred women my age to wear a bra or a T-shirt, a covering, something to leave what were fabulous two decades ago to my imagination. The dying octopus experience with the old woman on Cyclonos was a cruel reminder. Perfectly nice woman, slim even, but the expiring breasts depressed me.

I pull Ola closer. These are twenty-one-year-old breasts, upbeat, tight, no play in them.

Nearby, Matt is grinding with his two chubby girlfriends, Tara and Ivy.

The song ends. Ola lifts her head from my shoulder and we look into each other's eyes. I feel the spirit of the wind, or something along those lines.

In college, I dated a black woman, but she was African American, light-skinned, decaf with two creams. Ola is African African, double-espresso, sweet sensory overload for a guy who rarely drinks coffee.

I press my lips to hers, tongues snake, wet, hot, and hoppy. We head back to our seats just as Steve is leaving the bar hand-in-hand with Naledi. Neither one looks back.

Ola and I sit out the next few songs and never mention Steve or Naledi. Ola tells me that she's a hairdresser and that she is vacationing in Cape Town for several weeks. She says she is staying with her sister, who lives about an hour away by cab. If that's true, returning to her sister's would cost about 200 rand, or thirty dollars. Ola must make a lot of money as a hairdresser.

The waitress brings more beers. I reach into the decoy travel wallet around my neck to pay.

"So," Ola asks, "Have you been robbed yet?"

I become aware of the real money belt strapped to my waist and stare out the window.

"I can tell by your expression that you have not," she says. "Let me offer some advice:

"You must be careful in Cape Town.

"People will rob you, stab you, and shoot you.

"They will put knock-out drugs in your drink.

"They have HIV.

"Don't trust colored people."

Does that mean I shouldn't trust her? I put down my beer, my lips still tingling from her kiss.

"See over there?" She points out the open window to a spot across the street. "That's where I was robbed." She adjusts her bra strap, and then points to a little scar above her right breast. The scar is tiny, barely visible, and looks as old as she is.

Why is she telling me all this?

Her cell phone beeps. She taps a few keys, and ignores me while waiting for a response. When it comes, she looks at the ceiling and closes her eyes. She doesn't share what's going on and I don't ask.

"I'm hungry," she says, reaching for my hand. "Let's find something to eat."

As we leave, she asks me for twenty rand, which she gives to the doorman.

"What's that for?" I ask.

"We're not allowed in here," she says.

We? Who is "we"?

Her phone beeps again. Tap, tap, tap.

On the street, she gestures for a cab. "I know a romantic restaurant by the waterfront," she says.

"What about the restaurants right here?" I point across the street to the Impala Bistro, the Mandingo Grille, and the Rhino Burger.

"They're filled with kids from university, too noisy," she says.

After all of Ola's "advice," I'm not about to drive off with her to some strange place.

We look at each other: South African standoff.

The secret to any negotiation is being prepared to walk. And so I do.

She follows, grabs my hand, and says, "OK, let's go to your hotel."

The universe loves me again.

But as we cross the street, my thoughts swirl like farm animals in a Kansas tornado.

South Africa's HIV rate is almost 20 percent, so the odds are one-in-five that she's infected.

What if the condom breaks?

What if the second condom breaks?

What if the third condom breaks?

At least she looks healthy.

Maybe fate brought us together—dashing guy, voluptuous girl, he from one world and she from another.

Her phone beeps again, but this time she ignores it.

Who the hell keeps texting her at three A.M.? Her sister? Her friend Naledi? Her hair salon?

Her pimp?

Nah. Cousin Joey once said that hookers never kiss on the mouth.

She puts her arm around me and the oxytocin flows again. I put my hand on her abundant hips, and then think of Naledi and her little cheetah hips. The flow of oxytocin slows.

In my room, we sit on the bed, thighs touching. "Turn off the light," she says. I comply. We sit in silence. I stare into the darkness, aware of her breast against my upper arm.

In my country, the land of the free and the home of the brave, when a girl is on your bed, you bust a move.

But what if she's armed? What if she robs me, stabs me, and shoots me. What am I going to tell the police?

I met this girl half my age in a bar.

We went back to my hotel.

And here I am in the emergency room.

Even if she doesn't rob me, once her clothes are off, will I be able to focus on the breasts and not the hips and butt?

Her phone beeps again.

I look over her shoulder. On the screen is an image of a child. Ola folds the phone into her cleavage.

"That is my son," she says. "He is six."

I flip on the light and sit, silent.

"What's your problem?" she finally asks. "You never had sex with a mother before? You think your mother never had sex? You think your mother never worked to feed you? You think you're better than me?"

"I . . . I . . . I."

"You what? *I* just spent the whole night with a man and didn't earn any money."

I can't do this, the big tush, the little kid, the disease, the crime. Too many variables. I stand up. Ola bursts into tears.

"This was Naledi's idea. A way to make money to feed my boy. He hasn't eaten in a week. My husband just left me for another woman. I am on the street. You got to help me!"

I really want to believe Ola. And so I do.

At the cab stand, I hand her my remaining cash, seventy rand, about ten dollars. Ola doesn't seem concerned about street crime and stuffs the bills in her pocket. She gives me a kiss on the cheek that could mean: "Bless you for your kindness." It could also mean: "Thanks, sucker."

Matt stumbles by alone, looks at Ola, and gives me a thumbs-up.

After Ola drives off, I watch a boy, who could be six, pick through a garbage can bolted to the ground. A teenager in a yellow smock chases the boy away. It's four A.M.

I've never paid for sex before but not because I have some lofty moral code. It's that I've always associated prostitution with streetwalkers, Saturday Night specials, and the movie *Taxi Driver*. And then of course there's the little matter of AIDS.

And karma.

I'm afraid that if I take a sleazy detour, I might hurt my chances of finding the right woman. Maybe that's why I'm still single: karmic payback.

Moody would disagree. Whenever I talk about karma, synchronicity, or fate, he talks about magical thinking, OCD, and fear. He says life is about managing fear without gimmicks. Magical thinking is a gimmick, a child's gimmick.

Moody could be right. But just in case, starting tomorrow, I vow to quit smoking, avoid bar girls half my age, and work out more often.

The next morning, a desk clerk at the hostel recommends a health club in an upscale mall. "It's a nice twenty-minute walk right now," she says. "But after dark . . ." She hands me a card for a local cab company.

On Long Street, the bars and restaurants are quiet. A few yellow-smocked boys are on patrol. The hostel kids must still be sleeping off last night. I bear left onto Klootzak Street. The area resembles a fortress: a narrow street, a narrow sidewalk, ten-foot-high cinder block walls topped with barbed wire. Behind the walls: a school, apartments, homes. The South African version of a gated community.

On the sidewalk, an empty Carling Black Label bottle. I have an inkling to pick it up and put it in the garbage, but don't.

Graffiti on a wall: "Welkom to the Rich World." Another empty Carling, another inkling. This time I pick it up.

Farther along the wall, a sign: "Security Provided by Skloof Protection, Armed Response." I imagine guard towers, machine guns, and floodlights.

A Subway sandwich wrapper. I pick it up.

Another wall. Above it, a dirty white rag or shred of T-shirt hanging from some barbed wire. I put my collection of trash in a can bolted to the ground. Good deeds, good karma.

I cross onto Meersloofer Street. A begging lady with straightened gray hair down her back. I give her ten rand. "Your kindness will be rewarded," she says. *A fellow believer.*

I reach the upscale mall intact. Inside the women are long, blonde, and sleeveless. The men wear polished, lace-up shoes. No ripped T-shirts, Tevas with safety pins, or yellow smocks anywhere.

After a workout, a long whirlpool, and a head and face shave, I go to the health club restaurant for a drink. The room is a fusion of mocha leather, exotic wood, and black pendant lamps.

I sit at the back bar several feet from a long blonde nibbling some tapas. She glances at my workout bag. "You win your squash match?" she asks.

"I was lifting weights. Can't you tell by my big, thick neck?"

"Cute accent. You from America?"

"Boston."

"I was in New York for the last year and—"

A crumb of potato cheese croquette flies from her mouth and lands on my bare thigh. She leans over and wipes it off with her hand. I flinch. She gulps down her martini and smiles, displaying her snaggly, European-style dental work. "Move over here, we don't bite," she says.

We?

A guy sitting on her left puts a hand on her shoulder and leans in. Unlike me, he actually does have a big, thick neck.

First Zofia and Aurek, then Sabine and George, now another bored couple is adopting me and looking to be entertained.

I move my stool a few inches closer.

"I'm Randy. I mean Randall."

"I'm Berty. I mean Beatrice," says the blonde, smiling.

"And I'm Dominick," says the guy. He has kinky hair and olive-colored skin. He looks Latin or Arab. His teeth are perfect.

"How are you enjoying your holiday?" he asks me.

"Great. But I think I've been a little too concerned about the crime around here." I recount Ola's real-life crime stories.

"She was probably just trying to shake you down for money," Dominick says. "But you *should* be concerned about the crime."

"I don't mean to sound racist," I say. "But she was black and kept telling me to watch out for colored people. I don't get it."

Bertie butts in. "In South Africa, native Africans are 'black,' mixed-race people are 'Coloured,' and whites are 'white.'"

"I'm Coloured," Dominick says, reaching for a marinated olive.

I feel my face flush.

Bertie holds her hand to my cheek and shakes her head. "Oh, honey. Everyone on this planet is racist; when are you Americans going to get it through your heads?"

I think of the Greek hotel manager who hated Turks, Charlotte who disliked Germans, and then back to Ola and the Coloureds.

"Americans blame all the country's problems on middle-aged white guys," she says. "When are the men going to stick up for themselves? I'd never date a white American, no self-respect, no balls."

Dominick smiles like a kid listening to his favorite bedtime story. Bertie kisses him on the mouth, and then slugs down the rest of his martini.

The frenzied eyes, the disregard for personal boundaries, the in-your-face opinions: Bertie reminds me of someone. Ricki.

Domenic is now massaging Bertie's bare shoulders. I am merely the middle-aged white guy in the audience.

I point toward the window at nothing and say, "There's my cab."

Bertie gives my shoulder a sloppy slap. "You know, Randall, you really need to relax."

I haven't thought this much about race since I was seven years old and my family moved from Vermont to Mount Vernon, a New York City suburb. At my new elementary school, half the students were black and many lived in a nearby housing project.

One day I was on the lunch line and a little black kid cut in front of me.

"Hey, I was here first," I said.

Before I could open my mouth again, he wheeled and punched me on the side of the face.

"Shut the fuck up," he said, baring his teeth. "I'm going to wait for your white nigger ass after school."

I looked down at him, tears filling my eyes, and didn't say a word.

I knew the "after school" drill because I'd seen black and white kids square off on the playground. Each combatant would balance a pencil, representing his mother, on his shoulder. Knocking the pencil off would initiate a fight.

For weeks after the punch, I raced home after school keeping my mother in my Scooby-Doo pencil box, out of harm's way.

Did those experiences turn me into a racist? Is that why I've never dated a black woman seriously? I don't know any white guys in Boston who date black women. I consider the unwritten rules for dating in my circle:

- Fat Jewish women are OK.
- Skinny *shiksas* are OK.
- Mysterious Asians are OK.

- Stacked Latinas are OK.
- South Asian Indians with rich parents are OK.
- But black women, no matter how skinny, stacked, or rich, are not OK.

Why?

Is it the lips? The nose? The hair?

No, it's the baggage: segregation, integration, affirmative action, busing, redlining, Black Power, White Supremacy, the Central Park jogger, Tawana Brawley, Rodney King, James Earl Ray, Jessie Jackson, Louis Farrakhan, Alabama state troopers, Watts, South Boston, Crown Heights, Howard Beach, Hymietown, the Mount Vernon elementary school lunch line.

Bertie is right: We're all a bunch of racists.

The next morning, I board the bus for a two-week tour along something called the Garden Route, a stretch of South African coastline sandwiched between mountainous rain forests and the Indian Ocean. According to Pittman's guidebook, the route is renowned for golden beaches and sheltered lagoons, soaring peaks and sheer gorges, and scrubland thick with fragrant vegetation. For decades, the scenery has been an inspiration to artists and writers. Have I mentioned how much I like sightseeing? I'm not here for the sights; I'm here for the party.

Steve is sitting alone, his constant companion, a coldie, in hand. He looks rested and sated. I sit across the aisle from him. He leans over to offer me a beer and gestures to the scenery outside the idling bus where a young black woman is kissing an old white guy. "He's a punter." I'm guessing Steve means a john and that somehow we're better than the old guy.

"You're headed for Thailand and Vietnam, right?" Steve asks. "Hands down, they have the best birds. You're going to have a time once you get there. But we should do OK in Bakvissie."

Bakvissie is our first overnight stop on the bus tour. The local hostel is renowned for mountain views and Mandrax parties. Mandrax are like Quaaludes. "When birds take them, they go crazy for a shag," Steve has told me multiple times.

The bus holds about twenty people, but is half empty. The two untouchable Dutch girls sit in back by themselves. Matt, Tara, and Ivy, the Americans, sit two rows ahead of us.

In the first row, a red-faced, Irish-looking guy sits by himself. Besides me and Steve, the guy is the only other person without hair. He appears to be in his fifties. He sits rigidly upright, stares straight ahead, and looks like an alcoholic or a priest or both. Steve offers another theory: "Pedophile. What else would a bloke that age be doing on this bus?"

Matt, Tara, and Ivy erupt into a freshman-style giggle fit: *They're probably thinking the same thing about me.* I swill my coldie and close my eyes for a sleep.

Four hours later we pull into a beachside town called Mompie Bay. Our lunch stop is Dogie's, South Africa's answer to McDonald's. I order a Double Dogie with cheese for thirty-three rand, about five dollars, and wait outside at a picnic table for Steve. The taller Dutch woman is sitting by herself at the table next to me. She's looking beyond the parking lot at a sheltered lagoon framed by a golden beach.

"Having fun?" I ask her.

"Sure thing," she says.

"That beach looks great."

She fingers a loose strand of blonde hair. "Yeah, it's awesome. I stayed here the last two years. This year I wanted to check out Bakvissie."

Her friend arrives. "Ciao," she says. They move to another table.

The alcoholic, pedophile priest is eating by himself at a table for four. Am I going to end up like that?

Steve comes outside with a huge bag of food and two attractive black girls. He hands one of the girls the bag and calls me to the side. "Want to stay and party? Can't do it alone, mate."

"Are they hookers?"

"No, part-timers like Naledi and Ola—they've got regular jobs, just looking for some fun and extra coin."

"What about the Mandrax party?" I ask.

"Look, mate, you know what they say about having a bird in hand."

I look at the girls: One is slim and attractive, the other, on second glance, not so much—below the table she is bigger than Ola.

Maybe for Steve this is an easy bird-in-the-hand decision. But at my age, I can't have sex with just anyone anymore. In recent years, I've learned the hard way that I have to feel some attraction or connection to sleep with a woman. It's not a moral issue, it's a performance issue—the little head, like the big head, isn't as reliable as it used to be.

The bigger girl smiles and pats the bench next to her.

"What do you say, mate?" Steve asks.

I catch the tall Dutch girl looking at me from across the picnic area. We smile at each other. She looks away.

"Can't do it, Steve. I know you can handle two," I say. "If you change your mind I'll be at the Mandrax party. Don't do anything I wouldn't do. Ciao."

Later, the bus seems much emptier. No Steve. No pedophile priest either. The driver starts the engine. Matt leaves Tara and Ivy in the front row and sits across the aisle from me. "So I hear you're a writer," he says. "I want to be a gonzo journalist, travel solo like you, write about shit. Truth is, I'm not crazy about traveling with two girls; they act like they're still in high school and a man needs his space."

He lowers his voice. "I'm banging Tara, the one with big tits." As if on cue, Tara turns around in her seat and gestures for Matt to come up and join her. "Later, man," he says.

Was I a knucklehead like Matt at his age? Have I changed? What kind of grown man keeps a spreadsheet of women? I stare out the window at the sandy shore and try not to think about anything.

Midafternoon, we pull into the Bakvissie hostel, a meandering farmhouse with a porch and spindly rocking chairs. The Swartberg Mountains undulate in the distance like clay-colored waves. Instead of warnings about taxis, the wall behind the front desk lists local attractions, group trips, and hostel job openings.

A guy about my age checks me in. He has a deep tan, an earring, and blond, poodle-style hair down to his collar.

"You requested a single room, mate, but we're sold out," Mr. Blond says to me. "So we put you in the honeymoon suite. I trust you will use it for good, not evil. See you at breakfast." He winks, pats my shoulder, and sends me on my way.

As I'm leaving the lobby, I hear him address a clutch of young women. "Gooood afternoon ladies," he says in a precious South African accent. "Checking in? Join us tonight for the Bakvissie Boom-Boom Party, hey?"

At the Boom-Boom party, Mr. Blond plays pool with the Dutch girls. Other hostel kids I haven't met stand at the bar and giggle. Matt and his sidekicks giggle. Must have missed the Mandrax hors d'oeuvres. If I had a job like Mr. Blond's, I'd be partying with giggling chicks every night. If I had listened to Steve, I'd be partying with two Dogie's birds tonight. My mood plunges like a mallard full of lead shot.

Action item: Stop thinking about birds all the time.
I head back alone to the honeymoon suite.

Over the next few days, I sample a few other local attractions.

Ostrich Ride

Promotional brochure: "An ostrich can run at speeds up to sixty miles per hour and can disembowel a man with a single kick."

Riding the ostrich is like riding a 250-pound feather duster mounted on a grocery cart with a broken wheel. I steer and brake by yanking its bony wings while praying it doesn't get mad and kick me.

Disturbing thought: This is the most action I've gotten from a bird in months.

Cave Trek

Promotional brochure: "Twenty-million-year-old cave system composed of hidden grottos cut into limestone."

It's like hiking through a giant skull. Fifty-foot-high chambers resemble sinuses and stalactites hang from the ceiling like mucous from the world's worst case of post-nasal drip. The Americans giggle incessantly. All I think about is my medication stash back at the hostel.

Boom-Boom Party #2

Boom-boom is a bust: just me, Matt, Tara, and Ivy. We play pool. They joke about their former boss: "The old perv," "the bipolar geezer," "wanted to kick him in his junk."

"He sounds like a real dick," I say. "How old was he?"

"I don't know," Matt says. "Maybe forty. But he was probably an asshole when he was ten."

And so goes the rest of the week: No Mandrax and no action.

On Friday, our little tour group, which unfortunately still includes me, checks out of the hostel. As Mr. Blond swipes my credit card, I notice that the shorter Dutch girl is behind the counter assisting him. They both look rested and sated.

"Hey, mate," he says to me. "You're a writer. Will you look at my novel?"

Before I can answer, he addresses a new clutch of chickies waiting to check in. "Hello ladies, coming to our Bakvissie Boom-Boom party tonight?" The Dutch girl is still by his side. He may be a dick, but he's not a settler.

Blog Entry: October 7
Bakvissie, South Africa

Please FedEx me a new liver . . .

Met a woman on red-eye flight to Cape Town. Drank too much.

Been staying in hostels with college kids the last two weeks. Shots till two A.M.

Also, met a couple of decent guys my age:

• An Australian physician named Steve showed me the sights in Cape Town. He's here on a humanitarian mission at a nearby beach town called Mompie Bay.

• Hostel owner in Bakvissie offered me a job running his website. Money was decent, but had to decline, having too much fun touring and sightseeing.

Sampled some delectable South African cuisine:

• Ostrich egg: One egg feeds ten people. Tastes like egg.

• Meat pie: Tastes like a Twinkie filled with ground skunk.

• Biltong: Dried meat snack that tastes like a cream-filled Slim Jim.

Did I read somewhere that the Red Sox are doing well? Abe? Lenny? (All we get on TV here is rugby—what a pansy game, just a bunch of guys trying to pull down each other's shorts.)

And for all you folks who've forgotten how to write, here's the e-mail address again: rburns@rburnsworld.com.

Heading up the coast to a town called Lekker Anties. Will report in later after detoxing.

—Burns

Outside the Lekker Anties hostel, I'm preparing for a jog. The guidebook recommends a five-mile route into the Tsitsi-kamma rain forest past soaring yellowwood, hard pear, and stinkwood trees.

As I'm stretching, Anika, the taller Dutch blonde, comes out and begins picking nearby wild flowers. She smiles. This is the most interaction we've had since Mompie Bay. I play it cool and acknowledge her by saying simply, "fynbos," refer-ring to the pink and green flowers she's holding.

"I used to work for Reed Elsevier in Amsterdam," she says. "The big technical publisher. I just got laid off. But I am not a writer."

Anika talks about publishing and computers and unem-ployment and flowers. I'm bored. So I start lying: I tell her about the short stories I had published, my readings in Boston book stores, the writing courses I taught.

She's wearing black running tights. Cheetah hips. "I like to jog too," she says. Then the untouchable one squeezes my arm as if we have some deep, mysterious connection. I flinch. I'm not sure why she's being so friendly, but I have a hunch.

"I didn't see your friend at breakfast," I say. "Everything OK?"

"She took a job in Bakvissie. So now I am traveling alone. You want to meet later?"

At dinner, Anika saves me a seat next to her.

"How do you like it here?" she asks.

"Great. The food's decent, the running trail is nice, and I've got a king room with a shower."

The word "king room" seems to hover between us.

"Ah. I am in the dorm," she says. "That is all I can afford."

I feel her leg brushing against mine. "Want to meet later for a hot tub?" she asks.

"I'll bring the wine," I say.

As I'm showering after dinner, I imagine rolling Anika around in the fynbos. I imagine traveling up the coast with her for the next week. I imagine us living in the Netherlands on a street with a goofy, skloofy Dutch name.

The hot tub is on a raised deck. Anika is in the churning water and she's not alone. She's with some guy named Peter, a British medical student, in his early twenties, scrawny, pink, and without chest hair. A needle dick. I can probably kick his ass.

Anika motions for me to sit next to her. Peter pours me a glass of wine from an open bottle near him on the deck. I put my bottle near me on the deck.

Amongst the bubbles, Anika squeezes my hand, and then turns to Peter and raises her wine glass. "As I was saying, if you don't look into my eyes when we toast, you'll have seven years of bad sex."

They toast. I sit there like a bump on a stinkwood. Peter looks past Anika into my eyes. He smirks. I consider leaving.

Anika hops onto the lip of the hot tub. Black bikini, full balconies, high-relief abs. I reconsider.

Peter hops onto the lip of the hot tub alongside Anika. Black swim trunks. The outline of a geoduck clam, a python with a Portobello ski cap. Needle dick has a monster schlong. I try not to look.

I think of initiation night at my college frat. I was blind-folded and naked. The pledge-master said, "Burns, you call that little thing a dick?"

"Sorry, sir, it runs in the family." Everyone laughed but me.

Anika is now talking about her former job at Reed Else-vier. Peter leans over to offer me more wine.

When Anika abruptly says good night and leaves, I hand over the wine I brought and say to Peter, "Got an opener?"

Back in my room, I pace the floor. In less than two months, I've struck out with women on three continents and been hit on by guys on two.

I want to feel sad or angry or anything. But instead, I'm just misty, fogged in, numb.

I drop to the floor and do twenty-five push-ups, a dozen leg raises, and side planks. But it's no help.

For years, Moody, has said that when the Dark Place looms, I should stop fighting it and just visit. "Don't move in," he said. "Just visit."

The foyer of a split-level ranch in Mount Vernon, the New York town where the kids would just as soon knock a pencil off your shoulder as look at you. I am seven years old.

Upstairs, a bedroom door that is always closed since my mother remarried after divorcing my biological father whom she never talked about. "Adults need their privacy," she told me. I always assumed privacy referred to her bedroom and any discussion of my biological father.

Another bedroom belongs to my stepsister, Harriet. I used to go in there, but not anymore.

Nearby is the bathroom. This is my safe room. It has a black oval rug where I kneel to pray for luck playing sports and for protection against tough kids at school. When I can't sleep, I read the labels on vials, bottles, and cans in the medicine cabinet.

One day when I am eleven, the girls at school create a loose-leaf "slam book" that ranks boys by attractiveness. My page says stuff like "shy" and "weird dresser," in other words, I'm a zero. That night after praying and reading labels, I stand at the toilet watching my poops drift like dying goldfish. I get this inkling to touch each one three times, the magic number.

After several months of following this compulsion, I stop. Touching my poops has not changed my luck or my slam book ranking.

In the basement there's a playroom, the land of failed distractions: a weight set, a chemistry set, fly-casting gear, snorkeling gear, an empty fish tank, an empty terrarium that once housed a chameleon that looked like a little monkey, a saxophone in a dusty case. And the fail-proof distraction: a Motorola television.

Under the Ping-Pong table, a crate-sized cage covered with a tarp. Whimpering emanates from inside. I lift a tarp corner and something stirs against the metal bars. An empty water bottle, a food dish with a few pellets of food covered with ants, an untouched baby toy. More whimpering. When I lift the tarp higher, the house's central air-conditioning system rumbles like the footsteps of a giant space monster coming to get me.

Visiting hours are over.

Later, on the hostel computer, there's a note from Pittman:
Dear Mr. Burns,
Our sincerest apologies.
While we make every effort to be factually accurate in our books, we do make mistakes. We rely on readers such as yourself to help us keep our materials up to date.

As a gesture of our appreciation, we have contacted the hostel in Bangkok and arranged for a 50-percent discount on your room. Please visit us in Saigon, so we can make further amends.
Stay the course,
Wallace Pittman,
President, All-American Language School
Author, Solo Salvation: Travel the world on your own

I hit "delete."

Back in May, just in case, I calculated return flights from all my stops back to Boston. A return from Cape Town was $1,300.

I zip over to farescrooge.com and type "Cape Town to Boston." While the site is calculating fares, I pace the room until I feel something firm, like a power cable, under my sandal. It's an eight-inch millipede. The bug is curled up like a kitten with 200 pairs of legs. It looks like it wants to play. I wrap it in a tissue and throw its black ass out the door. If there's a flight for $1,500 or less, I'm out of here.

The computer stops churning. The cheapest flight on an airline I can pronounce is $1,920. I search for flights to Boston from Bangkok where I am heading in three days. The cheapest one-way is $1,530. Close enough. I click "Buy Now" and the price immediately jumps to $1,750. Fuck it, I just want out. I enter my credit card number. The computer churns. And then crashes and I'm fucked again.

The next morning, my hostel room is cold and dank; getting into my clothes is like climbing into a wet gym sock. Outside, it's about fifty degrees. Tall weepy trees drip rain on everything.

My hostel-mates are assembled at the front desk reviewing a blackboard listing the local attractions: abseiling, kloofing,

shark-cage diving, skydiving, and bungee jumping. Peter
avoids looking at me; maybe he thinks I'm a tease. The Americans are not giggling for a change, and Anika and her friend,
who must have just reappeared this morning, are busy ignoring everyone. Apparently life as Mrs. Blond didn't work out.

"What's abseiling?" Matt asks the desk clerk.

Peter responds: "It's what you Americans call rappelling."

"What's kloofing?" Matt asks, ignoring Peter.

Peter responds: "It's what you call canyoning, following a
mountain stream down its course. It can involve abseiling and
jumping from great heights. It's quite dangerous."

The desk clerk cuts in: "Sorry mates, due to the weather,
the only activity for today is bungee."

Matt turns to me: "We doing this for the fucking US of A?"

Without thinking, I high-five him. "Fuck yeah," I say.

The Lekker Anties jump site is about 700 feet high, the
equivalent of two Statues of Liberty stacked on top of each
other.

On the way to the site, Peter the med student provides a
litany of possible whiplash injuries incurred by those who've
survived a jump: retinal hemorrhage, broken neck, severed
carotid arteries, shoulder dislocation, spinal damage, and
blackouts caused by strangulation from the bungee cord. And
then there were those who simply soiled their knickers.

In the bungee check-in area, we fill out liability forms that
are remarkably brief and free of legalese. Basically, it says, "If
you get hurt, tough *scheisse*." A local guy, who appears to be
in his teens, straps me into a body harness while another teen
weighs me and Magic-Markers my wrist with the number seventy-three, that's seventy-three kilos, about 161 pounds. I've
put on six pounds in the last month. *Scheisse.*

Tara is being harnessed next to me. She starts to hyperventilate, "Ohmygod, Ohmygod Ohmygod." The teen who weighed me looks in my eyes, "You don't have to do this, if you don't want to, mate. You can watch from the observation deck."

The observation deck is across the ravine. Peter and the Dutch girls sit there in comfy chairs with glasses of red wine. Peter toasts in my direction. I ignore him.

To get from the harness area to the jump platform requires tottering along a metal-grate catwalk that provides a view of rocks and boulders that drop away underfoot to a thread of river 700 feet below.

The catwalk ends on an open concrete platform suspended beneath a bridge that spans a ravine. Techno music booms. A girl from another hostel starts jumping up and down to the beat. A few others join her with tight, nervous smiles. Matt walks alone in circles, exhaling deeply. Tara and Ivy must have bailed.

I pace focusing on the lines and stains on the concrete slab floor. One stain resembles a fractured femur, another, a gravestone. A guy working the platform calls out names in the order in which we'll jump. I'm going third.

Matt approaches and then looks across the way to where Peter again toasts us. Matt gives him the finger. "That British guy is the biggest fucking pussy."

Matt looks around at the other jumpers on the platform. "You know, we're up here with a bunch of twenty-year-old girls." He drums on the railing in front of us.

"I guess that begs the question: Do we have the balls of a twenty-year-old girl?" I ask.

He points to his "I'd Rather Be in Mississippi" T-shirt and says: "A Southern man don't do fear." Matt slaps a metal no-smoking sign above us. "I want to try skydiving next."

"I've been skydiving," I say. "This is much hairier."

"No way."

"Jumping out of a plane, you're so high up, the ground looks soft and fuzzy. Here you can see every rock and tree, any one of them could take you out." I slap the sign. "Just like that."

Matt glances over at his girlfriends, who are now sipping wine on the observation deck, as if he wishes he were there too.

He opens his mouth to talk and I cut him off: "Listen, Matt, no more talking, we need to focus."

When I'm called to the platform, Matt makes a fist. I make a fist. We bump fists. "For the fucking US of A," we say.

A girl in a Lekker Anties Bungee T-shirt tells me to sit. She binds my ankles together with a padded collar that attaches to a white bungee cord as thick as a sink pipe. She has skin that's at least 80 percent cocoa and a sweet-sounding accent like Ola's.

She and another assistant maneuver me to the edge of the concrete slab. I repress the urge to ask how long they've been in this line of work.

I feel a hand under my chin. The girl tells me not to look down. She's either a mind reader or she noticed that I've stopped breathing. I stare straight out at the horizon and can feel tears in my eyes.

I think of my family and suicide and my mother's brother, Uncle Woody, who jumped off a building at age forty-two. "Didn't feel a thing," my mother always said.

The assistant rubs my shoulder to calm me. A little oxytocin flows, but not enough. "Mr. Burns, where you from?" she asks.

"The US."

"You have good rugby team, hey?" I hear the other staffers laugh, and somehow recall that the US team was creamed by the South African team two nights ago.

"OK, Mr. Burns. We gonna count to three. You bend your knees and do a nice swan dive for us, arms out, hey?"

I nod without looking down.

"One, two . . ."

I'm humming a line about Billy Joe McAllister on the Tallahatchie Bridge, when I feel a gentle push.

During a bungee jump your body accelerates from zero to ninety miles per hour in five seconds. A $200,000 Lamborghini goes from zero to ninety in eight seconds. I drive a Honda Civic, which goes from zero to ninety if I'm lucky.

As I'm falling, I feel like I'm in a plane hitting the world's biggest air pocket. Only there's no seat belt, emergency floatation device, or drink service. There's a yanking sensation in my stomach, as if someone has grabbed it and is trying to pull it out through my ears. I keep waiting for an explosion of ground skunk deep inside my colon or a seeping wetness in my pants.

Gradually the collar tightens, noose-like, around my ankles and the falling stops. I open my eyes as I bounce back up toward the sky. The numbness recedes and the only wetness I feel is from the soft mist around me.

The next day, our tour returns to the Bonobo in Cape Town.

Lucky me, there's an e-mail from Ricki:

Hey Burns,

Should I send you a new liver? Give me a break. I bet you're depressed as hell. Guess that misogynistic, head-fucking shrink didn't help you much. Still can't believe you dragged me to see him. Do you do that with all your girlfriends? No wonder you're still single.

So, your so-called friends aren't writing. Shouldn't be a surprise, what a bunch of schmucks. Abe the fat fuck with the porky wife. I bet he still hates me because I told him off for making fun of you. Why are you still friends with that ass? Oh, and Lenny the poon-hound who hit on my seventeen-year-old cousin. Then he kept bugging me to set him up with my friend Valerie with the eating disorder. And let's not forget Josh, your other wingman, who ditched you the minute he got a girlfriend.

Good luck to you.

—RRRRR

And another from Ricki:

Hey Burns,

Sorry if some of my previous e-mails were a little edgy. My therapist says I have an anger problem. Who me? Ha! We're trying a different medication, something that's supposed to boost the sex drive. Eat your heart out.

You remember my dachshund, Wiener, with the little wheelchair for his paralyzed back legs? The dog you called Ironside? He died yesterday. Hope you're happy.

—RRRRRR

Why does she keep writing? And why am I attracted to women like her?

I know why: Fish genes.

In a session with Moody two years ago. I'm looking at the wall clock. At $125 for fifty minutes, I'm paying this guy two dollars and fifty cents a minute.

Five dollars pass. Moody breaks the silence. "So, Randall, why do you think you're still single after all these years?"

"I'm at a loss. That's why I'm here."

"You must have some theories. Give me a metaphor, tell me a story."

He takes out a fresh legal pad, pen poised.

"Ever been fishing?" I asked.

"Sure."

"So you know, fish aren't attracted to bait that is healthy and moving smoothly through the water. Fish are attracted to bait that jumps, quivers, and zigzags due to some type of distress. I must have some fish genes because I'm only attracted to erratic, ziggy women who have moods that flop around like a mackerel on a hot sidewalk."

He scribbles and underlines. I wait and burn through another two dollars and fifty cents, and then continue.

"Over the years, I've dated some stable women, but I just never got hooked. Like Dani and then Karen."

"I remember Karen."

"After two months, I was fed up with Karen's constant cheerfulness, which seemed phony. Her moods never zigged or zagged. You kept telling me to stick with her and sit with the discomfort. But being with her was like trying to see how long I could hold my breath, which brings us back to the fish genes.

"Anyway, when she put her arm around me, I didn't feel a thing. After sex, I had nothing to say to her. I felt guilty, angry, and was having trouble sleeping. But you kept saying to 'give it another week' and wrote me my first prescription for Ambien."

"I remember."

"So I gave Karen another week and another and another and she still ended up on my spreadsheet with the rest of them."

He put down his pen. "Having a thing for volatile women doesn't explain anything. Lots of crazy people marry. I treat them. Marriage is no barometer of mental health."

"Are you calling me normal?"

"I'm calling you a high-functioning neurotic who seems to have problems with relationships."

Tonight at the Bonobo, halfway around the world, I'm still single and at a loss. I think about flopping mackerel and death and dogs in wheelchairs. I think of myself on the bungee platform, looking at the rocks and trees below. There's only one way to go from here, Billie Joe, and it's not up.

Ricki: Cell A46
First encounter: Barbecue, Cambridge, Mass., August '03

She was petite with straight shoulder-length black hair, a barbed-wire tattoo around her right bicep, and black jeans and red high-top Converses. She moved like someone who exercised regularly. The little lines around her mouth indicated she was probably about my age, too old for Converses.

The barbecue was in Cambridge, so it was a vegetarian, gender-neutral, low-carbon-footprint affair.

I noticed her because she had brought a huge, bloody porterhouse that looked like a prop for a slasher movie. I watched as she wrestled it onto the grill.

She glanced at me. She glanced again. "Having fun?" I asked.

I don't remember what she said but when I looked into her eyes, it seemed like she'd been crying. Or laughing. Or laughing and crying. Or maybe she just had indigestion. Looking deeper still, I could sense a disturbance, an electrical storm. I imagined her brain cells flashing, twitching, and jumping like herring chased by a large predator. I wanted to be that predator.

On our first date, she showed up an hour late wearing Ray-Bans on an overcast day.

"Apologies for my tardiness," she said. "I'm a little hung over. I was up late at a Caribbean-theme party last night. I was the only white person there."

She had my attention. We went Rollerblading. Halfway down Oxford Street, I heard a loud "ka-thunk" followed by "Ah, fuck!"

Ricki had slammed into a parked car.

I was hooked.

Our second date was a blur. Indian food, French movie. A handicapped bathroom. She locked the door. Two layers of toilet paper on the seat. My kind of girl. Jeans down. The burble and gurgle of pee. I kissed her. A double helix of tongues. When I peed, she aimed. A tightening grip, vanilla hand cream, a gluey handkerchief she saved in her purse.

After a few months, we hit the inevitable plateau and began arguing. She had a list of complaints, the catalog of atrocities. I only had one complaint: her complaining. She yelled, I became passive aggressive. Eventually we crossed the 50 percent mark, where the bad times outnumbered the good ones. I made an appointment with Moody and she agreed to go.

"What seems to be the problem?" he asked.

"He's a neat freak," she said. "And a hypochondriac. And he's got the worst taste in clothes and music."

She was wearing a snug black skirt that I'd never seen before.

"And he's a cheapskate. And he's weird. Did he tell you he sleeps with a blindfold and mixes his food together like a four-year-old? Or that he's obsessed with smells and refuses to poop in my bathroom?"

Her eyes moistened and I thought back to our first encounter at the barbecue.

"He's so provincial and refuses to travel anywhere. I can't stand it anymore. Please medicate him!"

She turned to me and glared. I smiled, distracted by her wet lips and tan legs.

"What would you like from Randall?" Moody said.

"There you go taking his side! That's the kind of patri-archal attitude that used to get women locked up in mental hospitals. I knew this was a stupid idea."

After the session, I called Moody. "Should I bail on this relationship?"

"You know I can't give you advice like that."

"If I said I wanted to bail, would you suggest I sit with it for another week?"

"Probably not."

Outside the hostel, the Cape Town streets and balconies are packed with kids. I turn left on Long Street and pass an African tchotchke shop advertising authentic Zulu war axes, ceremonial dance hoes, and Ngulu execution swords, all 50 percent off. A block later, a familiar gaunt, black man with rheumy eyes and a red ski cap calls out to me from an alley. "You want some crazy, good fun?"

I pause and scope the area: a black woman with Ben Wallace afro, a black guy with zebra-striped baseball hat. Orange keffiyeh. Purple fez. Paisley top hat. I spot a white guy, but he has dreadlocks and doesn't count. I am well outside my comfort zone.

On the next block is a place called Dele's Sports Pub. An oblong light fixture shaped like a rugby ball hangs from the ceiling. A couple of old white guys with white moustaches and silky dress shirts unbuttoned to their navels sit at the bar watching a match. Two black kids in yellow security smocks are playing pool.

I take an open bar stool as a group of black guys comes in off the street. They hassle the yellow smocks playing pool. The smocks leave. The black guys peck at their cell phones and swing the pool cues at each other as if they were Zulu war axes.

I stare ahead at a blackboard behind the bar: "Slap Chips, Bunny Chow, Sarmies, Peri Peri, Bobotie." I'm guessing that's food.

A thirty-something black guy sits down next to me. He's wearing a white dress shirt. I can't stop myself from thinking: Oh, crap. A carjacker on his day off.

A Coloured barman asks for my order. "Windhoek, please," I whisper. The guy next to me orders a Windhoek too. I stare up at the overhead TV so hard my eyes start to burn.

Our beers arrive at the same time. The guy catches my eye and gives a little nod. He swills. I swill. We swill together.

He pounds his empty beer on the counter two gulps ahead of me and smiles. "One more time," he says.

As we're halfway through our second beers, he yells out, "Ag, no man" and smacks the bar with his hand. I flinch without taking my eyes off the TV. He's going to put a pencil on his shoulder and dare me to smack it off.

He points to the TV. "Ag, Ag." Apparently, there's been some kind of penalty. One player probably smudged another player's mascara.

While he's distracted, I down my beer. He laughs. "You cheat, man. One more." The alcohol starts to kick in, my eyes start to clear, and I notice he has put on reading glasses.

"What just happened?" I ask.

"High tackle."

"Is that like a nuggie?"

"Nuggie?"

I open my mouth, wrap on my skull with my knuckles, and produce a sound like an empty coconut.

"You funny, man."

"And you're a fast drinker."

"Ag, I'm going to meet a woman I'm supposed to marry."

"Congratulations."

"How you marry someone you only meet once? You married?"

"Funny you should ask." I take a sip of my beer and look up at the TV. "Looks like a penalty for a wedgie."

He stares at the label on his Windhoek. "She's supposed to be big and healthy and obedient."

"Obedient means fewer fights over who's supposed to take out the trash."

Suddenly I'm no longer funny.

"I am twenty-eight," he says. "I had it with courting."

"Tell me about it."

And so he does.

His name is Chata and he sells authentic Nigerian throwing spears made by his family in Zimbabwe to the local tchotchke shops. He doesn't explain how Zimbabwe family members make authentic Nigerian products and I don't ask. He says owning a business should make him a good catch, but Cape Town women keep dumping him. For months, his parents have been sending photos of marriage prospects from Zimbabwe. He's says he's done waiting for love. He's ready to settle.

I offer Chata a beer. He accepts and offers me an opportunity to invest in the family business. I decline.

As we sip and watch the match, some teenage boys run into the bar and bum cigarettes from a mustachioed guy in a half-unbuttoned dress shirt. They seem to know each other.

Chata finishes his beer, stands to leave, and points to the mustachioed guy. "You should know that later on, this place fills up with gay people."

He gives my shoulder a sloppy slap. "Relax, man, you'll be fine."

My mood lifts. I'm leaving South Africa tomorrow for Bangkok, the promise of someplace new.

Pittman says solo travelers often fall into a pattern. Leaving and arriving become the high points of any destination. Arriving, everything is new and fascinating. Leaving, you're optimistic about the next place. The problem can be the time in between when, inevitably, you get bored, lonely, and depressed. Sounds like most of my relationships.

The Chronic Single's Handbook
Chapter Two
Personality Test: Are You Marriage Material?
I. Give yourself one point for each item that applies.
1) You can tolerate boredom:
- *After sex.*
- *After lithium.*
- *Fuck you.*

2) Your nesting instincts:
- *I have no furniture.*
- *I have college furniture.*
- *I once went to Pottery Barn for a free wine and cheese reception.*

3) Your girlfriend asks you to get a video for her preschool daughter's birthday party. You choose:
- Borat.
- Death Wish.
- Caligula.

4) You miss your ex most when:
- *Eating alone.*
- *Watching a movie alone.*
- *Paying the mortgage alone.*

5) If a significant other says "no" to sex, you:
- *Take her to her favorite restaurant because she's probably having a difficult week.*

- *Take her college-aged daughter to her favorite restaurant because you're having a difficult week.*
- *Visit Yvonne, the double-jointed masseuse.*

6) *Your ideal frequency for seeing a significant other:*
- *Once a week.*
- *Once a month.*
- *Once a year.*

7) *Your mother:*
- *Call her once a day.*
- *Call her once a year.*
- *Her body is lashed to a rocking chair in the attic.*

8) *Your last relationship failed because:*
- *You forgot her birthday.*
- *You forgot her phone number.*
- *You forgot her name.*

9) *It's your anniversary and she is expecting something special, so you:*
- *Go drinking with the boys.*
- *Go skiing with the boys.*
- *Visit Yvonne, the double-jointed masseuse.*

10) *How well do you understand women?*
- *When a woman says, "No" she means, "Feel my breasts."*
- *When a woman says, "Let go of my throat, you're hurting me" she means, "Feel my breasts."*
- *When a woman says, "Get out now or I'm calling the police," she means, "Feel my breasts."*

II. Scoring:
- *One to five: Clueless*
- *Six to ten: Hopeless*
- *Ten or more: The next NFL commissioner*

CHAPTER FIVE: BANGKOK

Life's journey is about finding your place on a beach with kind eyes.
—W. PITTMAN

Bangkok.

Bang. Cock.

The name alone sounds skeevy, and from the moment I get off the plane, I'm on high alert. The guidebook warns about transsexual ladyboys, tuk-tuk scammers, and locals that play volleyball using their feet. The decor in the airport isn't helping matters: smirking Buddhas, sneering Buddhas, a gang of Buddhas pummeling a giant, three-headed snake.

I just survived South Africa and my third red-eye flight in a month. Now, outside the Bangkok terminal, a statue of a willowy, female Buddha beckons with four arms. Her belly button is at half-mast, sleepy, peaceful. Her eyes are at half-mast, knowing, welcoming. Kind eyes. I imagine a sloppy slap on my shoulder: *Relax, you're meant to be here.*

An airport bus drops me downtown on Sukhumvit Road, a boulevard that's supposed to be two blocks from my hostel. On the corner stands a local woman wearing a T-shirt that says "University of Nepraska." That's Nepraska with one "p."

The street is peppered with food carts selling noodles and soup for thirty baht, or about one dollar. Most people are wearing flip-flops. I'm wearing my Keens and stand a head taller than the crowd. The sooty, humid air stings like a lungful of red ants.

I approach a guy with a mossy, blond beard growing down his sternum. He's wearing a fishing vest and shorts, and the chinstrap on his wide-brimmed hat is pulled tight across his jowls. The air is still, but he looks like he's bracing for a typhoon.

"Excuse me," I ask. "Do you know how to get to a street called Soi 28?"

He points down the block. "You from the US?"

"I'm from Bost—"

"Yeah, I'm from Texas. I was an MP back in Saigon, one of the last guys out, last guys out."

"Saigon. Wow," I say, taking a step back. "Is it OK to eat at the food carts around here?"

"You don't want to hang around here. Soi Cowboy is just a few Skytrain stops, Skytrain stops." He tugs twice on the travel wallet around his neck.

The Skytrain is Bangkok's subway, which is supposed to be clean and safe. Soi Cowboy is a red-light district, which is supposed to be neither. Cousin Joey said the Cowboy is worth seeing. "Bring rubbers, if you have any left," he said.

The man from Texas looks off in the distance. "This whole Sukhumvit area is built on a swamp. I'm going to retire here, retire here."

He exhales into his hand and sniffs his breath.

In less than two minutes, this guy has confirmed my worst fears about Southeast Asia. This place can do things to you, permanent mind-warping things. But I'm only in Bangkok for three days, a pit stop. I can hold a sooty, humid breath that long.

I put on my hat, tighten my chinstrap, and walk away, walk away.

Five blocks later, I spot a concrete blockhouse with a gnome-sized bamboo garden and a koi pond large enough for three fish. The Sukhumvit Hostel.

The Sukhumvit is the guidebook's pick for budget accommodations in Bangkok. It's centrally located, which can mean either close to everything or near nothing. The simple, clean decor is supposed to appeal to the Buddhist in you. The thirty-dollar-a-night single rooms appeal to the Jew in me.

My room is on the second floor and includes a bed, a lamp, and a wall tapestry, but few other distractions. I drop off my bag, head down to the front desk, and confirm the additional 50-percent room discount Pittman promised.

In the lobby, I meet a group of twenty-somethings, including:

• Adler, a nervous little German who recites from a Bangkok guidebook as if it were a bible. "Thai people eat tarantulas, lizards, and rats," he announces to the group. They ignore him. Adler probably got picked on at school and scored poorly in the class slam book. He's young enough to be my son. I adopt him.

• Pam and Peggy, two American girls wearing T-shirts that say "University of Stanfurd." I point to their shirts: "I hear that's a good school, except for the English department." They laugh. Pam has cheek bones. Peggy has chins. But I don't care: After my adventures with Ola and Anika, I'm done with women in their twenties.

• Two annoying British guys, probably not gay. They don't offer their names and I don't ask. After my T-shirt joke, they turn their backs to box me and Adler out of further conversation with the girls.

Adler, unfazed, blurts out, "Thai people don't like it if you touch them on the head or point at them with your feet."

I say, "Thais have a thing for the king too. Use his name in vain and you go to the slammer."

I turn to the Brits and wave a disapproving finger: "Never refer to the old boy as a shitehawk, arse bandit, or nancy boy. OK?"

The Brits look me in the eye, expressionless.

The girls laugh. Pam points to my UMass T-shirt: "Hey, my brother goes to UMass." She is long and blonde. She probably has a sparkly navel. Not that I care.

I suggest we all grab dinner on Khao San Road, Bangkok's version of Long Street, the backpacker district, a must-see shit hole, according to Pittman.

Khao San Road is a thicket of high-volume restaurants, yellow neon, and street vendors. There's a fish and chips place called "Oh, My Cod" and a food cart selling "pan cake with eeg." The moist air smells sweet and sour like a Chinatown dumpster. Street signs are written in Thai, which uses characters that resemble Greek letters crippled by arthritis.

We settle on The Smiling Thai, the first restaurant with the name spelled correctly. Pam and Peggy sit first. The Brits act as if someone just shut off the music and snag seats on either side of the girls. Adler and I sit on the other end of the table.

I order the green curry extra, extra spicy to impress the group. The waitress is not impressed and trots off to the kitchen.

Our meals arrive. My curry has as much zip as a bowl of Cream of Wheat. "Mine rots. How's yours?" I ask our group.

Grumble, grumble, grumble, grumble, grumble. A unanimous five-grumble rating.

Adler recites from his guidebook: "Thailand is known as the Land of Smiles and displaying anger is a sign of mental illness. The smile can be used to convey different emotions: happiness, hostility, or hatred."

"Thanks for the info, Adler," Pam says, winking.

She asks about my trip. I say I'm traveling around the world for four months. I mention *clausurado* in Venezuela, Beaufort 7 in Greece, and bungee jumping in South Africa. She is impressed. The group is impressed. I am impressed. I enjoy a moment of serenity and self-acceptance. Pam takes my photo for her blog. I think about my blog and spoil a nice moment with one question: "Do your friends from home ever call or write?

Girls: No.

Brits: Speaking of shitehawks . . .

Adler: My mother writes every day.

One of the Brits puts his arm on the back of Pam's chair, claiming her. He smiles. I smile.

The waitress returns. We all put on our "the-food-sucks-in-this-country" smiles.

I realize I have a lot in common with kids this age: apathetic friends, weird grooming habits, constant partying, and trying to get laid. These common interests may serve me well applying for jobs at companies populated with twenty-somethings. On the other hand, my interests haven't changed much in twenty years. Maybe this is why women my age call me immature. I order another beer.

Back at the hostel, everyone disperses except for Adler, who hovers near me.

"Want to visit the National Museum tomorrow morning?" He's still clutching his little guidebook.

"I've got some stuff to do," I say. "But thanks anyway."

As I walk toward my room, he calls out: "How about Chinatown in the afternoon?"

I feel bad blowing him off. But I'm wiped out. It's not just jet lag. For the last eight weeks, all I've done is try to meet new people. Wooing and entertaining strangers is like making cold calls around the clock. ABC: Always be closing. I pour energy into people who vanish after an hour or a day.

The next morning, I consult the hostel front-desk manager: "Is there a gym, a health club, nearby?"

"Siam Health Adventure on Soi 7, very close, twenty-five baht taxi."

Outside I flag down a cab.

"How much to Siam Health Adventure on Soi 7?" I point to the meter on the dashboard.

"Meter no work," the driver says.

"The guy in the hostel said it would be twenty-five baht."

"OK, thirty-five baht."

"He said twenty-five baht."

"OK, we use meter."

"As long as it's under twenty-five baht."

"OK, thirty baht."

"Forget it, I'll get another cab."

"OK, OK, twenty-five baht."

I write the price, twenty-five baht, in my pocket notebook and show it to the cabbie. He smiles, nods, and off we go.

Instead of watching the road, the driver watches me in his rearview mirror. I flip through Pittman's guidebook to a section on Bangkok transportation. "Vehicle accidents are a leading cause of death for foreign tourists." I close the book and look out the window at the street signs for Soi 33, then Soi 37, then Soi 40.

"Excuse me, are we going to the Siam Health Adventure on Soi 7?"

"Today king's anniversary, much traffic, we go this way."

I hold up the piece of paper to the rearview mirror and point to the price.

"OK, OK, twenty-five baht," he says.

The driver pulls over on Soi 42, gets out, and opens my door. The sign on the store in front of us says, "Lik Lik Jewelry: Diamond Sale Today Only."

"You want diamond for wife? Lik Lik, very fair, very cheap. Come, come."

"I don't want any diamonds. I want the gym."

He closes the door and off we go.

Soi 40, Soi 33, Soi 22, Soi 15.

The cab pulls over in front of Lik Lik Soapy Massage. He opens the door.

"Is this the Siam Health Adventure?"

"Many beautiful girl. Special massage for special customer."

"If you don't take me to the gym, I'm going to call the police."

He points down the street to a sign: Lik Lik Muay Thai and Romantic Foot Massage.

The guidebook includes a warning about the Bangkok taxi hustle.

"I'm not interested in kick boxing or massage or anything else from Lik Lik," I say. "I want the Siam Health Adventure on Soi 7."

"Same, same," he says. "Siam Health closed for queen's birthday."

"The emergency number for the tourist police is 1155, right?"

I hold up the guidebook, which has the phone number listed in large bold type.

"OK, OK, Siam Health Adventure."

Five minutes later, we pull up in front of a building called Ginger Towers that advertises luxury apartments, a shopping mall, underground parking for 700 cars, and four floors dedicated to Siam Health Adventure.

The driver gets out, opens my door, and smiles. I offer my I-feel-guilty-for-something-I-can't-explain smile and give him thirty baht.

The cab ride is only a warm-up. Bangkok scammers are waiting for me at every turn.

Scam #1: Siam Health Adventure

The decor is polished steel with pink and blue neon. Techno music throbs in the background. A sign says, "To Your Healths." The reception desk is manned by a half-dozen young women with name tags that say, "Member Relations Officers."

One of them peels off to take care of me. She says the one-day rate is 800 baht, about twenty-six dollars, almost two nights at the Sukhumvit hostel.

I counter: "How about 800 baht for twenty-four hours, so I can come in tomorrow morning too?"

"I check my manager," she says.

After ten minutes, she returns and takes me to a room of small tables, the deal-closing room. The officers and other customers are Thai. I'm the only *farang* in the place.

"We have male and female steam rooms," says the member relations officer. She caresses her ring finger, which is devoid of a wedding band.

"We first club to offer pole-dancing classes." She makes a pole-climbing motion with her hands.

"Our spa give Swedish massage." She smiles a smile that could mean many things.

"Look, I'm only in town for a couple of days," I say. "But I might come back to live, and if I do, I'll join this club, and you'll get a big commission and be able to buy an apartment in Ginger Towers."

"OK, 800 baht."

We've agreed to something, but I'm not sure what, so I ask for that something in writing. She whips out a business card and scribbles something about two days.

In the free-weight area, I talk to a local guy with an expensive-looking haircut.

"Mind if I ask how much a membership is here?" I ask.

"Six-hundred-thirty baht a month."

Scam #2: Soup

Outside the hostel there's a soup cart. The hostel manager says a bowl should cost thirty baht, about a dollar.

The wooden soup cart rests on a pair of dusty mountain-bike tires. The proprietress ignores me and pets a mangy dog. A shelf open to the Bangkok air displays greens, cellophane noodles, and balls the color of mushroom caps. The food preparation area is wooden, worn, and covered with deep gashes. *In Thailand, take Azithromycin.*

In the center of the cart sits a boiling stock pot filled with dark liquid. *Only eat food that is thoroughly heated.* I decide if she accepts twenty-five baht, we'll have a deal.

"*Sa-wa dee krab,*" I say with a little bow. "How much?"

"Forty baht."

I smile. "Twenty baht."

She smiles and returns to the dog.

No deal, no soup.

Scam #3: The Kid

A block from the food cart, a little kid offers to read my palm. Instead of giving him cash that he will no doubt spend on drugs and hookers, I offer him something that he really needs: a cookie from a nearby bakery shop.

He goes right for the most expensive item in the display case, a sixty-baht éclair. The counter guy wraps the pastry and smiles. The kid smiles. I smile.

Outside, I stand with the kid waiting to see the joy on his face when he bites into the pastry. We stand in silence. "Eat, eat," I say. Suddenly he doesn't understand English. He points to a hole in his shirt and then points to a Lord & Taylor's across the street. I smile. He smiles. "Good luck to you," he says. "You will have many wives and childrens."

"Good luck to you too," I say.

As I walk away, the kid stands on the corner and waves to me. He still hasn't opened the package. Probably going to share it with his little friends.

I mention the pastry incident to the hostel desk clerk. He shakes his head. "Him return cookie to store and share money with counterman. But your intentions good." He flashes me a "you've-been-had-by-an-eight-year-old" smile.

Blog Entry: October 17
Bangkok

Loving the land of Singha and sex-change surgery. Imagine me showing up to my college reunion as "Randi" instead of "Randy." I'd be a hit.

Some of the language I've picked up:

Sa-wa dee krab: Hello, I'm a Westerner, please charge me double.

Kap kuhn krab: Thank you, carrying all that cash was straining my wallet.

Pet-pet, mahk-mahk: Hot and spicy. Proper usage: "Can I get the Swedish massage, pet-pet, mahk-mahk?"

In Bangkok another night, then off to Vietnam.

Still haven't received my new liver. Let's get on the stick, people.
Again, that e-mail address: rburns@rburnsworld.com
—Burns

When I awake the next morning, the linoleum floors in my single room seem lumpier. The rusty window bars seem rustier. The Buddha-themed wall tapestry looks as if it was a door mat in a previous life.

After using a nail clipper to trim a splinter on the head-board, I open my day planner and review today's options:

• Wat Pho, a temple that houses the humongous, remarkable, serenely luminescent, 150-foot-long Reclining Buddha.

• Snake zoo with Adler.

• Sex show at Soi Cowboy.

Sights, snakes, or breakfast strippers. Nothing appeals to me. But what would appeal to a woman on Match? I imagine updating the travel section of my profile with "the Garden Route of South Africa, the Olympian Zeus in Greece, and the giant Reclining Buddha of Thailand." Adventurous, cultured, spiritual. The women will be all over me.

I hop the Skytrain to a ferry up the Chao Phraya River, and in an hour, I'm standing outside a large walled compound. Wat Pho spans twenty acres and has sixteen entrances. But that seems to be the only two things the guidebook, my tourist map, and the hostel desk clerk agree on.

Pittman recommends an east entrance on Sanam Chai Road. The tourist map recommends a west entrance on Maharat Road. The hostel deskman recommends a south entrance on Chetuphon Road. I'm standing on a road called Thai Wang facing east or north or maybe south. My eyes start to burn from the sooty air.

To my left, a tour leader addresses a crowd of Western tourists.

"Wat Pho, or Wat Po, is sometimes abbreviated Wat Phra Chetuphon Vimolmangklararm Rajwaramahaviharn." He laughs at his own joke and continues. "This wat is home to ninety-one religious structures called stupa and chedi."

My guidebook says there are seventy-one structures known as pagodas. The tourist map says there are ninety-nine structures, including some called *prang*.

The tour leader continues: "The wat includes a main chapel, called Phra Uposatha or Phra Ubosot or simply bot."

The crowd starts to rub their eyes, thumb through their guidebooks, and scratch themselves.

"The Reclining Buddha is housed in a sanctuary, pavilion, shrine, or temple called a *viharn, vihara, vihaan, wihan,* or *wihaan*." The crowd looks as confused as I am. I follow them through a nearby entrance.

Inside Wat Pho, the tour leader rattles on about stone monuments called Lan Than Nai Tvarapala. I scan the grounds: sword-wielding statues; dragon-faced statues; multiroofed temples with curlicue spires; corncob-shaped monuments festooned with burnt orange and sea-green tile. The tour leader refers to the grounds as "wondrous" and "magnificent." A less erudite person in a fussy mood might call the place "garish" and "cheesy."

I pay fifty baht and follow the group to the hall of the Reclining Buddha. Everything about the exhibit is long as advertised, starting with the line and the humongous, remarkable, wooden shoe rack. "Please find a cubby for your footwear before entering the hall," the tour leader says.

Do I really want to leave my ninety-dollar Keens in this rack? A uniformed guard is watching over the shoes, but what if he's in cahoots with the local shoe thieves like the little kid and the pastry clerk? Everyone in the group puts their shoes in the rack. I do what they do.

Just then, a Westerner exits the exhibit, gives the rack a once-over, and stomps over to the security guard. "My blue Crocs are gone," he tells the guard.

"Look again," the guard says.

The Westerner combs the rack. No blue Crocs.

"Look again," the guard says.

The American spots a pair of orange Crocs—in another section of the rack—looks around quickly, and takes them. I immediately retrieve my Keens from the rack, hide them in my daypack, and get back in line.

Behind me: a young Western couple, and behind them, a young Asian couple. Another couple in front of me and another is exiting the exhibit. All young. All paired off.

I put on my Keens, head for the exit, and walk away, walk away. I came. I heard. I saw enough for a Match entry.

The Chao Phraya River is the muddy color of a thirty-baht soup. Small craft zip around like water bugs swirling murky water in their wake. From the dock, I watch a couple in a gondola-shaped boat with a canopy. The man puts his arm around the woman and kisses her ear. Their Thai boat driver steers using the six-foot handle of a *Mad Max* contraption that chugs and spews like an old V8. The woman brushes the man's throat with a long-stemmed rose.

Enough already with the couples.

The only other person on the pier is a young Asian woman wearing a frilly, yellow dress. Perfect breasts jockey under the frills.

"Excuse me. Do you know which boat goes to the Central Pier, near the Skytrain stop?" I ask.

She flips her hair, straightens a pleat, and answers in a dark brown voice, "This one does, honey."

I take another look at her. There's something boyish about this lady. Or rather, there's something ladyish about this boy. I look the other way.

As the ferry departs from the dock, I find a spot on the railing next to a Western woman wearing a T-shirt that says "Colorado Buffaloes" with all the words spelled correctly. Her Tevas are tapping to imaginary music. Long hair, long legs, long everything—what Pam, the American twenty-something, will look like in twenty years if she's lucky. The woman glances at me. Then she gives me a second look.

"Having fun?" I ask.

She points to another gondola-shaped boat ferrying yet another couple on the river.

"They're having fun," she says. "Reminds me of Venice."

"Me too." I give her the once-over: no earrings, no watch, no adornments of any kind. She must have read the tips about not wearing flashy jewelry around Bangkok. Or . . .

"Are you an artist?" I ask.

"Well, I did study art history." She turns toward me and gives me the once-over: plastic sports watch, worn daypack, tropical-weight painter's pants. "Don't tell me you're a painter," she says.

"During my Renaissance phase, I dabbled in matte, satin, and if the muse was with me, high-gloss."

"You've never been to Venice, have you?" she says.

"Does this mean you're not going to loan me 500 baht?"

"I already blew today's budget at Wat Pho." She turns to watch the couple in the gondola. *The lonely, romantic type. This could work.*

"Hope you didn't fall for the old Wat Pho disappearing shoe trick," I say.

"I hired a guide who told me not to put shoes in those racks. He said people from Cambodia go there to steal stuff."

"Not just from Cambodia."

She says she's from Denver, likes to ski, and works for a software company. I double-check her fingers for a ring or a tan line. She's clean.

Now what? Ask her out for a drink when we dock or maybe dinner later? *Hey, I know a really crappy restaurant on Khao San Road.*

She eyes another gondola boat with another happy couple and resumes tapping her Tevas. She's starting to drift; I'm losing her.

I try to recall a past experience to apply to this one. The Greek ferry encounter didn't turn out so well. Anika and the hot tub? Another maritime disaster.

Maybe I just need to be more forceful, more confident, like the Brits who wanted Pam and went after her. I think of the Thai taxi drivers, the member relations chick, the eight-year-old kid with the pastry. Bangkok isn't for nancy boys. Bangkok is for closers.

I tap her on the shoulder. "So, how long you traveling for?" I ask.

"Two weeks."

"Do you have a job waiting for you back home?"

"Yeah, job, dog, husband. The whole nine yards."

This is the second ringless woman with a husband in a month. Married teases, hostel birds, part-time hairdressers, and mad Russians. What's with the women on this trip? I still have an unopened thirty-six pack of rubbers. Pittman's guidebook has been wrong about a bunch of things, but he couldn't have goofed about something this major. Is it me?

Across the Chao Praya, another gondola boat glides by with two men arm and arm. I glance over again at the ladyboy:

restless breasts, slim with biceps as large as mine. He's really not bad.

I've never had a homosexual experience, but I've come close. In third grade, I slept over at cousin Joey's house. Early in the morning, we woke up and started wrestling. Then he challenged me to a duel. In our variation of mano-a-mano combat, each warrior had one weapon, a half-inch penis. We rubbed the tiny heads together until one got so red that its owner (me) surrendered. But this was a one-time event, never to be repeated. Too painful.

Then, in my early twenties, I hitchhiked from Boston to LA, and went right to the beach. Four hours later, I was sunburned. This was no cute little pink New England-style sunburn; this was the real deal. I developed huge blisters on my legs that sloshed when I walked. The next night, I felt worse rather than better, so I started hitching back to Boston.

The first car that stopped was a poppy-yellow VW Beetle. The driver had long, blond hair and a beautiful face like Sharon Stone's. Except the driver was a guy, a pretty guy. I got in.

He glanced at my legs and said, "That doesn't look good, my man, why don't you stay with me and my girlfriend for a couple of days."

At his place, the girlfriend made dinner and went to bed. Then he took out some beer, and then he took out some weed. As we partied, I thought: This guy is OK. He's sharing his home, he's sharing his food, and he's sharing his party supplies. So I took out a bottle of Percodan that I had been saving for special occasions. Percodan was a prescription pain-killer known to induce feelings of well-being and camaraderie.

The next day, he went to work, the girlfriend went to work, and I sat on the couch and watched TV. At the end of the day, he came home without the girlfriend.

After dinner, he took out the beer, then the weed, and I took out the Percodan, which was known to induce feelings of well-being and camaraderie.

We partied for an hour, and then he said, "Ever been to a gay bar?"

I took another hit of beer and another hit of weed, and thought: Why not?

At the bar, guys were checking me out and buying me drinks. I thought to myself: This is what it must be like to be a hot chick.

The next day, he went to work and I sat on the couch and watched TV. At the end of the day, he came home without the girlfriend. After dinner, he took out the beer, he took out the weed, and I took out the Percodan, which was known to induce feelings of well-being and camaraderie.

We partied for an hour, and then he said, "I bet that couch is uncomfortable. Why don't you sleep in my bed with me?"

I took another hit of beer and another hit of weed, and thought: Why not?

His bed was the size of a swimming pool. I considered his long blond hair and beautiful Sharon Stone face. Then I noticed the sheets were bunched up and sprinkled with little white crusty stains. I thought to myself: I don't think I want to be bunched up and sprinkled with little white crusty stains.

"Thanks, but my sunburn is still pretty bad," I said. "Probably best for me to stay on the couch."

The next night after dinner, he took out the beer, he took out the weed, and I took out the Percodan, which was known to induce feelings of well-being and camaraderie.

We partied for an hour. We partied for another hour and another and another. There was no mention of gay bars and no mention of sleeping in his bed.

This continued for two more nights, but my sunburn didn't get any better.

Finally he came home with a plane ticket for me: Turned out the guy was a travel agent.

The next day, he drove me to the airport, where a gate agent met us and said, "Mr. Burns, I understand you're not feeling well. We're going to put you in first class."

I considered Mr. Sharon Stone with his long blond hair and beautiful face. I gave him a hug, a kiss on the lips, and then the rest of my Percodan.

Since then, I've maintained my gay virginity but acquired some suspicious tastes:

• I like mouthy, ballsy women who lace their conversation with words like "asshole," "cocksucker," and "scumbag."

• I don't like curvy girly-girls. I prefer slender, boyish women who look good in Under Armour.

• I flirt with men. If a friend is dressed nicely, I'll say, "You're going to break some hearts tonight." If a friend compliments my outfit, I'll say, "I bet you say that to all the guys."

• I develop crushes on new male friends and during our getting-to-know-each-other stage, we'll talk on the phone several times a day. At some point in the relationship, one of us will say, "If you had a cunt, I'd marry you." The other one will respond: "I bet you say that to all the guys."

Maybe I just don't like women.

But I'm not exactly attracted to men:

• I don't like facial or body hair on women or men.

• I don't like anuses, sphincters, dingle berries, fartel berries, *culo* cranberries or any of that scene back there.

• I have no desire to touch a *schlong* other than mine.

Maybe I just don't like other people.

To have successful relationships, Dr. Moody says you have to learn to ignore a lot of things about other people. You also have to learn to tolerate boredom. If you have to spend most of your time bored or ignoring other people, why bother with them?

Oh, right, you need the oxytocin.

So, say you meet some people you like, and you go out to eat with them all the time, which is expensive, but you do it because that's what people do, and then these people wonder why they're fat, and you listen to them complain about their weight, but you endure the complaining and get to know them, and then you establish boundaries, but then you spend all your time defending those boundaries because these people start asking for favors, and the one time you say "no" their feelings get hurt, and they pout and won't say what's wrong, and soon you spend all your time worrying about their feelings and have no time for yourself, and then, when you go on a trip around the world, which is like the biggest thing you've ever done, the fuckers don't write.

I admire the ladyboy's toned legs. A woman outside and a man inside. *Too confusing. I'm going to die alone.*

Back at the hostel, I look in the bathroom mirror at my wide, anxious eyes. When the Dark Place beckoned in South Africa, I followed Moody's advice and didn't resist. It was bad advice then, it's probably bad advice now. Off I go.

I'm in the foyer of the split-level ranch. The smells: Salisbury steak, pine disinfectant, and a hint of cigarette smoke. By the door, four pairs of galoshes.

It's two A.M. I'm seven, awake, and wandering. The door to my parents' room is locked.

The door to my stepsister Harriet's room is open. I shake her:
"I had a bad dream. Can I sleep with you?"

"Fine."

She yanks back the covers. She is fourteen and tall for her
age. Her bed smells powdery like cupcakes unlike my bed, which
smells like a wet dog even before we have a dog.

"I'm thirsty."

"Be quiet."

"I'm bored."

"Shut up."

"I can't."

"If you promise to shut up, I'll show you how to play the egg
game."

I lie on my back.

"Close your eyes. Now, pretend I have a giant egg in my hand
and I'm going to crack it. Imagine the yolk dripping over you,
only it's warm and soft, not gooey."

Above my head, I hear the clap of hands, the smell of vanilla
hand cream. Spidery fingers graze my hair, my cheeks, my neck.
I feel chills, prickles, a flush, warm and floaty. Over my paja-
mas she traces my chest, nipples, ribs. My thoughts wander, drift,
evaporate. I'm a feather, a droplet, mist. She circles my tummy. I
feel myself dissolve into warm sheets, a cushy mattress. I'm awake
but can't move. Her hands slide side-to-side under my waistband,
the pads of her fingertips against my skin. My body tingles like a
sleeping arm that just woke up.

"Eeew," she says. "Gross. Get out of here!"

A paneled den, a month later, Harriet is babysitting me. Her
friend Myrna is over. We're watching TV.

"Randall, Myrna wants to play the egg game with you."

I don't like Myrna. She's mean and Harriet acts mean around
her. Harriet met her on the volleyball team. Myrna weighs more
than most of the boys.

"No egg game," I say.

From behind me, someone grabs my wrists and pulls me down. My head thumps on the carpet. Myrna sits on my chest, knees on my arms.

"Get off, you fat pig!" I yell.

Harriet jumps on my shins and tickles me. I thrash, spit, squeal. I slam and bang my head against the rug.

"Come on, Randall, show us the little pocket rocket," Harriet says.

She tugs down my pajama pants. I shriek till I'm out of breath. Soft fingers drift across my belly, probe my belly button. The scent of warm vanilla, a warm heartbeat between my legs.

"Look Myrna, the little pervert is loving it."

In bed that night, my head and wrists ache, I lie awake feeling the warm heartbeat, the buzz of a sleeping arm, the twitch of a phantom limb.

I can't sleep and go to Harriet's room.

"Get out you little perv."

Soon after, my parents buy me, in succession, a chameleon, a gerbil, and a dog.

At fourteen. Same house, same foyer. By the door, three pairs of galoshes. Harriet is off at college or pregnant somewhere, I don't really care.

In the kitchen, "The Way We Were" is on the radio. A fridge covered with photos of Harriet and me and a magnet that says, "Insanity is hereditary. You get it from your kids."

Downstairs in a finished basement, another bedroom. Harold the basset hound wags its tail and jumps on the bed. On the dresser, a stacking turntable. On the wall, a Roger Dean black-light poster. On the windowsill, a loaded BB gun. Outside, the neighbor's window riddled with little holes, a wounded blue jay on the ground.

Across the hall, the playroom, that land of failed distractions. Under the Ping-Pong table, the large cage covered with the paint-spattered tarp. Whimpering emanates from inside. I lift a tarp corner and something stirs against the metal bars. Around the room: a beanbag chair leaking stuffing onto the floor, a hole in the wood paneling where I hide my stash. I pull off the tarp: clinging to a wire hanger covered with cloth, a baby monkey. The baby has wide, anxious eyes that never blink.

Like mine now in the mirror.

I imagine the monkey's voice: "Why do you keep coming here?"

I hear myself answer: "I don't know."

When I told Moody about Harriet, he took out a fresh pad of paper.

"So what?" I said. "I was diddled by my older stepsister. I got a boner, so I must have enjoyed it. My cousin Joey says he's jealous."

In the hostel computer room, I check e-mail. There are three messages.

From Match.com:
You caught her attention! She finds you intriguing.
You both enjoy a drink or two in social settings.
Like you, she exercises regularly.
Find out who she is.

I click to find out and the next screen asks for my credit card number. I hit delete.

One person commented on my blog.
Abe, Lenny, Rachel?
No, it's my old pal, Anonymous:
Dear Friend,
Try this weird trick for better sleep without drugs.

The text is accompanied by a photo of a barely legal girl in a bikini holding a leather strap. I consider clicking but hit delete.

From Ricki:

Hey Burns,

Figures you're loving Asia. It's the perfect place for you and your obsessions with germs, smells, bodily functions, and all things weird. Just read a book about a condition called "counterphobia" that made me think of you. Seems there are a lot of fucked-up people who are attracted to things they're afraid of.

I bet you're saving money by staying in another hostel filled with college girls. Take a break from stealing their hand lotion and visit some place other than the gym.

And in other news, I'm going in for surgery, so you won't hear from me for a while.

Safe travels, Ha ha.

—RRRRRR

I begin to type.

Hi Ricki,

Thanks for writing.

Sorry about Wiener.

Sorry to hear about your surgery.

Sorry, sorry, sorry.

Instead of hitting send, I hit delete, and then hit the road: Skytrain, ferry, Chao Phraya, boys and frills, couples and roses, temples and statues. Eventually, I'm face-to-face with the giant Reclining Buddha of Wat Pho. I'm not sure why I'm here.

The Buddha is long and serene as advertised. I give the gold-plated Gigantor the once-over:

One-hundred-fifty-foot body lying on its side like a napping blue whale. Check.

Sacred headgear that resembles an old-time, leather football helmet covered with acorns. Check.

Peaceful Buddha smile, the smile of one who is about to depart this world for nirvana. Check.

Feet with mother-of-pearl etchings representing Buddha's 108 auspicious characteristics, whatever that means. Check.

While pondering the Thais' obsession with feet, I hear ca-chinking, like the sound of a cash register. I follow the noise to a row of metal bowls that is about as long as the Buddha himself.

Tourists are buying bags of coins to drop in each of the bowls for good luck. There are 108 bowls, how auspicious. My inkling to drop in some coins is interrupted by a more profound inkling—in my bowels.

The shoe guard directs me across an open courtyard. I pass a row of stupas or chedis or prangs. No bathroom.

A helpful local guy in a linen suit approaches and says that all Wat Pho bathrooms are closed for the king's coronation day. The guy recommends a bathroom on the other side of town, conveniently located near a bespoke suit store: Lik-Lik herself will measure me. He gestures toward a cab stand near an exit.

"Should I bring my rich, senile father?" I ask. "He loves clothes. He's talking to one of the stone statues. I'll get him."

I excuse myself, and then walk in the other direction and keep walking. I cross a street and enter another compound with orange-robed monks walking around, but no tourists. Deep in my bowels, the inkling has graduated to a boiling. Instead of asking for directions and risk being told to leave the grounds, I pretend to know where I'm going and follow the sound of voices and shuffling feet.

Around the corner, two metal posts spaced about eighty feet apart rise from the ground. Each post is more than ten feet high and supports a fan-shaped sheet of metal that resembles a giant flyswatter. Attached to the flyswatter is a metal hoop. I hear the bouncing of a ball. Someone with a Thai accent yells, "Three pointer," and then someone else yells, "Brick." Everyone is wearing orange robes and sandals.

I am considering how to describe this scene in my blog, when a monk exits a small, tiled building and adjusts his robe. The building is the size of an outhouse.

Inside the building, I reach for a light switch and can't find one. I reach for the door and can't find one. In one corner, there's a hole in the floor surrounded by raised porcelain foot rests. In the other corner, a sauce pan floats in a plastic barrel filled with water.

I stare into the soupy, brown hole of the toilet and imagine a hand raising my chin and a voice urging me not to look down. I imagine myself squatting over the hole. *You don't have to do this if you don't want to.*

I imagine Peter, the Dutch girls, and Pam from the Sukhumvit hostel watching me. I imagine the ferry woman from Denver raising her hand for a high five and saying, "We doing this for the fucking US of A?"

Something with legs and a tail skitters up the wall and onto the ceiling.

A faucet protruding from the tiled wall drip-drips into the plastic barrel. The boiling sensation intensifies in my colon.

I think of Ricki and counterphobia and the rush, the electroshock jolt, I get from doing something scary or repulsive.

I swallow three times, drop my pants, and hover my butt over the hole. I grab the rim of the barrel with one hand for stability. The other hand points my penis back like a little hose. Money starts to slip out my pockets. As I go to catch the cash, my penis springs free and sprays my sandals, feet, and pants. All I can do is let it all go.

After I'm done, I look around for toilet paper. *Nothing.* Not a shred, not a newspaper, not a magazine, not a parking ticket, not a movie stub. I check my pockets. I have some wet cash and a copy of my passport, which is too small for a mess like this. The floor is covered with leaves, possibly used by previous patrons instead of toilet paper.

My thighs are getting tired from squatting. A monk is walking toward the loo. I try to think of a past experience to apply to this one. I think of the Dark Place and touching my drifting poops. An image pops into my head: a butt with a protruding whip. What would Mapplethorpe do?

I grab the saucepan, fill it with water, and pour it along my butt crack and into the squat hole. Then I put my left index and ring finger together, wince, wipe, and rinse my digits over the hole with another sauce pan of water. Wince and repeat.

I fling a last saucepan of water into the hole, which causes a soupy mess to bubble onto the floor. I run for the exit and pass the monk on my way out. He smiles. Kind eyes.

Back at the hostel, I receive some bad news: My single room has been given to a couple and I will have to sleep in the guys' dorm. "Not so bad. No charge," says the desk manager.

He leads me to the room and opens the door halfway until it hits something springy. He turns on the light. The six-person dorm is smaller than last night's single room and includes three double-bunks. Four of the beds are covered with grimy backpacks and an assortment of wrinkled clothes, nondescript tubes, and Nalgene water bottles. The room smells cedary and acrid like a gerbil cage. I sidestep a Teva sandal held together with duct tape and head for an empty top bunk by the only window.

I haven't had a roommate since college. Recently, I've had problems sleeping with a woman in my bed, even after sex, even after Ambien. I imagine trying to sleep in the same room with the two Brits, Adler, and two other kids I've yet to meet.

My only hope is to exhaust myself before bed, but it's too late for the gym. I'll have to go for a walk, a very long walk, to the one must-see sight left on my list: Soi Cowboy.

I'm too embarrassed to ask anyone to join me, so at eleven thirty that night, I start the half-hour *schlep* to Soi Cowboy, an outdoor sex mall renowned for go-go bars, prehensile vaginas, and the Boston backpacker salesman's top pick, Tug's Asian Massage.

As I walk, I practice a little Buddhist serenity and let State Department warnings about Bangkok nightlife drift by like imaginary clouds.

Bar workers and prostitutes have been known to lace beverages with sedatives and rob tourists. Do not leave drinks unattended or go alone to unfamiliar establishments.

I cross under a concrete overpass onto Sukhumvit Road. The sidewalks are well lit, tree-lined, and populated.

Alcoholic beverages may be stronger than those in the US. Every year Americans die of apparent premature heart attacks after imbibing.

After thirty minutes, the streetlights, trees, and crowds thin out. An attractive woman bops by, earphone wires dangling from her head. Soi Cowboy must be close. I make a deal with myself: I'll hit one go-go bar and then back to the hostel.

Some clubs charge exorbitant, unadvertised cover fees. Failure to pay can result in violence.

Another thirty minutes pass and I'm lost and surrounded by asphalt. It's too late to take a train and I've sworn off cabs.

*Police have been known to raid bars and force patrons to
provide urine tests. Anyone who tests positive for drugs is arrested.*

Now we have a real problem. My blood is 50 percent
Lunesta. I decide to turn around and walk back to the dorm.

I reach the hostel at one A.M., sufficiently tired, and hop
into my bunk. One guy I don't recognize is asleep on the
bunk below me. An hour later, two guys come in talking in
their outside voices:

"Shitehawk."

"Wanker."

They slam the door behind them and scramble into their
bunks. One coughs, then sneezes. The other yawns, then
scratches. Each moves around in his respective bunk bed
trying to find a comfortable spot that he's never going to
find. The metal beds creak like door hinges, click like ratchets,
clink like chain link, clang like metal coat hangers, and ca-
chink like coins dropping into a metal bucket, an auspicious
metal bucket. Fucking Brits.

I lie there waiting for the snoring to begin. I don't care
what it costs. This is the last time I sleep with strangers—at
least ones I don't choose.

At five A.M., another roommate cracks the door open,
rummages around in his backpack, grabs something, and then
leaves, slamming the door. Adler?

I go to the bathroom to take a leak. In one of the stalls,
I hear someone breathing. I look at his sneakers. Too large
for Adler. More likely a Brit. Then I hear "vvhhht, vvvhhht,
vvvvhhht," like something being squirted from a tube. I finish,
flush, and hurry toward the door, not wanting to hear another
"vvhhht, vvvhhht, vvvvhhht."

I'm grateful to the State Department. If I had made it to
Soi Cowboy, I'd probably be broke, incarcerated, or snapping
the rooster in a hostel bathroom like this guy.

I think of my spreadsheet of women and the droughts, the longest of which was a year with no sex, a record I equaled this morning.

No job.

No friends.

No luck with women.

Recently Moody mentioned something called "middle-age drift."

"Fifty is a weird age," Moody said.

"But I'm only forty-eight."

"For some people it starts earlier."

"What does?"

"Apathy, detachment, and isolation. Singles give up on dating. Relationships die of natural causes. Friends stop calling. Middle-age people hibernate to gather their strength for the fourth quarter."

Sounds like a plan.

The next afternoon, I pack, and then check the hostel computer to confirm my flight to Hanoi: twenty dollars for a two-hour flight that leaves at nine P.M. Then I see an advertisement from farescrooge.com: Bangkok to Boston, $1,100 for a twenty-five-hour flight that leaves at nine P.M. Either way, I've got time to decide.

Outside the hostel, there's a new soup establishment, a metal cart surrounded by several bar stools. Lined up to order is the tallest Asian woman I've ever seen. She's arm in arm with a little blond guy holding a guidebook. Adler.

"How's the soup," I ask him.

"Great, and it's cheap, twenty-five baht. Can I buy you one?"

"I got it, but thanks anyway."

The woman and I both wait for Adler to introduce us, but he doesn't.

"I'm Randy," I say and reach to shake her hand. She has perfect breasts and a firm grip. She says nothing. Adler says nothing.

I break the silence. "I'm flying out of Bangkok tonight and . . ."

Adler cuts me off: "We're really sorry for kicking you out of your single room last night. I hope you got some sleep. It was great meeting you. Have a good trip."

I watch the two of them walk off with their soups.

The soup proprietress motions to me. "*Sawadi,*" she says.

I look into her pot of dark, boiling liquid. It has a musty smell I can't place. There's no menu or sign.

Let's do this.

"How much? I say.

"Forty baht."

"Twenty-five baht," I say.

"Thirty-five baht."

I try Pittman's travel tip: negotiating down instead of up. "Twenty baht," I say.

She smiles, clucks, and turns to another customer.

"OK, OK," I say.

I try to justify my fleecing: This cart has metal counters— fewer bacteria.

A local guy in his twenties serves me. The soup contains noodles with gray, chewy, fishy balls. I eat and slurp and fume because I know I'm being overcharged.

I finish the meal, and the guy collects my bowl. The proprietress is nowhere in sight.

"How much?" I ask him.

"Twenty-five baht," he says.

I pay quickly and leave.

On the way back to the hostel, I pass the proprietress. She smiles. I smile.

That's right lady, Bangkok is for closers.

The Chronic Single's Handbook
Chapter Three: Personality Test: Are You Better Off Alone?
I.   Give yourself one point for each answer that applies.
*1)   As a child, when other kids were out playing, you spent
your time:*
- *Shoplifting.*
- *Wetting your bed.*
- *Running away from home.*
- *Setting fire to roadkill squirrels.*

2)   Your favorite comedy movies:
- Caligula.
- The Exorcist.
- Leaving Las Vegas.
- A Clockwork Orange.

3)   Your favorite celebrities:
- *OJ.*
- *Fatty Arbuckle.*
- *Tonya Harding.*
- *Nurse Ratched.*

4)   You favorite quote:
- *"So it goes."*
- *"Everybody lies."*
- *"Hell is other people."*
- *"Stop me before I kill again."*

5)   If you had a boy, you would name him:
- *Ebenezer.*
- *Holden.*
- *House.*
- *Sue.*

6)   Favorite foods:
- *Steak tartare.*

- *Carpaccio.*
- *Sushi.*
- *Vicodin.*

7) *Favorite colors:*
- *Black.*
- *White.*

8) *At a friend's dinner party, you typically:*
- *Open the refrigerator, take one bite of every item, and put it all back.*
- *Stuff a used tissue in the spinach dip.*
- *Steal the salt shakers.*
- *Ask for a doggy bag.*

9) *Which best describes your social style?*
- *Aloof.*
- *Reticent.*
- *Boorish.*
- *None of your fucking business.*

10) *You invite your elderly mother to dinner in a bad part of town. You show up:*
- *Fifteen minutes late.*
- *One hour late.*
- *Five hours late.*
- *Never.*

II. True or False:
Give yourself one point for each True answer.

1) *You need time alone, the way you need sleep: At least eight hours a day or you get grumpy.*
2) *You shun perpetually cheerful people: kids, reformed alcoholics, and anyone who sells real estate.*
3) *Your closest friend is the one buried under your floorboards.*

III. Scoring: Add up Multiple Choice and True/False

- One to Five points: Introvert
- Six to Ten points: Misanthrope
- Eleven to Fifteen points: Sociopath
- Sixteen points or more: Verizon customer service rep

CHAPTER SIX: VIETNAM

In darkness, be not unkempt by life's cacophonous hex.
—W. PITTMAN

Two hours after leaving Bangkok, my flight lands at eleven P.M. in Hanoi's Noi Bai airport. Like Thailand, Vietnam is a Buddhist country. But when I scan the terminal there are no smirking deities or sexy, welcoming statues. The decor is late Soviet Union: no billboards, advertising, or color. The walls are painted in a palette of olive drab and olive drabber. Exposed metal beams adorn the ceiling. The room looks like a hangar or a detention center.

A grim, uniformed man scrutinizes my papers. According to the guidebook, my passport will be popular reading in Vietnam. When I check into a hostel or hotel, I'll have to surrender it for review by the local authorities. When I check out, it will hopefully be returned.

Unlike Thailand, Vietnam is a communist country. I think of police states and labor camps. I think of China and North Korea. Creepy. Invasive. Titillating. I feel an adrenaline rush. Counterphobia.

Exiting immigration, I spot an Asian guy holding a sign that says "Burns." In Venezuela, I was "Mr. Randall Burns." In

South Africa, "Randy Burns." Now I'm just "Burns." A reflec-
tive person might think: I'm just a vestige of the man I once
was. I think: Let's do this, Charlie.

I follow the guy outside the terminal.

He points to the curb. "You wait me here."

There are few lights outside the building and fewer people.
Leaves rustle, humidity swirls. Beyond the parking lot, I imagine chest-high elephant grass, rice paddies, and palm trees, lots
of palms trees. Not the clean-cut, lawn ornaments that grow
in Florida. Southeast Asian palm trees, jammed together and
unkempt, fronds shooting off in all directions like a punky,
jungle hairdo. I imagine running around in this jungle with
cousin Joey, flamethrowers on our backs.

As kids, Joey and I played war after school. Our jungle
was the woods behind my house. We were heavily armed with
air guns, cap guns, squirt guns, ray guns, tommy guns, guns
that could shoot around corners, guns that launched Styro-
foam grenades. We watched *Combat* and *The Rat Patrol*.

For my tenth birthday, I got a chemistry set. The gunpow-
der recipe didn't work, so Joey and I filled the Pyrex beakers
with household chemicals and lit them on fire. For his tenth
birthday, Joey got a model rocket kit with engines and fuses.
We lit the projectiles on fire and launched them flaming into
the woods. Take that, you Krauts. Eat shit, you Japs.

No one in our family had ever seen action in the military,
but we were going to be airborne rangers, parachuting into
enemy territory, dispensing death from above. But along the
way to our eighteenth birthdays, we got distracted with daring
daylight raids of his parents' medicine cabinet for Valium and
Seconal and that was it. But to this day, Joey and I never miss
a war movie.

In addition to the war, Vietnam has other attractions:

• Wine made from fermented cobras.

• Six-hundred-pound catfish that locals catch using dead dogs for bait.

• The most beautiful women in the world. The guidebook says so. Steve from Sidney says so. Joey says so: "The chicks are all wands, thin as reeds, just the way you like them." Too bad I'm taking a break from women.

I check my watch: Ten minutes have elapsed. The driver was supposedly sent by the Hanoi hostel I prebooked. I amuse myself humming a few bars of the *Ride of the Valkyries*.

A car pulls up and a tired Asian guy gets out. I don't recognize him. He's smaller, lighter-skinned, and for lack of a better word, squintier than the Thai cab drivers.

He opens the trunk and grabs my backpack.

"Me hepp you."

"How much to Phu Vu Street in Hanoi?" I ask.

"Sorry, sorry." He opens the car door.

"How much? How much?"

"Sorry, sorry."

"Are you from the Loose Goose Hostel?"

"Sorry, sorry."

"Are you from the Hanoi Hilton?"

"Sorry, sorry."

According to the guidebook, the Vietnamese are sensitive to the "colonial attitudes" of condescending Westerners, so diplomacy and politeness are essential when dealing with locals.

I check my watch: midnight. I don't see any other cabs, so I do the diplomatic, polite thing and climb in.

He stomps on the gas. The taxi careens onto a poorly lit highway crammed with hundreds of little motorcycles that dart across lanes, in and out of traffic, and between trucks.

Some motorcycles carry four people. Some carry bales of hay. Some carry plump, pink, pig corpses strapped across the backseat. Don't these people sleep?

The drivers honk constantly using a staccato series of blasts. No one is wearing a helmet.

Twenty minutes pass and I've yet to see a stoplight, a traffic signal, or a sign for a town I recognize. I notice the driver watching me in his rearview mirror. His eyes are small, black, and lifeless.

Pittman says to trust your gut in dangerous situations. But my gut isn't feeling very trustworthy because I'm in a country we bombed and invaded. If interrogated, I'll say I'm from Newfoundland.

I see the driver looking at me again in the mirror.

My gut churns. What would John McCain do?

The next time this guy slows down, I'm going to bolt. He probably has an AK-47 under his seat. Good thing Joey and I trained for something just like this. I'll run in a weaving motion like a drunken wide receiver. AK-47s aren't known for their accuracy.

I tie and retie my shoes, and then move my wallet and passport into a zip-up pocket. He can have my backpack.

There's an accident up ahead.

The driver slows down.

I finger the door handle.

We pass a sign that says Hanoi.

"Hanoi, Hanoi?" I ask in the squeaky voice of someone who wouldn't last one night in captivity without his Ambien.

The driver smiles in the mirror and says, "Yes, yes."

A more evolved person might think: OK, sometimes I overreact.

But I think: Was this Vietcong joker messing with me the whole time?

Loose Goose Backpackers is located on a narrow street in Hanoi's Old Quarter. The three-story building is pastel yellow with scrolly metal balconies that would be ideal for throwing

Mardi Gras beads. The scene reminds me of the Bonobo in Cape Town without the teenagers in security smocks.

By now, when I check into a facility with a Saturday-morning-cartoon name, I know what to expect. The Loose Goose lobby: Sweaty kids in cargo shorts and beige ski hats. A guy in a T-shirt that says "#Twat." A girl in a hoodie that says "#Dickhead."

A blackboard lists activities, including kayaking in Ha Long Bay, a coastal bus tour, and a rooftop barbecue. I surrender my passport to the desk clerk and head upstairs.

My room is spare, Sukhumvit-like, and Soviet-inspired. The floor and walls are concrete. By the bed stands a mirror with a jagged crack. Above the bed a ceiling fan spins. Whirling fan blades. Whop, whop, whop. Vietnamese miscellanea ricochet inside my head like small-arms fire: Tonkin, Khê Sanh, Da Nang, Mekong, pongee sticks, spring rolls.

I sleep till ten the next morning, miss the free hostel breakfast, and hit Phu Vu Street, a guidebook recommendation, in search of food. The signs are in Vietnamese, which uses English characters with Jackson Pollack spatterings around the letters. Stores sell red dragon kites, purple silk lanterns, and lacquer rice bowls. Bicycles and little motorcycles whip around the two-lane street. Female drivers wear opera gloves to protect their skin from the sun and surgeon-style masks to protect their lungs from the pollution.

In Bangkok, I developed an appreciation for particulate matter. Taking a deep breath was like having a cigarette whenever you wanted one—for free. Hanoi seems less polluted. I inhale a few times. No Bangkok coughing fit, just a relaxing buzz, a soot-light.

A few blocks away, a local woman on a corner squats next to a covered wooden bucket. She's wearing a conical straw hat that obscures her face. Her tush is almost touching the ground.

Some guys might notice her champion squatting form, reed-like figure, or snug Vietnamese pajamas pants. Have I mentioned that I'm done with women? I focus on the food and brace myself for yet another Southeast Asian transaction.

The woman opens the bucket cover and flashes a rice mixture that includes small green things that could be raisins, peas, or aphids.

I take a hit of sooty air, exhale slowly, and then give her a little bow. "How much?"

She opens her hand wide: Five fingers.

Does she think I was born yesterday?

I counter with four fingers.

She nods OK.

That was easy, but what did we agree to? Four dollars or 4,000 Vietnamese dong?

"Dong?" I ask, a little embarrassed.

She nods in agreement.

Four thousand dong, twenty cents for lunch. She's speaking my language.

I whip out my dong and hand her four bills.

She scoops some rice with her bare hands and wraps the mixture in a page from today's edition of *Nhan Dan*. A wet spot forms on the single sheet of newsprint. I open the paper and wolf down the flavorless mixture. During the walk home, I run the numbers: eighteen dollars a night for a queen room at the hostel, three meals a day for less than a dollar. For $7,000 I could live here for a year. What's a little emphysema at those prices?

Later that afternoon, the lobby is crowded with beige ski hats. The air temperature is eighty-five degrees. A group of kids is signing up for the bus tour down the coast to Saigon.

That's 1,100 miles, the distance from New York to New Orleans—for twenty-five dollars, the price of a Boston cab to the airport.

The tour leaves at six thirty tonight and stops at noon tomorrow at a coastal town called Hoi An.

That's nearly eighteen hours on a bus.

Pittman's guidebook describes this bus tour as "rough and tumble, the cheapest way to see Vietnam."

"Cheap" is always good. "Cheapest" is always a concern. But since arriving in Southeast Asia my pricing metrics have changed. Yesterday's *concern* has become today's *good*. I've discovered that rock bottom has a bargain basement and I like it down here: Red-eye flights and five-hour layovers? Half the price of a direct flight? Buy now. Rooms just wide enough for a bed? Fine. No TV? No windows? A few bugs? Did I hear twenty dollars a night?

That evening, a bus pulls up in front of the hostel and I think: greyhound. Not Greyhound as in the bus company, but greyhound as in the sad, anemic, former racing animals that end up in public school lunches if no one adopts them.

Greyhound buses have two sets of wheels in the back for a smooth ride. This greyhound has only one set. Greyhound buses have large tinted windows. This greyhound has small, rusting windows that look like crusted eyes in need of an antibiotic. I'm in.

As we board, the bus driver swills a small can of what is hopefully an energy drink. The bus emits a grinding noise and accelerates. I grab a seat in an empty row. Once we reach cruising speed, I hear empty cans clinking in the trash bag by the driver's feet. Minutes later, the tires hit something and the windows rattle.

Boom! Boom! Bash!

Eyeball-shaped lights and air-conditioning fixtures fall from the ceiling into my lap. I hold my hand up to the openings where the fixtures used to be: Hot air is blowing into the cabin.

Outside the window, vehicles ricochet through the highway potholes. Our driver drafts, or more precisely, tailgates, the cars in front. To pass, he swings out into oncoming traffic, honking frantically at the motorcycles that scatter like insects exposed to a kitchen light.

Boom! Bash! Boom!

I can't bear to look out the window and I can't read because the overhead lights are rolling around on the floor. I distract myself by counting the fingerprints on the headrest next to mine.

Bash! Bash! Boom!

In the row next to me, a girl wearing a *Clockwork Orange* bowler and a guy in a pink mortarboard sit quietly. The only sounds from them are the crashing cymbals from their earbuds. They are both gripping the handrests. From behind me, I hear the occasional cough. Otherwise the other riders are silent.

The girl in the bowler looks toward the back of the bus where a bathroom isn't. "Seventeen more hours?" she says to no one in particular. "I'll never make it." Even in the dim light, I can tell she's an endomorph, soft and round, not my body type, which is fine by me.

The guy in the mortarboard next to her is also an endomorph, a bearded version of her. He looks out his window. "Nutters, all of them," he says in a British-like accent similar to hers.

After another round of potholes, I open a two-dollar bottle of Vietnamese rice vodka I bought for the trip.

Asian booze, like Asian food and milk, is rumored to contain formaldehyde. Though formaldehyde is great for preserving food and corpses, ingesting it can cause nausea, liver damage, and death. Works for me.

"Anyone for a toddy," I say to the couple in the hats.

"Brilliant," says the guy. "We've got a carton of peach juice and plastic cups."

I mix a round of drinks. We toast and swill.

The girl hands me her cup for more: "This is my only hope for survival." I pour another round. We introduce ourselves. They're from London, a brother and sister, Alfie and Elizabeth. I finally got a foreign accent right.

The bus hits another pothole. I offer drinks to two guys sitting behind me, and then propose a toast, "To Vietnamese drivers."

Another round of potholes, another round of drinks.

"I need to have a pee," Alfie says, glancing at the back of the bus where a bathroom still isn't.

I point to his empty cup. "Plan B?" I say.

During the night, the bus makes three pit stops. Each time, we all get off to eat and piss. Neither Alfie nor I remember any of this in the morning. I add another item to the list of things I'm done with: Vietnamese liquor.

At noon the next day, the bus pulls up in front of a Hoi An hotel called the Bang Su. The name sounds familiar. I look at the side of the bus: Bang Su Bus Company.

The four-story hotel has a soaring entrance supported by six lacquered pillars the size of telephone poles. As we stumble up the hotel steps, young Asian women in silky uniforms stream out to greet us. It's like we've disturbed a giant hive.

"This way. This way. You room, this way."

Alfie, Elizabeth, and the other kids surrender their cash and credit cards. Clever sales tactic: Deprive chumps of sleep

for eighteen hours, then drop them off at your hotel where
high-pressure salespeople lie in wait.

"This way, this way." A young woman in uniform
approaches with a smile that could mean many things. She's
also a wand. I can see how a guy might find it hard to resist
her invitation to see a hotel room.

"How much is a good room?" I ask.

"Twelve dollar."

"Let's have a look."

The room has a queen bed, air-con, a TV, a writing desk,
and a full bathroom. There are no cracked mirrors or ceiling
fans. A room like this would go for $200 a night in Boston.

I ask to see a better room. This one is twice the size with
two beds and a view of the swimming pool. Bill Marriott
would be impressed.

"How much?" I ask.

"Fifteen dollar."

"How about twelve dollars?"

"OK, for you only, twelve dollar."

That was too easy. Either I'm getting better at haggling or
Vietnam is not Thailand.

After checking in, I check out the rest of the hotel. In the
lobby, Alfie, Elizabeth, and several ski hats from the bus mill
around.

"Hey, Randall," Alfie yells over to me. "I owe you a shout,
mate." A "shout" is a round of drinks. Alfie is a good guy.

As soon as I join them, I regret it.

Elizabeth is reading out loud from a travel brochure:
"More than 200 tailors dot Hoi An's quaint, narrow streets.
Eager to create the garment of your dreams, these bou-
tique shops can whip up a custom-fitted suit in no time for
$125 US."

"I don't have money," says one kid.

"I'm hungry," says another.

"Why don't we go for cao lau?" Elizabeth asks. "That's the local dish. It says here the noodles are made with water from a special well."

"My stomach is not getting on so well," says one guy.

"Right, right," Elizabeth says. "How about a tour of the town? 'Hoi An oozes charm and history. This World Heritage Site offers a well-preserved example of a Southeast Asian trading port of the sixteenth century.'"

"It's raining."

"I like the tacky clothes idea."

After a few minutes of this, I find myself looking around the lobby: shiny black pillars, shiny oxblood beams, lacquered this, lacquered that, a wall crowded with flags from a dozen different countries.

I start to feel crowded. One of the benefits of traveling alone is that the only indecision and whining you have to deal with is your own.

Next to the flags hangs a sign for the hotel gym. "I've got to sweat out some formaldehyde," I say to the group. "I'll see you guys in a bit."

Walking away, I hear:

"I don't have a gym costume."

"I need a ciggie."

The Bang Su gym consists of three pieces of equipment probably left over from the French occupation. The gym attendant suggests a health club at a beachside resort called The Marlowe, five kilometers away.

On my way out of the Su, I see Elizabeth and the group in the lobby arguing. I sneak by them. Outside it's overcast, drizzling, and probably sixty degrees. The street is lined with one- and two-story buildings with tiled roofs. The town's roots as an ancient trading port are still evident: A tailor advertises custom-made suits in four hours; a restaurant offers cao lau and a Bia Hanoi beer for three dollars; a hair salon offers massage. Across from the hotel, a local woman in a ski vest and gray hoodie calls out to me: "Hey you, rent motobike?"

Her rental stand reminds me of the soup carts in Bangkok: mountain bike tires, worn wood, scratched metal. She looks a little old to be a hoodie hipster.

"Motobike special today," she says.

"It's raining," I say.

"Where you go, me drive you."

I turn back to the lobby and see the gang heading my way.

"How much to The Marlowe?"

"Four dollar."

"How about two dollars?"

"Three dollar."

"If we arrive in one piece, I'll give you one dollar."

"OK, OK, two dollar."

This chick wouldn't last an hour in Bangkok.

We hop on her little motorbike and go.

Every Vietnamese woman I've seen so far has been stunning and petite. Until now. I anchor my hands on her ample waist.

As we speed off, I take in the scenery:

   Tailor, tailor, tailor,

   cao lau joint,

   tailor, tailor, tailor,

   hair salon offering massage,

   hair salon offering cao lau,

   tailor offering cao lau,

   another hair salon offering massage,

   tailor, tailor, tailor.

The woman turns her head over her shoulder to face me as she's driving. "Where you from?"

"Canada."

"How old you?" The bike drifts into the lane for oncoming traffic.

"Twenty-five. How old are you?"

"Me twenty-five too."

OK, we're even.

"You marry?" The bike weaves back across the road, narrowly missing three kids hanging off one bicycle.

"Nope."

"Why no?" The tires spin on a patch of sand.

"I got intimacy issues."

"Eh?" The bike skids but doesn't go down. "Me, no marry, either. You like Hoi An?"

"It's a very nice town. Do you think we should go slower?"

"You should get marry and buy house here."

She turns her head over her shoulder and makes me an offer:

- We get married.
- I buy her a big house in Hoi An for $30,000.
- I leave town and visit periodically.

As I'm considering whether to haggle with her, we arrive at The Marlowe.

"One piece, two dollar," she says.

I give her three singles.

"Me wait you here."

"No, thank you. Like I said, I have issues. You take care."

She drives off and I'm left with a disturbing thought: That's the closest I've come to getting married in years. I review the marital success rate in my family. Of fifteen aunts, uncles, and cousins who married, nine have been divorced—a 60 percent failure rate. My stepsister, Harriet, was divorced three times. Maybe I'm the lucky one.

At ten thirty that night, I forage around the Bang Su for dinner.

- Rip-off hotel buffet: closed.
- Cao lau noodle joints and tailors across the street: closed.
- Hair salons offering massage: closed.
- No sign of Alfie or anyone else from the bus.

A quarter-mile walk from the hotel, I see lights—it's a large garage or a small hangar or a function hall. Inside, twenty or so Western guys are seated at long folding tables. Empty beer bottles are scattered on the tables, plastic chairs, and floor.

A cart with a boiling pot is set up in the corner. Noodles, greens, and unrefrigerated meat sit on the counter. Cases of 333 brand beer are stacked on the ground. I walk over and point to the pot, point to the 333s, and hold up one finger. Before I can ask the price, the proprietor hands me an open beer. He grabs ice from a cooler and puts it in a plastic cup. I shake my head, "No! No! No, thank you."

I'll eat aphid rice and breathe particulate-filled air, but I won't touch Southeast Asian ice.

I sit near a lone guy sipping a soup.

He is wearing a black ensemble: a long-sleeved pullover, wool slacks, a large gold watch, no socks, and leather buckle shoes. A clump of gray chest hair protrudes from the neck of his shirt. He looks like he's ready for a date—in Paris. I'm wearing my Keens, a blue quick-dry T-shirt, and olive river pants. I look like I'm ready to go white-water rafting.

"How's the soup?" I ask.

"No English." He shakes his long, gray coif. I know this accent.

"*Vous êtes français?*" I ask.

"*Oui. Vous êtes americain?*"

I speak basic French and introduce myself. He says his name is Guillaume. I'm too self-conscious about my language skills to say much more, so I listen. And squint. And listen harder.

I'm able to catch a few phrases:

"Forty-nine years old.

"Anarchist.

"Sarkozy and Bush, idiots, broke the world."

Guillaume is talking too fast for me. "*Lentement, s'il vous plaît,*" I ask. He probably thinks I flunked third-grade French or that I'm dumber than Bush.

After we finish beer number one, he is talking slower and my comprehension improves to that of a fourth grader.

"Hate politics . . . Television . . . fake experience . . .

"Career change . . . degree in social work . . . drug and alcohol counselor.

"I want to experience life with the mind." He points to his head.

"With the heart." He points to his heart.

"With the passions." He points to his crotch.

I point to the two empties in front of him. "*Encore?*"

I return with my soup and a beer for each of us. Halfway through 333 number two, my comprehension reaches fifth-grade level and his monologue turns to poverty.

"No retirement pensions . . . Vietnamese families care for old relatives . . . Old women selling trinkets on street probably have no family."

I finish my beer and he continues. "I give elderly street women one million dong, about sixty-five of your American dollars. That's a month's salary for some. These people are poor but nice. Haven't been ruined by capitalism like the Thais in Bangkok." He points to my empty bottle. "*Encore?*"

I think back to the moped woman. Because of her homely appearance, she may never get married and end up on the street. I may never get married and end up on the street. I can't even count on my friends who have barely written. I make a note to be nicer to Joey's daughter, Jan. Maybe she'll visit me when I'm old and in the home.

Guillaume returns with four bottles and slides two across the table to me.

We chug the first beer and start on the second. He asks in French: "Want to go visit some local bars?"

Isn't everything around here closed?

I point to the street. *"Toute fermé."*

Is toute *masculine or feminine, singular or plural? Who gives a* merde?

He points his half-empty beer bottle at a little red motorcycle. I gulp my last gulp and have to grab a chair to stand up. He grabs a chair to stand up, mounts the bike, and points to the backseat. *"Allons-y."*

I steady myself with the chair and consider the situation with drunken detachment.

State Department warning: In Vietnam, at least thirty people die each day from transportation-related injuries and many more are hospitalized, often with traumatic head injuries.

The ride with the Vietnamese woman wasn't so bad and I got a marriage proposal.

"Allons-y!"

State Department warning: Drivers should exercise extreme caution when driving at night. Road signs and streetlights are few, and buses and trucks travel at high speed with brights that are rarely dimmed.

He must be a good driver, he's European: Grand Prix, Le Mans, autobahns, dressed in black.

"Allons-y, Monsieur Bush."

State Department warning: International health clinics in Hanoi and Ho Chi Minh City can provide acceptable care for minor illnesses and injuries, but more serious problems will often require medical evacuation to Bangkok or Singapore.

I hear Singapore is nice this time of year. *Vive la France.*

The crosstown bar is run by a Vietnamese woman who recognizes Guillaume. The waiters are young guys who recognize him. He starts tickling and horsing around with them. Friendly, these French. In the back room, a local woman in short-shorts plays pool with a Western guy twice her age. I buy two beers, and Guillaume and I wobble onto the patio.

I ask if he's traveling alone.

He says *"oui"* and tells me about his two grown children.

I tell him that I'm single, traveling solo, and have never been married.

He says he's never been married either. He lived with the mother of his children for twenty years, but they decided not to marry. They split up three years ago. He says he's not cut out for marriage.

Then he says something about *"les prostituées."*

Then I say something about *"le HIV."*

He reaches into his front pocket and produces a handful of condoms. Then he shows me a text message on his phone. It's from a *prostituée* he met down the coast in Nha Trang. He says she's one of five women he's *"fait l'amour"* with since arriving in Vietnam a week ago. He didn't fuck, bone, or hose these women; he made love to them. Classy, these French.

But I didn't see any prostitutes in Hanoi or Hoi An. Where is he meeting them?

The hair salons.

Ola was a hairdresser; the world is starting to make sense.

But I'm still missing something: Do you request a massage at these "hair salons" and the women automatically provide the *coucher-coucher* treatment?

He leans in and offers the following advice:

• If you're getting a massage and want more, try to massage the masseuse.

• If she starts talking money, you're in.

• If she slaps your face or calls the police, you're out of luck.

• And don't hire multiple women at once because while one is grabbing your unit, the other may grab your wallet.

Guillaume calls over the waitress and whispers something in her ear. She reappears with two busboys carrying a jug large enough to refill a watercooler. Inside the jug, there's a hooded snake, a cobra, as thick as a forearm. The cobra is coiled several times and fermenting in a yellow liquid. A scorpion is crammed into the snake's mouth like a gag, a gag with pincers and a stinger. The Vietnamese version of tequila with the worm.

The waitress pours Guillaume and me each a shot. "Good for the manhood," he says in French. The snake brew smells like high-school biology and leaves a rubbery aftertaste. My manhood remains uninspired. I think of the black hooch on Mojito Island that was also supposed to stir the passions. Maybe it's just me and my passions are too old to stir.

On the ride home, Guillaume takes a shortcut and gets stuck in the mud. We dismount and regard the situation: An overdressed Frenchman, a mechanically impaired Jew, and the little red bike that couldn't.

"*Mince alors. Zut.* Holy shit," I say.

"Holy shit," he says.

Guillaume tiptoes back into the muck to restart the engine. His black shoes are now brown up to the buckles. I wade in. He guns the engine and I push, forcing mud into my Keens and between my toes. After ten minutes, we wrestle the bike free and exchange high fives.

He pulls up in front of my hotel, shuts off the engine, and gets off the bike.

"Our paths will cross again," he says in French.

"J'espère," I say, unconcerned with whether I've conjugated the verb correctly.

We exchange hugs and I watch him ride off.

Across the street, there's an empty spot where the moped lady hawks her wares during the day. I decide that the next time I see her, I'll give her five dollars.

Blog Entry: October 28
Hoi An, Vietnam

Partied with a cool Parisian guy. Reminded me of a slim Gérard Depardieu. Got a marriage proposal from attractive young Vietnamese woman. Her family owns a chain of car dealerships. Should I go for it? Cast your votes now.

I erase and start over.

Blog Entry: October 28
Hoi An, Vietnam

Tip of the Day: How to Send Overseas E-mail

It's identical to sending e-mail in the US. Here's a five-step refresher:

1) Make sure computer is plugged in.

2) Press ON switch.

3) Open e-mail program: Google Mail, Yahoo mail, Hotmail— you name it.

4) Type: "Dear Randy, I am deeply sorry for not e-mailing before now. I realize that you have been a great friend. To show

my sincerity, I have wired $100 into your bank account. Please
buy yourself a beer, a wife, or a town in Vietnam."
5) Press SEND.

Before I sign off, a message appears from W. Pittman:

Dear Mr. Burns,
We appreciate your thoroughness and will certainly correct
the latest factual errors you noted on pages 145–147, 165, 173,
186–189, etc. We rely on feedback from thoughtful readers to
correct future editions. We hope that you will visit us when you
are in Saigon.
Onward,
Wallace Pittman
President, All-American Language Schools
Author, Solo Salvation: Travel the world on your own

I Googled Pittman back in Boston, but I decide to Google
him again. Nothing has changed: He still has a Wikipedia
page, a web page, but no blog or presence on Twitter, Face-
book, or LinkedIn. I still can't believe a guy named Wally
scored one of life's trifectas: A book deal, a successful business
in an exotic locale, a beautiful, young wife. I have to see this
guy for myself in Saigon.

The next morning, I check out of the Bang Su at seven
A.M. for the eight-hour bus ride south to Nha Trang. From
the lobby, I see the row of bikes and mopeds secured with a
rusty chain. The moped lady is nowhere in sight.

Nha Trang is known for its beautiful beaches, Vietnam's
Riviera. Among the city's many sights: The Yersin museum
devoted to a French researcher who traced the bubonic plague
to rats. The town was also a notorious R&R spot for American soldiers during the Vietnam War. Alfie and his fellow kids

are staying at another Bang Su hotel, the cheap hotel option. I'm going with the super cheap option, which charges eight dollars for a queen room with a full bath. "Sounds dodgy," Alfie says. Alfie is still young, but he's probably right.

At 1400 hours, I exit the greyhound and detect an airborne agent that could be mustard gas or a burning squid factory. The curbs are piled with smoking garbage. Rats frolic in the streets. *Yersin museum, rats, fleas, bubonic plague.*

I've read that untreated, the plague progresses like this in less than a week:

• First: Fever, chills, aches; you lose interest in online dating.

• Later: Lymph nodes in armpits fill with stinky pus, swell to the size of an apple, and turn black. You cancel the upcoming ski trip to Jackson Hole.

• Finally: Body turns blotchy purple, limbs turn black with gangrene, and then things get really unpleasant.

I cover my nose with my hat and move out.

One klick from the bus stop, hustlers overtake me. Several men brandish DVDs and travel books. A woman offers what appears to be the local specialty, boom-boom with Vietnamese girl.

"That's very kind, but no, thank you," I say. *"Non, merci."* "No boom-boom." *"Bonne journée."*

1430 hours: At my destination the Hotel Dong II Long, I encounter resistance from a local couple manning the front desk.

"How much for a room with a large bed?" I ask.

"Eight dollar," says the man.

"I'll give you six."

He shakes his head, "No."

I turn as if I'm going to leave. The man turns to answer the phone. The woman walks away. A Western tour group floods the lobby and the man checks them in. I hang back until he's done.

"Any more eight-dollar rooms?" I ask.

"You again?" he says. "One left."

I register, collect a key, and ascend six flights of stairs. The room has two large beds and a view of a construction site. The pillows are heavy and hard; a blow from one could send someone home in a body bag. The toilet paper rolls are wet and crumpled like papier-mâché. I switch on the bedside lamp but nothing happens.

Six flights later, I'm back at the front desk.

"You again?" the man says.

"I'm having a little problem with my room and was hoping you could help me."

"What problem?"

"My lamp doesn't work and the toilet paper is wet."

He makes a phone call and talks in Vietnamese. What I hear: Cluck, squawk, cluck. Squawk, squawk.

I wait.

He makes another phone call. Cluck, cluck, cluck, squawk.

I wait.

The woman appears and hands me a soggy roll of toilet paper.

"We go." He points to the stairs.

In my room, he turns on the ceiling fan; its blades whirl inches from my head. Whop. Whop. Whop. Then he holds the lamp switch for several seconds. It goes on.

"All fix." He marches out.

1530 hours: I put on a bathing suit and head to the beach for afternoon PT. Thirty feet from the hotel, I'm back in the shit.

"Travel book?" "DVD?" "Boom-boom?"

"No, thank you." "*No melónes.*" "*No, gracias.*"

The beach is long and gray. Local teenagers sit fully clothed on the sand. That's weird, the waves look perfect for body surfing.

I spread out my towel in the sand and run into the water. After lining up in front of a modest wave, I start paddling to shore. A surge grabs me and I zip toward the beach, hands outstretched, a middle-aged torpedo. The wave breaks, flips me over, and slams me neck first on the sand. A stinging pain shoots down my spine.

Zut, merde, mince alors.

I wiggle one foot, then the other. I turn my head gingerly. Another large wave crashes on my chest and starts dragging me into the surf. I crawl to my towel and lie there panting.

I hear Singapore is nice this time of year.

Back in my room, I search for the ibuprofen. Underfoot, I hear: crunch, crunch, crunch. The floor has been overrun by fingernail-sized beetles. After gobbling three 200-milligram pills, I stomp the bugs until the linoleum is covered with black, gooey carcasses. Suddenly I'm in the mood for a bean burrito.

2300 hours: No luck securing a burrito, I settle for two twenty-two-ounce Tiger beers at a beachside pub. On the way back, I'm bushwhacked again.

"DVD?" "Travel book?" "Boom-boom?"

"No English." "*Danke,* no." "*Kap Kuhn krab,* no."

Inside, the deskman and his family are asleep on single-sized mattresses lined up on the floor. The guidebook says many Vietnamese hotel owners sleep in the lobby to save money on a security guard. I think about all my haggling over a few dollars with Vietnamese people who have no money.

Merde.

I scout the building for another entrance. No luck. I tap the gate. Nothing. I bang the gate.

The man appears wearing the same clothes he wore during the day. "You again?"

"Sorry, sorry," I say.

I climb the stairs double-time, and flip on the room light. Several platoons of ants are gorging on beetle entrails. Suddenly I'm in the mood for tapioca pudding.

But I'm not bothering the deskman and his family again tonight. I wipe up the mess with soggy toilet paper, flush it, and go to bed.

0100 hours: I'm awakened by screaming, gunshots, and explosions through the wall. I cover my head with the rebar pillows. Fucking TV.

0200 hours: The battle rages next door. I pop three more ibuprofen and rap on the neighbor's door. Nothing. I pound the shit out of his door.

Someone stirs inside. "Grunt, groan, grunt."

I imagine a guy with a room full of boom-boom girls.

I yell through the door: "Sorry to bother you, but would it be possible to turn the TV down a little?"

The door opens. An elderly guy. Alone and uncircumcised.

The horror! The horror!

0600 hours: I awake to the chirping of pile drivers and jackhammers. It smells like the burning squid factory has been doused with cat urine.

I leave the Dong in search of breakfast and encounter the usual.

"Video?" "Travel book?" "Boom-boom?"

I abort the breakfast mission and fall back to the hotel.

"You again?"

"I'm really sorry about last night. Could you please book me a flight to Saigon?"

"For today?"

"How about right now?"

About eighty dollars later, I land in Ho Chi Minh City, or Saigon to anyone who watches war movies. For accommodations, the guidebook lists a cheap option for fifteen dollars a night and a super cheap option for twelve dollars a night. For the hell of it, I look at the midrange options, which start at thirty dollars a night. No way.

I settle on the fifteen-dollar-a-night Rising Son hotel in a quaint-sounding part of town called District 1. The price includes a room with a queen bed, continental breakfast, and Internet access. A steal if there are no beetles.

The front deskman checks me in. He doesn't ask for my passport and I don't offer it. I collect my key and scope out the room.

Bathroom: no tub or shower, just a spray nozzle on the wall and a drain on the floor next to the toilet.

Decor: a framed wall plaque with a note from the local police. "Foreigner and Vietnamese woman must not stay in room without marriage certificate. You can rent other room fur lady."

Pillow: covered with the small, hopping insects.

I visit the desk manager.

"Excuse me. There are little bugs all over my pillow."

He smiles. "Yes, may I hepp you?"

"Are they fleas?"

He smiles harder. "Bug no bite."

I look up at the lobby ceiling fan. Whop, whop, whop. A breath lodges in my lungs. I feel my hands grip the check-in counter. I'm having a Nha Trang flashback. I need to exercise.

"Is there a gym, health club, within walking distance?" I flex my arms as if I'm lifting weights.

He flexes back, smiling a smile that can mean so many things, and opens a tourist map. He draws a small circle on a street called Cach Mang Thang in District 10 and traces a line from the hotel to the circle.

"Three kilometer," he says.

That's almost two miles, a forty-minute walk. No sweat.

Outside I take a few deep breaths. The sooty air calms me like a nonfilter cigarette.

Across the street, idling buses surround an expanse of green. A large sign says, "Peoples' Triumph Over Colonial Oppressors Park."

The traffic makes me feel oppressed. It's like New York City during rush hour, but with no stop lights, stop signs, or traffic cops. Instead of yellow cabs, there are thousands of honking motorcycles spewing across six lanes.

The tourist map includes a page of instructions for crossing Saigon streets that I distill to the following:

• Walk slowly and steadily, and the traffic will part like a school of fish.

• Don't do anything stupid like change your mind or direction.

I walk to the curb and watch as motorcycles and the occasional bicycle, bus, or car jostles for position. A middle-aged local woman on a motorcycle separates from the pack, veers onto the sidewalk, and heads toward me. She weaves around a few pedestrians and stops a few inches from my sandals. She guns her bike and smiles. "You like boom-boom with Vietnamese girl?" She points to an attractive, twenty-something on the back of her bike. "One hour, fifteen dollar US."

The twenty-something has long dark hair and wears jeans and flip-flops. She looks like a Western college kid, but without the ski hat, tattoos, or slutty clothing.

I decline diplomatically and politely: "I'm almost fifty years old, I'll never last an hour with her," I say.

"OK, OK. Ten dollar, one hour."

"Let me think about it and have my people call your people."

She frowns and drives off. I stutter-step into the street and then retreat to the curb. Another middle-aged woman on a motorcycle locks onto me, separates from the pack, and drives onto the sidewalk. She's wearing plenty of makeup.

"Why you no walk?" She smiles and points to the young woman on the back of her bike. "You like boom-boom with Vietnamese girl?"

"Actually, I like older women," I say. "How much for you?"

"Me? Same price."

"Maybe another time. Let's be in touch."

She watches me stutter-step on and off the curb, shakes her head, and then drives off.

I give up and retreat to the hotel. I shower, grab a fresh pillow from the closet, and get into bed. As I start to doze, my eyelids start to itch. I adjust my sleep blindfold. My eyelids itch some more. I adjust again. The itching turns to skittering, crawling, twitching, burning. I feel the lash of a thousand eyelashes, the puss of a thousand sties. I whip off the blindfold and run to the bathroom mirror. My face is covered with little hopping insects.

I shower again and crawl back into bed, my head wrapped in a hand towel soaked in 30-percent DEET insect repellent. The bugs gambol freely on the exposed part of my face.

After dressing and repacking my backpack, I head down to the front desk.

"Excuse me. Those bugs in my room *do* bite."

"May I hepp you?"

"Can you move me to another room?"

"Hotel full." His eyes are small, black, and lifeless.

I take out Pittman's guidebook and point to a page recommending the Rising Son. "*Traveling Solo* gave you guys a really good rating. That's why I came here. Is there anything you can do for me?"

"Fuck Wally Pittman!" The deskman slams his hand on the counter. "You friend him?"

"No, I only bought the book."

"Then shut up about book."

I slam my hand on the counter: "OK, I'm checking out and want a refund."

"No refund."

"I've only been here three hours and the room is infested with insects."

"No refund."

"I paid for the room with a credit card. I'll have my credit card company cancel the charge, and you'll get a bad credit rating."

"Bad credit rating to you."

The ceiling fan wobbles and creaks. Here I am again, haggling with a poor local over a few bucks. Have I learned anything in the last week? Apparently not.

I slam the counter, "Well . . . Fuck you!"

"I call police."

I run out the door dragging my backpack along the ground.

Outside I take a few sooty breaths. I've finally reached my threshold for squalor. No more cheap hotels. No more twenty-five dollar bus rides. No more hanging around with unwashed hostel kids. I have money. Time to throw it around. Give me West Palm Beach, adults in linen shorts, and potable ice.

Two blocks away on Pham Ngu Lao Street, The Saigon Breakers Hotel.

Lobby: chandeliers, paisley carpets, Breakers piano bar, employees wearing shoes instead of flip-flips, free bottled water, bell staff that expects a tip.

King Single Room: ceiling sprinklers, radio/alarm clock, entertainment center with surround sound, Breakers bath amenities, bathroom telephone, full-length mirror, walk-in closet, cleaning staff that expects a tip. On the bed, chocolates and a clear package with a new sleep blindfold.

Breakfast Buffet: tablecloths, cloth napkins, salad forks, Breakers eggs benedict, Swiss cheese omelet, spring rolls, deep fried cheesecake, wait staff that expects a tip.

Dinner Buffet: candles, flowers, wine glasses, steamship round, sole in butter sauce, chicken in cream sauce, asparagus in cheese sauce, spring rolls, deep fried cheesecake, after-dinner chocolates, free bottled water, hostess that expects a tip.

I spend the next two days eating, sleeping, using the hotel gym, and never leaving the premises. It's like a vacation from traveling. And I love my new blindfold. But my hotel bill has reached $150, the equivalent of two weeks in a hostel.

That night, I take a seat at the Breakers piano bar next to a couple in matching North Face fleece vests. They're probably spending their Saigon vacation indoors as well.

The bar menu is in small type. I hold it close. I hold it far. It's still in small type.

"You need longer arms or reading glasses," says the woman next to me in a familiar, *kvetchy* accent. New York Jews, my people.

"I'm in denial," I say. "I'd rather not see than get glasses."

The bartender hovers.

"Do you have 333 beer?" I ask him.

"For light lagers we have Heineken and Budweiser, both imported." The bartender is Asian, but speaks English without an accent.

Glass shelves behind him sport Kentucky bourbons, French vodkas, clear tequilas, and no Vietnamese booze of any kind.

"I'm in the mood for an import," I say to the bartender. "A Budweiser would be great."

"Where you from?" the woman next to me asks. Her eyes wrinkle as she smiles. Her hair is unnaturally black but her eyebrows are graying. She was probably attractive at one time. I'm guessing she's in her midfifties.

"Boston," I say.

A guy on the other side of her leans in to join the conversation. "We live on Long Island." He runs his hands along his scalp where hair used to be. He has a carpal-tunnel wrist brace on one hand.

"I grew up in Westchester," I say.

"We have friends who grew up in Westchester. You're probably too young but we'll ask anyway."

She names people I don't know: "Pritzker, Goldfarb, Weintraub."

"When did you graduate?" she asks.

"Mount Vernon High, class of '77," I say.

"We're class of '80," the guy says. "You're well preserved. You must not have kids."

They ask about my trip.

I begin a Budweiser-fueled monologue: three red-eyes in four weeks, black-market money-changers in Venezuela, street hustlers in Bangkok, bugs and rats, rats and bugs, hostels and hostel kids.

"You've been traveling with kids the same age as are our kids?" the woman asks, gray eyebrows arched.

The guy looks at me with pity and then jealousy.

I loosen up with a second Budweiser: formaldehyde wine, marriage proposals, Parisian sex tourists, motorcycle madams, Australian punters.

"What's a 'punter'?" the woman asks.

"It's a john," the guys says. "Honey, we have to get up early tomorrow. We should probably get to bed."

"You can go to bed," she says. "I'm ordering another round of drinks. Another Bud?"

I know I should probably stop, but I can't: Hookers, black hookers, hairdressers disguised as hookers, hookers disguised as hairdressers, Nha Trang boom-boom girls.

The woman interrupts me. "You know, I read somewhere that one in seven American men has paid for sex."

"I'm going to bed," the guy says.

Some private, unspoken code must have passed between husband and wife, because she decides to go with him after all. I'm left to my thoughts and a half-filled bottle of Bud. I'm feeling hungry and sociable and cheap. I'm in the mood to hit the streets again.

Three blocks from the hotel, I find an open-air noodle joint. The place is packed. An old local guy points his cigarette to an open plastic seat across from him. Once I'm seated, the cook comes over for my order. My seatmate points to his soup and his beer. I nod OK and the cook leaves.

My seatmate offers a cigarette. I accept, and he lights it for me. I point to myself "Randy" and put out my hand and we shake. His hand is sticky and has tobacco stains between two fingers. He smiles but doesn't say anything.

My order arrives.

He gulps his beer. I point at him with my beer.

"You're a party animal," I say.

He taps my beer bottle with his, and reaches into a bowl of greens on the table and drops a handful into my soup. Then another handful. Then he squeezes a wedge of lime into my bowl. I think about where his hands may have been. Then I stop and tap my beer against his.

He smiles, nods, and says nothing.

A few feet from us on the sidewalk, a gray-haired man is dressed as a witch. He stops and chats with my new mate in Vietnamese.

The witch turns to me: "Where you from?" he asks in a Southern accent.

"Boston."

"Where's your costume," he says.

"What for?" I ask.

"It's Halloween. *Laissez le bons temps roulez*, man." He slaps my back, waves to my seatmate, and runs off into the crowd.

The witch isn't going quietly into middle age. I think of the New York couple back at the hotel: carpal tunnel brace, paunchy, unsteady on their feet, early to bed, and younger than me.

"*Bons temps*," I say to my seatmate. He taps my beer with his.

I e-mail Pittman the next morning. Minutes after hitting send, I receive an invite to see him that afternoon.

After lunch, I put on my best outfit, which I've been washing by hand for the last two months: quick-drying khaki pants, a maroon collared-shirt with hidden security pockets, and brown urine-stained Doc Martins. I want to reek of success, but I worry that I just reek.

I thumb through my worn copy of Pittman's book, *Solo Salvation: Travel the World on Your Own*. So far, the book *has* been 60 to 70 percent accurate, with some notable exceptions, such as the Rising Son. I've added yellow stickies to pages indicating more changes Pittman may want to make in the next edition. Maybe he'll offer me a job. Maybe we'll coauthor a book. Maybe his publisher will ask if I have a book in me and *The Chronic Single's Handbook* will sell millions. Maybe I'll stay in Saigon. Fuck Boston.

It's midday and the traffic is light and nonthreatening. The motorcycle mama-sans are nowhere in sight. On my way to Pittman's All-American Language School, I pass the Cultural Park, the Reunification Palace, and turn left onto Glorious Victory Street in a part of Saigon known as District 3. The guidebook claims the Vietnamese have forgotten about the war. I add another correction.

In the All-American reception area, four local women in suits and headsets sit behind a long red desk. One of them looks familiar, but I can't place her.

The walls are decorated with framed posters:

"More study, more fun! Joyously together!"

"Learning with a comfortable feeling!"

"Celebrate the Halloween. How lively!"

I introduce myself to the familiar-looking woman.

"Hi, I'm Randall Burns. Mr. Pittman is expecting me."

She hands me an envelope. Inside there's a note.

Dear Mr. Burns,

You're one of the few readers to make it this far. You're on your way to the 5-percent club.

Keep going!

—Wallace Pittman

I scan the reception area for a surveillance camera. "Is this a joke? When do I see Mr. Pittman?"

"No joke. No Mr. Wally."

"What do you mean 'No Mr. Wally.' Is he out of town?"

"No Mr. Wally."

"What about his e-mail today?"

She smiles and dismisses me with a little bow.

The blades of a ceiling fan catch my eye. Whop, Whop, Whop.

As I consider pounding her desk and yelling, I notice her wedding band and think about the picture of Pittman and his hot, young wife. I think about travel books and middle-aged trifectas and the fools who believe in them. I think about life's cacophonous hex and English language schools that barely understand English.

Out on Glorious Victory Street, I give a homeless guy a dollar for a cigarette. I don't even haggle.

After walking and smoking and walking some more, I find myself in front of a travel agency.

Inside a local guy sits behind a long card table that has one leg propped up on 5¼-inch floppy disks. Cigarette butts bury an ashtray. I detect the familiar scent of burning squid.

I'm holding Pittman's guidebook.

"I know this book," says the local guy.

"You know Wally Pittman?"

"No."

"I heard he's around here. Is he?" I ask.

"No."

"It's kind of important."

"What I do for you?"

"I want to go to Cambodia."

The guy points to a sign on the wall advertising a flight to Phnom Penh and three nights in a deluxe hotel for fifty dollars. "Chapter Seven in book," he says. "You stay Bang Su, Hoi An?"

"How'd you guess?"

"I book you Bang Su, Phnom Penh, with nice airlines. Leave tonight."

I slide the tickets into my pocket, throw the book in the garbage, and head out.

The Chronic Single's Handbook
Chapter Four
Tips for Spending Your Life Alone

- *Accept that relationships come and go, but mostly go.*
- *Enjoy free porn, but invest in good antivirus software.*
- *Use plenty of hot sauce.*
- *Accept that moods are cyclical; if you're happy now, wait a few hours.*
- *Accept that some people grow up to be professional athletes and some people die of horrible wasting diseases. Similarly some people get married and some people—like you—don't.*
- *When someone calls you a commit-a-phobe, counter with the number of friends you've had for more than a decade, the number of years you've had the same car, or the number of years you've had the same career—all numbers that will no doubt exceed the length of most marriages.*

CHAPTER SEVEN: **CAMBODIA**

If at first you don't succeed, remember kind words better no tree frogs.
—W. PITTMAN

My third hour in Cambodia, I'm sitting alone in a Phnom Penh restaurant, if you can call it a restaurant. It's a corrugated roof on tent poles with no doors or windows or name. Three-panel accordion dividers are scattered around an asphalt space that's probably a parking lot by day.

The menu is written in what I'm guessing is Khmer, the Cambodian language, a series of square roots, caret signs, fishhook swirls, and dots like lizards' eyes. The servers and customers are darker-skinned than the Vietnamese—more like the locals in Bangkok. No one pays any attention to me. A waitress in a black skirt and narrow Morticia Addams hips dodges my table for the second time.

Cambodia is the one place Ricki was afraid to visit, something about typhoid, Japanese encephalitis, and street gangs disfiguring each other with battery acid. The guidebook said that since the average monthly income is fifty dollars, if you tip generously, Cambodia offers "lots of sketchy fun." I had to come.

I use the menu to fan myself. The waitress stops short and comes over. "Do you have any specials tonight?" I ask.

No answer.

"I can't read the menu, can you recommend something?"

Her eyes widen as if I had asked to borrow fifty dollars.

"Chicken, chili, hot, hot?" I run a finger up and down my menu.

She steps back as if I might run a finger up and down her next. A busboy plunks down a glass of water and races away without looking at me.

An Asian couple at the next table calls out to the waitress who gives up on me and rushes over.

They talk in what must be Khmer. What it sounds like:

Moon bong, prawn long.

Climb on, climb on.

At the hostess stand, I consult the woman who seated me. "Excuse me. I'm having a problem ordering. Do you have an English menu or a waitress who knows English?"

Same wide eyes.

"Parlez-vous français?" I ask, recalling that Cambodia was a French colony.

Ditto.

I retreat to my table and glance at what other diners are eating: soupy curries, brown stir-fries, rice, and more rice.

I use the menu to swat at a fly drinking from my water glass. The hostess, the waitress, and a busboy stop what they're doing and pay me a visit. They look concerned. I point to something soupy on the next table and make a squawking noise while flapping my arms. Then I point to a can of Angkor beer.

Everyone nods. Meeting adjourned. We have a plan.

Minutes later, a beer appears, followed by a plate of fried chicken wings sporting a few singed feathers.

A waiter circulates with a large platter. I hope it's a dessert tray so I can order something without plumage. I scan his platter for pastry or fruit but the tray is stacked with tiny corpses, like the aftermath of some medieval battle: baby snakes on skewers, broiled frogs on sticks, fried crickets on toothpicks, and kabobbed beetles, the same fingernail-sized bugs I crushed underfoot in Nha Trang.

"No, thank you," I say.

The waiter looks at me, smiles blankly, and moves on to the next table. I twist a feather off one of my fried chicken wings.

This is the first country in which I couldn't perform a basic task like ordering food. And this is Phnom Penh, Cambodia's most modern city. But I've been worrying about the same crap in every country: the food, the water, the drivers, guinea worms, dengue fever, armed robbery, torture. It's getting old and boring, and I'm hungry.

The guidebook, now spotted and greasy after I retrieved it from the trash in the Saigon travel office, gave this restaurant three stars. I consider throwing it in the garbage again, but for some reason, I'm not yet ready to part ways with Pittman. I toss his book into my daypack and take out *The Insider's Guide to Phnom Penh*, a booklet I picked up at my hotel. In a section called "Just for Westerners," I find no restaurant recommendations. There's a roundup of hostess bars, whatever those are; a review of Bazooka Joe's Shooting Range, where you can shoot chickens with a Soviet-era machine gun or cows with a rocket launcher; and a public service announcement featuring a Western guy, head down, gripping the bars of a prison cell. The announcement offers a reminder for people who need reminding: "Having sex with a child is a crime."

A fly lands on the page and scratches itself. The ceiling fan wobbles overhead. Time to hit the bathroom, find a quiet stall, and regroup.

On the way, I pass a middle-aged Westerner sitting with a group of Asians. The table is piled with curries, stir fries, rice, and cans of beer. Everything I want and need. I pause and address the Westerner. "Excuse me, do you speak English?

"How's it going?" His accent sounds Midwestern.

"Not so well, actually," I say. "I'm having a hell of a time trying to order. I've been here for an hour and all I've got is some hairy chicken wings."

"Sit yourself down." He points to the empty chair next to him. "We've got plenty. Where you from?"

"Randy Burns from Boston."

"Ah, Red Sox country." He extends his hand. "Ned Downey, Minneapolis."

Ned appears to be in his midforties and has a horseshoe fringe of brown hair circling a bald spot the size of an ostrich egg. He's wearing new, white walking shoes with Velcro closures and white socks up to his shins. He's as fat as my ex-best-friend Abe.

Ned introduces me around. Jorani, his twenty-something Cambodian girlfriend, sits to his left. Her yellow-and-white striped polo shirt matches his. Everyone else at the table is related to her: a younger sister; two teenage male cousins; her father, who looks overworked and underfed and could be sixty or ninety; and her plump mother. Both parents have dark skin that they probably didn't get from golfing. Jorani and her younger sister both have lighter skin probably from covering up in the sun and using skin-lightening cream. Young Cambodians like young Vietnamese consider light skin to be fashionable.

Jorani says, "Please to meet you."

After nodding hello to me, the rest of the table returns to their conversations: "Moon bong, prawn long. Climb on, climb on."

Ned offers me a platter of brown stir fry. "Your little city keeps stealing all our good players: Moss, Ortiz, Garnett."

"Who in their right mind wants to spend the winter in Minneapolis?"

"Fair enough. Can't stand it myself. I've been coming here the last couple of winters. I own an Internet business—you know, novelties, inexpensive jewelry, and the like. Last month, we sold a load of Freudian slippers with little bearded faces to keep your toes warm." He slips me a business card for Horsestail.com. "Check it out some time."

"Thanks," I say.

"Jorani here is in school," he says.

Jorani gives me an inscrutable Asian smile. "Study the business, the accounting, the English."

Slender arms, slender neck, a wand. Ned has done well for himself.

"Eat," she says, handing me a beer.

I take a few sips and then dig into a stir fry of green stalky vegetables and spongy brown ovals the size of my pinky. Inside each oval is a soft bone that reminds me of a fingernail.

"This is interesting," I say. "What is it?"

Jorani points to her mouth. "Tongue of the duck," she says.

I say nothing.

"You can leave it be," Ned says. "Jorani, want to pass him the pork?"

She spoons more food onto my plate. "Drink," she says.

Ned answers his cell phone: "Hi, Ma . . . Eating dinner with Jorani and her family . . . Yes, we're wearing the shirts . . . The dishwasher kaput? . . . Oh, for gosh. I can't do much from here . . . A new one will be spendy . . . Emergency number's on the fridge . . . OK, Ma. I'll give a jingle-jingle in a few."

Later the check comes. Cambodia bars and restaurants are supposed to accept American dollars so I throw in a ten. Ned tosses it back to me, whips out a wad of singles and twenties, and throws down one of each. "How about joining us for a drink and some dancing?" he asks me.

A Midwestern guy who loves his mother, picks up the check, and is accompanied by a local college girl and her family. Why not?

At Jorani's former employer, the Luau Bar, Ned, Jorani, her two male cousins, and I sit at a long bamboo and lacquer table. The decor is nouveau Khmer, lots of red and black. Red awnings, black stools, red and black floor tiles. The windows are covered with black security bars shaped like Asian characters. Several little red motorcycles are parked inside the bar near our table.

The servers are local women, who appear to be in their early twenties, dressed in modest shorts and polo shirts. Their waists are tiny; sweet Morticias as far as the eye can see. I'm still taking a break from dating, but these women are hard to ignore.

Most of the customers are Western guys with leatherneck haircuts and military tattoos: scorpions with bayonets, bulldogs with machine guns. Most have British-like accents, smoke nonstop, and wear sweaty tank tops. There's a striking absence of ski hats and irony. These are not kids.

The bar menu is in English and includes a list of beers, spirits, and sodas. The most expensive item is a three-dollar beverage called a "Lady Drink." I order a one-dollar can of Beerlao. Jorani and her cousins each order a Coca-Cola.

"Mr. Ned, the James, no ice?" the waitress asks.

"Yes, honey."

"The James?" I ask Ned.

"Jim Beam. He and I go way back, so I call him 'James.'"

The waitress returns, serves Ned first, then me, and then everyone else. Jorani dips a finger into Ned's drink, and then dabs behind each ear. They smile at each other. The cousins look bored.

Jorani chats with the waitress and points to me. "Moon bong, prawn long."

I lean toward Ned. "What's a 'Lady Drink'?"

Before he can answer, the waitress saunters over and sits on my chair arm.

"Waz you name?" Her black hair drifts past her shoulders.

"Randy."

"Where you from?" She smells like cinnamon.

"The US. What's your name?"

"Me, Betty."

She has slender brown legs. I imagine her rubbing them together to produce a chirping sound.

"Where *you* from?" I ask.

"Phnom Penh." Everyone at the table is watching us.

I can't think of anything else to say, so I dust off my usual pickup line. "Having fun?"

"Eh?"

At the table next to us, a waitress is parked on the lap of a Western guy chugging a Beerlao. She takes off his baseball hat and puts it on her head backward. She pokes his ample gut and says something that sounds like "Tohm. Tohm." She tickles him. He tickles her back. She kisses him on the head and then stands up to go. He yanks her back, and she lands in his lap again. She laughs. "You bad boy."

Another guy at the table snaps a photo of them. "The next pint's on you, mate, or I send this to Phoebe."

The lap girl laughs again: "You marry? You very bad boy."

I sense Betty perched quietly by my side, waiting. My arm is pressed against her thigh. *Chirp, chirp.* But I'm not really in the mood. I'm still on hiatus from women.

Moody introduced me to the dating hiatus five years ago. I was in a dry spell and hadn't had sex in months.

"Finding a girlfriend has been too high a priority for you," Moody said one day. "For the next three months, I want you to give it a rest. Instead of going out, go home, read, find a hobby. No spreadsheet, no dates."

Four months later, I was still on hiatus. I liked the discipline, the depravation. It was like dieting, jogging, or saving money. A week later I met Maxie on Match.

Since then, it's always been clear when to start dating again: A slender, edgy woman would come in over the gunwale like a flaming game fish.

Betty gets up and drifts away. I let her go.

"Another Beerlao?" Ned asks me, winking. "Don't worry. There're plenty of others."

"Sure, thanks," I say, both for the beer and the promise of plenty of others. "So what's a 'Lady Drink'?"

"It's a drink you buy for the girl if you want her to hang around with you. She earns a dollar for each one."

Jorani is sipping a red can with a black straw. How many lady drinks has she had in her career? How many has Ned bought her?

I join Ned and toast with the tohm-tohm guys.

At midnight, Ned suggests moving to a bar called The Apocalypse for some dancing. "Same owners, same menu, same cheap prices," he says to me.

"I'm not really dressed to go out," I say.

"Where you staying?"

"The Bang Su."

"Got to love that name. No problem. We'll visit Su and you can change into something more comfortable—we can wait in the tuk-tuk."

Jorani grabs the check and pays. I overhear Betty at another table, "Waz you name?"

It's after midnight and the Bang Su lobby is secured by a locked metal gate. I can just see a night watchman snoozing in a hammock draped with a ripped mosquito net. I tap on the gate. The man jumps up to let me in. I tip him a dollar. He gives me a little bow and climbs back into the hammock. As I start toward the darkened stairs, something lumbers around a couch, bolts past the hammock, and settles under a melamine end table. The creature is too large to be a squirrel and too small to be a Rottweiler.

I crouch for a better look: It's a half-bald rat.

I follow the guidebook's advice for encounters with Cambodian wildlife and look for threatening gestures: teeth gnashing, hair bristling, back arching, foot drumming, growling, ear flattening, tail between the legs, backward earth flinging with hind feet.

The night watchman snores. The rat remains still, watching me.

I check for foaming mouth, cowering pups nearby, teardrop tattoos around the eyes. All clear, but the bald spot bothers me.

I rub my smooth-shaven head and tiptoe to the staircase, giving the rat a wide berth. "Sit, stay. Moon bong," I whisper.

The night man doesn't stir.

When I return in a collared shirt, Ned says: "You look pretty sharp."

"Handsome mans," Jorani says.

The two cousins, as usual, say nothing.

I mention the bald rat.

Ned says. "Yeah, I heard The Su has all the charm of a kennel. You should move to my hotel, the Tamarind, tomorrow. It's new, clean, cheap, and near the waterfront where all the action is. I'll let them know you're coming."

Ned's scalp glistens under a streetlight. His knee socks and Velcro shoes seem whiter. Who is this guy? Is he a pushy scammer or a friendly Midwestern weenie?

The doorman at The Apocalypse recognizes Jorani and invites us to the front of the line. He runs his walnut-colored hands around my sides, down one leg, and up the other. He gives the head of my penis a little tweak and waves me in. I give him a little wave with my index finger. "You very bad boy," I say. He winks.

Once inside, the sound system jolts me like a rifle butt to the chest. The crowd is a seething mix of overmuscled white guys, sullen locals, and stunning Asian women in lacy tank tops and short-shorts. Any minute, I expect people to start fighting or fucking.

We shuffle through to a corner. The walls are made of large stones, the kind found in medieval prisons. Jorani points to some locals playing pool on the other side of the room. "No go there."

Ned shrugs, "There was a stabbing in here a few years ago. But it's OK now." I decide not to let Ned out of my sight.

Jorani slices through the crowd and returns with a twenty-two-ounce beer for me and a James Beam for Ned. Then she and her two silent cousins hit the dance floor.

Ned's cell rings. "Hi, Ma," he yells into the receiver. "He's coming to fix it tomorrow? . . . Here's one for you: We met a guy from Boston and we're showing him the sights . . . Yeah, I'll tell him the Patriots only win because they're lucky . . . And the Celtics . . . And the Red Sox . . . And the Bruins. It's kinda loud in here. I'll jingle-jingle tomorrow."

Ned gives my wrist a squeeze. "I got divorced in 2003. Then a buddy invited me here on a trip. That's when I met Jorani. Amazing, no?"

The dance floor is wand after wand after wand; sleek, fast, and tight. Sweaty collarbones, little-boy butts, heart-shaped calves in tiny flip-flops. Nothing sags, droops, or jiggles. If Lenny could see this.

"Compared to what I'm used to back home," I say, "this is like being in some kind of alternate universe."

Ned pokes my arm. "I hear you. I tried online dating, InaHeartBeat.com. The women outweighed me. Then I came here and thought: Why am I banging my head against the wall in the US? Sure Jorani's a bar girl, so what? I was married; let me tell you, the guy always pays for sex, one way or the other. Here you just get more for your money."

Jorani appears with another round of drinks and heads back onto the dance floor.

I watch a girl dancing alone. She has delicate features except for Angelina Jolie lips that give her a naughty, feral look. She smiles. I smile. I try to imagine visiting Cambodia a couple of times a year.

"Yeah, life can be good," Ned says. "Anyhoo, I brought a bag of cheap jewelry for Jorani to sell to her bar-girl friends. We plan on hitting the classier clubs this week," he says. "You should join us."

"I'm in," I say.

Back in my room, my stomach and the duck tongues are having a disagreement. I decide to start a daily Pepto-Bismol regimen, something I should have been doing since I landed in Southeast Asia three weeks ago.

In the morning, my stomach feels better, but my mouth tastes bitter and rubbery like a bicycle tire or a pickled cobra. I head out for a palate-cleansing breakfast.

A nearby bar advertises a "Western Special" of eggs, toast, bangers, and a can of Beerlao all for six dollars. The bartender is clearly a Westerner: rolling gut, pink face, and pointy gray beard. He takes my order, puts his burning cigarette in an ashtray, and clomps off to the kitchen. A few bar stools away, another Westerner, who looks slightly younger, reads a Khmer paper. His arms are adorned with large angry tattoos, the kind found on Polynesian warriors preparing for battle. He's smoking a cigarette; two cans of Beerlao sit open in front of him. It's ten A.M.

When he glances in my direction, I ask, "Is there a health club or gym around here?" realizing too late that he might not be the best person to ask.

"I belong to the Mekong Club by the Japanese bridge. Nice accent." He sticks out a hand to shake. "Mickey from Alabama."

"Randy from Boston."

"I lived up north for a while, Alaska, that is, and then moved here ten years ago. I run motorcycle tours to the Cambodian countryside for Western visitors. You interested?"

"Maybe another time."

"No problem." He hands me a business card.

He goes on to tell me that he's married to a Cambodian woman, has learned to speak Khmer, and has a child. "I didn't meet her in a bar if you're wondering," he says.

I *am* wondering, but don't admit it.

"Do you miss the US?" I ask.

I am conscious that Mickey is staring at my mouth. He smiles. "Did you spend last night licking some bar girl's asshole?"

"What?"

He points to my mouth. "Your tongue, it's black. Either lay off the bar girls or lay off the Pepto-Bismol."

Before I can come up with a response, the bartender reappears, and then Mickey asks, "Serge, do I miss America?"

"Your wife is better looking than any Miss America," the bartender says.

"Serge, do I miss hanging out with soft, saggy guys who have to be fiddling with some toy every minute like a four-year-old?"

Serge heads back to the kitchen. I get the impression he's heard this rant before.

Mickey turns up his volume. "Serge, do I miss a country where you can't say 'boo' to someone without violating their civil rights, but kids can say 'fuck you' to their parents and teachers?"

Serge returns, serves Mickey another Beerlao and says, "Remember, you told me to shut you off this morning after four."

Mickey ignores him: "Besides, if I took my wife back to the States, she'd just spend money like every other American woman. That would be it for our cheap and easy Khmer lifestyle."

"So did you give up your American citizenship?" I ask Mickey.

"No way."

On the half-mile walk from the Bang Su to the Tamarind, I observe the cheap and easy Khmer lifestyle. On Srei Krom Street, a mother holds her toddler's penis as he pees on the sidewalk. Turning down Samnang, a wild-lipped girl calls out from a karaoke bar, "Hey handsome mans, come sing me." On the corner of Street 140, tuk-tuk and motorbike drivers mill around, smoking. One shouts to me, "You want Cambodian girl, small-small?" He makes a tiny OK sign with thumb and index finger to indicate the size of the woman's vagina.

The area around the Tamarind is populated by middle-aged Western guys like me. Out front, a middle-aged guy is patching out on a little motorcycle. On the balcony above, a middle-aged guy is eating breakfast. Across the street several middle-aged Western guys are shopping at an outdoor market. A few are accompanied by young, pretty, local women, their money-honeys.

The night Ricki and I got back together after our first breakup, she made me dinner and served my favorite beer. During dessert, she leaned over and whispered into my ear: "Daddy, can you loan your baby a hundred dollars for contact lenses?"

Ricki was a terrible credit risk. A month earlier, she had maxed out her charge cards and began swapping the balances to banks that offered interest-free deals. And she continued to shop. "This is my take-no-prisoners number," she'd say, modeling an Armani jacket for me.

"Is there any more beer?" I asked.

"Don't be cheap. I'll pay you back next week."

"Like when? Like exactly when?"

"Like next Monday, high noon. I'll stop by your office. Here, you can check my credit scores." She pulled up her tank top.

Her breasts were orange halves with dusky nipples the size of figs. Perfect size, perfect shape, and I often told her so. I lent her the money.

Later that weekend, I noticed a new pair of shoes in her closet.

Monday, I didn't mention the cash and neither did she. Tuesday, still no money. Wednesday morning, I answered her phone call with an e-mail: "Buried at work." She stopped by my office that afternoon.

"You look awful, what's the matter?" she asked.

"Stressed, got a big deadline tomorrow," I said. "How are the new contacts?"

"Are you going to bug me about that money? You're such a cheap fuck, I can't stand it!"

I think of Jorani paying for all the drinks. I bet she would never call Ned a cheap fuck. Maybe the Mickeys and Neds of the world know something about women and money that I don't.

The Tamarind is a block from Phnom Penh's Sisowath Quay, a boulevard along the Tonle Sap River. Restaurants, shops, and bars line one side of the quay; the other side has a two-mile promenade with palm trees and flags from countries considered friends of Cambodia.

I opt for a twenty-dollar room without a view or even a window. It is slightly larger than its full-sized bed. But the room is clean and new and, so far, rat-free. While I'm unpacking, someone slides a note under my door:

Hey, Tom Brady

Meet us in the lobby at 8 for drinks and dancing at a classy club.

—Fran Tarkenton

That night at eight, I find Ned and Jorani in the lobby as he is handing a wrapped gift to the front-desk girl. She smiles and traces the package corners with her finger before unwrapping it. Inside there's a stack of Hershey's chocolate bars.

"Oh, Mr. Ned, you nice man. Jorani, you lucky girl."

Jorani smiles and grabs Ned's arm. They're wearing matching Hawaiian shirts.

Ned turns to me: "Hey, Randy, you ready to rock?"

Out at the curb, a tuk-tuk driver swings around. "To the Gin Club, Mr. Suk," Ned says.

The entrance to the Gin Club is an accordion-like garage door located on a side street. The doorman frisks us, but this one doesn't try to cop a feel. Nearby a legless man rocks in a small wheeled cart and begs for money. Ned gives him a dollar and a high five. I give him a dollar and a high five.

Inside we pass a corridor of food stalls with the words "Pizza," "Chinese," and "Hamburgers" scrawled on them. Patrons circulate among the stalls and vendors call out bazaar-style.

I follow Ned and Jorani to the disco room. Along one wall is a long bar and a large-screen TV. Instead of local toughs, the pool tables are occupied by Western guys and Asian girls. Not exactly classy, but a step up from The Apocalypse.

A tall woman with Texas-sized breasts and muscular shoulders is ripping up the dance floor in time to Michael Jackson's "Billie Jean."

"Ladyboy," Jorani whispers to me.

Ned leads us to a high-top table. He pulls out a chair for Jorani and then another for me.

Instead of sitting, I go to the bar for a round.

When I return with the drinks, Ned is holding a stack of bar napkins.

Jorani giggles, pointing to her tongue, and then to my mouth.

"Black," she says.

Ned hands me the napkins. "Pepto-Bismol, right? Son, you'll never get a date with that tongue. Stop taking that shit."

"Actually I'd heard that some women like this look," I say, recalling the Boston vaccine nurse in her black hoodie.

I use a napkin to swab off my tongue and then open wide to show off my work. Jorani gives me a normal-size OK sign.

I ask Ned, "How does this bar girl thing work?"

He offers a five-minute discourse, punctuated with wrist squeezes and arm pokes.

The gist:

• In hostess bars like the Luau, you buy the girl a couple of Lady Drinks, negotiate a price with her, and then pay the bar five dollars to take her for the night.

• In freelance joints like the Gin Bar, if you click with a freelancer, you buy her a real drink, and then negotiate a price. There's no bar fee.

• Want something longer term? Wire the girl $300 a month so she doesn't have to work in a bar. When you visit Phnom Penh, she will barter at hotels and stores to get you the local prices. This is Ned's arrangement with Jorani and the reason she typically buys the drinks. "We don't talk about what we do when we're not together," Ned says. "It's all good."

• What do young Asian girls want with middle-aged Western guys? Money, mostly, but the girls also think our white skin and long noses are exotic. According to Ned, Khmer men don't make good husbands: They gamble, beat their women, whore around. And young Western guys have too little dough and want too much sex.

One of the girls drags an old Western guy onto the dance floor. The guy's bifocals hang on a neck lanyard and bounce in time to the music. Soon the dance floor fills with old Western men and hot Asian girls.

When I make eye contact with a girl standing alone by the bar in jeans that must be size 00, she immediately comes

over and puts her arm around mine. Her skin is smooth, soft,
and warm.

Click.

Jorani exchanges smiles with the girl on my arm and
reaches for Ned's hand. Ned prattles on ignoring the girl on
my arm, like she's supposed to be there. "These girls aren't
like New York streetwalkers," Ned says. "The girls kiss on the
mouth, act like a girlfriend. And if you talk fast, they can't
understand a thing."

The girl smiles vacantly and rubs my back. Ned talks faster.

"Think about it. Isn't it better for them to work in a bar
than to spend nineteen hours a day in a sweatshop for two
dollars?"

Concerns about sex tourism, sex trafficking, and *60 Minutes* special reports recede as I look closer at the girl on my
arm. Her cheekbones form little crescents when she smiles.
Her lips are thick and wild. She's wearing a sleeveless red and
black T-shirt and those jeans of mythical proportions.

Jorani says something to the newcomer in Khmer, and
then gestures to the dance floor. The girl takes my arm.

Once we're on the parquet, the girl pulls me close and
shouts into my ear, "Waz you name?"

"Randy. What's yours?"

"Me Mary. Where you from?"

"England." I'm not sure why I lie.

"Me Cambodia. You marry?"

"No."

"Why no?"

"I can never remember to put the cap on the toothpaste."

"Eh?"

The music pounds and Mary shuffles her black flip-flops.
I spin her around a few times. After one song, she points to
our high-top table. Mary is not much of a dancer.

"Want a drink?" I ask.

"Coca-Cola," she says.

Mary is not much of a partier either.

Jorani and Ned join us. Jorani talks to Mary in Khmer, and then suggests that we move to a quiet bar down the hall.

The quiet bar is filled with the usual Western-guy-Asian-girl couples. Everyone is seated at white plastic tables with white plastic lawn chairs. Eighties pop music plays softly in the background.

Once we're seated in lawn chairs, a waitress comes over and Jorani orders a round of drinks including a Coke for Mary, who is now caressing my arm.

Jorani shows Mary some of Ned's earrings. Mary picks a pair and tries them on. Jorani turns to me, "Pretty lady?"

"Very pretty lady," I say.

"You girlfriend her?" Jorani asks.

I think, anything for the team, but then recall that I've sworn off bar girls.

Mary offers two dollars for the earrings. Jorani offers an additional piece of jewelry. Mary adds another dollar.

"Two for one," Jorani says to me. "Girl say she from village in Battambang. Your girlfriend say she twenty-five. How old you?"

"Emotionally or chronologically?"

"Eh?"

One minute Jorani is calling Mary "the girl," as if she's a hooker; the next she's referring to Mary as my "girlfriend," as if we've been dating for months.

Mary starts massaging my right knee. The veins in her hands are like tiny blue serpents, rippling, swirling, and curious. She says in a voice loud enough for Ned and Jorani to hear, "Me go hotel you."

I feel blood rushing to my face and look around for our waitress, look over at the TV, look anywhere but at Jorani.

Carrying on with a call girl in front of another woman, even if that woman is also a call girl, seems pitiful, sleazy, and somehow wrong.

But this is probably how Jorani and Ned started off. This is probably how everyone starts off around here.

The drinks arrive. Jorani dips her finger in Ned's drink and dabs behind her ears.

"Why don't you just take Mary home," Ned says to me.

"She nice girlfriend," Jorani says.

I gently lift Mary's fingers from my thigh and stand. "I have to go fix my hair."

In the bathroom, sheets of wet toilet paper coagulate on the floor. Puddles of fluid have collected around the sinks. A local man smiles as he rubs the back of a middle-aged Westerner peeing into a rust-stained trough.

"Massage, 1,000 Cambodian riel," the masseur says, as I approach the trough. "Only twenty-five cent." He watches as I unzip. I inhale and exhale slowly. Nothing.

I give up and visit the toilet stall for some privacy.

During a recent dating hiatus that was stretching past six months, Moody said: "Don't stay on the sidelines too long or you'll get used to it, bitter about relationships, as if you're not already bitter enough."

Mary is no flaming game fish, but she's pretty cute.

She's also half my age and not even pretending to be a hairdresser—she's a real-deal hooker.

So what?

I review my past slutty behavior.

• I once worked in sales and marketing.

• I once worked in real estate sales and marketing.

• I have brown-nosed and sucked-up to get ahead.

• I have kissed women I disliked and slept with women I hated.

Jumping on Mary probably wouldn't cause further moral or karmic damage. But what about disease?

I try to recall the AIDS stats for Cambodia. Maybe it's the Beerlao or a misfiled memory, but I come up with no numbers, just an image of a man with a white Amish beard wearing a double-breasted navy jacket and standing next to an American flag.

Former Surgeon General C. Everett Koop.

If he had his way, Cambodian freelancers would probably carry warning labels. He'd probably advise me to smoke a pack a day rather than have sex with Mary. I would argue: Look, I've now been traveling for three months and struck out with women on four continents.

I feel a release and piss away.

Back at the table, Mary greets me with a smile. I sit down and her hand inches up my thigh.

Not bothering to lower his voice, Ned says, "Think of it as a very thorough checkup from a very friendly nurse." He pokes my arm. "You'll be fine."

Mary and I enter the Tamarind lobby arm in arm as if we were returning from the company Christmas party. A uniformed man nods to me, then Mary, and opens the door.

In my room, Mary mewls in my ear, "Me like you." She heads straight to the bathroom as if she's familiar with the place. The toilet flushes, the shower sprays.

I recall Guillaume's comments in Vietnam about bar girls who lift wallets and anything else of value.

My passport and wallet are already stashed in the hotel safe. While Mary's occupied, I stuff my watch, money belt, room keys, sleep blindfold, nail clippers, sleeping pills, and other valuables into the zip-up security pockets in my pants. Then, for good measure, I take the container of medications out of my backpack and hide it along with scissors and other sharp objects under the bed.

Mary emerges from the bathroom wearing only a towel. Coppery deltoids against white cotton. We exchange smiles. Her lips seem thicker and wilder. She jumps under the sheets, towel and all.

Fully clothed, I trudge into the bathroom, marsupial-like, cargo pockets sagging as if filled with offspring.

I shower and exit the bathroom wearing only a white towel. My clothes clang when I shove them beneath my side of the bed.

Now, we're both under the covers in our towels, sheets pulled up to our noses, staring at the ceiling.

We remain in this position, like two body bags, for several minutes, just long enough for my thoughts to start swirling.

She's the professional, isn't she supposed to initiate?

Since when is Mary a Cambodian name?

I wonder what goes on in curious-finger body spa?

I'm hard. I'm nervous. But mostly I'm hard.

Mary sighs and rustles under the sheets as if she might get up and leave.

The clock is ticking and she probably has other patients.

I roll over and look into her onyx eyes for some clue on how to proceed. She looks bored.

Something finally registers: The guy *is* supposed to make the move, even when he's paying.

I kiss the cornices of her collarbones, the cords of her throat, and the amazing lips. Her tongue is fleshy and sweet like a mouthful of raisins. I breathe through my nose and smell her skin cream.

I slide a hand along the curve of her belly, tease her belly button with my finger, and run my hands through her pubic hair. She follows my lead, and cups my balls.

Then she pauses.

"Long time or short time?" she asks.

Our first glitch. I'm not sure what she means, so I pick the option that sounds least expensive. "Short time," I say.

"Massage, massage?" she asks, running her fingers around the head of my cock.

"Does the massage, massage include a happy ending?"

"Happy, happy."

She spits into her palms, and I feel them on me, the blue serpents at work. Then I feel her mouth on my neck. As her tongue eases between my lips, my thighs tingle, my groin tingles.

"Cum for me, Randy."

And so I do. Months of waiting and frustration barrel through my body. Afterward, I give her a hug and say, "Me like you."

She laughs and heads to the bathroom.

I slip into a delicious oblivion. I doze listening to the water pulse against the shower door. But my idyllic moment is interrupted by one of life's big questions: What's this going to cost?

Mary exits the bathroom fully dressed.

"That was nice, Mary. How much?"

"Twenty dollar plus twenty dollar tip."

Her English has improved in the last five minutes.

I hand her two twenties and a five. She looks at the bills, puts her hands together, and gives me a little bow. "Me like you."

Three minutes after Mary leaves, the hotel phone rings.

Crap. I've been set up.

The phone rings again.

Mary was underage. Youtube. *60 Minutes*. Extortion.

And again.

They know I'm up here and the room has no windows or fire escape.

"Hello?" I say.

"Mr. Burns?"

"Yes?"

"Girl at front desk. OK her go home?"

"Oh. OK, yes, fine, thank you."

That night, I dream a sweet dream. I'm walking down a street in Phnom Penh. I am the world's most interesting man, a Manrico among men. Beautiful local women call out to me, "Hey handsome mans." Mr. Blond from South Africa, dressed in a linen suit, presents me with a big watch, a prescription for a lifetime supply of oxytocin, and a fortune-telling eight ball. No matter how I shake the ball, the same answer bobs to the surface: "You are done banging your head against the wall."

The next morning, I call Ned.

"How was last night?" he asks.

"Not bad. But I forgot to negotiate a price upfront and I probably got fleeced."

"This is the deal. For Western guys, it's twenty-five to thirty dollars for the whole night. Local guys pay five dollars. If the girl says, 'me like you' after you pay, you got fleeced. If she says, 'up to you,' she figures you don't know the local rate and will overpay. What did you pay?"

"Forty dollars, plus a five-dollar tip. She likes me a lot."

"Don't worry about it. I paid seventy dollars my first time and all I got was a hand job. What color is your tongue this morning?"

I go back to sleep and awake later to the sound of something sliding under my door:

Hey, Ted Williams,
Jorani and I are heading off to Siem Reap for a couple of
days. You should join us. Just ask the girl at the front desk to
book you the same ferry and hotel.
—Harmon Killebrew

Pittman's guidebook says that Siem Reap is the gateway to
Angkor Wat and renowned for a few other things:
  • Wildlife: chicken ranches, cat houses, a crocodile farm
twenty yards from a swimming hole filled with kids.
  • Disease: P. falciparum, the deadliest form of malaria.
  • Exotic Cuisine: Giddy Gordon's Pizza, known for its
specialty pies, such as the Giddy Giddy (topped with pep-
peroni and marijuana) and the Giddy Up (sharp cheddar and
magic mushrooms).
  I'm too old for mushrooms and a sleep doctor told me
to give up weed, but the local fauna sounds interesting. And
having Ned and Jorani as tour guides—even if they're starting
to annoy me—is reassuring. I decide to go.

An e-mail from my mother:
Glad to read that you had fun in Vietnam. I hear it's nice
this time of year. Uncle Heshie loves your condo.
Love,
—Mom & Dad

Heshie is a sixty-two-year-old doctor, a successful, responsi-
ble, grown man. Still I worry about how he's loving my condo.

Blog Entry, November 4
Phnom Penh
Made it to Cambodia, or maybe heaven. Friendly, colorful
locals. Lenny, these are our kind of people. Places to go, folks to
meet. Don't worry if you don't hear from me for a while.
—Burns

At a Siem Reap club called the Pohk Pohk Palace, Jorani introduces me to a girl sitting across from us at the bar.

The girl is a wisp, like all the others, but there's something else about her. Maybe it's her style: cowboy boots, short denim skirt, denim vest, and plaited pony tail, which she strokes with one hand. Maybe it's her mug of beer filled with ice—she's the first bar girl I've met who drinks. Or maybe it's her English, which is better than most. And maybe now that I've popped my punter cherry, I'm game for anything.

She says, "Hi" to Ned, sits down next to me, and puts her hand on my knee.

"Waz you name?" the girl asks me.

"Randy. What's your name?"

"Me Katie. Where you from?"

"Cambodia," I say.

"You no Cambodia." She holds her russet-brown arm against my blanched white one.

I point to the burning cigarette in her hand and nod, yes. She roots around in a tiny purse filled with green US bills, pulls out a pack of ARA, which I'm guessing is a local brand, and gives me one. She rubs my knee. I rest my arm on the back of her chair. We smoke together.

Katie points to a girl on the dance floor. "You like the dancing?"

"Sure," I say.

She stifles a laugh. Her eyes crinkle and a faint line appears across her forehead. I'm guessing she's in her early thirties.

"She ladyboy!" Katie slaps my thigh.

Jorani returns with another round of drinks including a beer on the rocks. Katie says, "Thank you," excuses herself, and heads to the bathroom.

Ned turns to me: "This one's a little old and she's got a space between her teeth. Let's find you someone with less mileage who doesn't smoke. The night is young."

Jorani smiles and says, "She nice girlfriend."

"Actually," I say, "I have a thing for quirky girls."

When Katie returns, Ned stands and swills his drink. "Suit yourself. Come on, Jorani, how about a Giddy Gordon's magic pizza? Catch you later, Randy."

Ned shuffles to the door while Jorani talks briefly in Khmer with Katie before joining him.

Once we're alone, Katie asks: "You marry?"

"Nope."

"Why no?"

"I drive a crappy car."

"Eh?"

"Are you married?" I ask.

"Pehh."

Billy Joel's "Just the Way You Are" starts playing. Katie grabs my hand and we join the other couples, mostly old guys, young women, and ladyboys on the dance floor.

Katie grinds against me. She's lean, as tight as a whippet. I grab her bare, sweaty waist.

She turns to face me, pulls me close, and yells into my ear: "Where you from?"

"Australia."

"I have Australia man one time. Him no have boom-boom long time. Him pay thirty dollar for five minute. Hah! Hee. Hee. Hee."

I laugh to be polite.

After another slow dance, she asks for the order: "Me go hotel, you."

"How much?" I ask.

"Up to you."

We leave the Pohk Pohk arm and arm. I put my nose in her hair and smell vanilla, my favorite scent.

Katie points to a food cart on the corner: little carcasses, bugs for sale. I buy her a bag, which she opens and shakes in my direction like peanuts at a Sox game. I grimace. She chows down. A little black leg lodges between her teeth. She goes to kiss me. I recoil. She kisses me anyway. Her tongue tastes smoky, nutty, musty like a mushroom.

The lobby of my hotel, the Angkor Princess, has a mahogany-colored front desk and a busty, full-sized statue of what is either a Khmer goddess or a Pohk Pohk ladyboy. Above the desk, four clocks display times for New York, Paris, Sydney, and Siem Reap. A step up from the Tamarind and, at twelve dollars a night, a deal. Jorani is a good negotiator.

The night guard gestures for Katie to open her purse, which is not much larger than a pack of ARA cigarettes. He roots around and takes things out: lighter, keys, cell phone. He examines each item and puts it back.

She stifles a smile.

"OK," he says.

I tip him a dollar.

My third-floor room has a queen bed, aircon, a rattan sitting table with chair, and a hand-crank casement window that opens above an overgrown yard. The stinging smell of insecticide permeates the air. Instead of chocolates, the turndown service at the Angkor Princess is a thorough spraying for mosquitoes. According to Ned, the cheaper hotels just hand you a mosquito coil to burn in your room.

Katie sniffs, removes her cowboy boots, and heads to the bathroom. I secure the premises, as I did with Mary, and then wash down a double-dose of antimalarial pill with bottled water.

The toilet flushes.

The shower sprays.

After fifteen minutes, the bathroom door creaks open, Katie stands in the wafting steam, a towel wrapped snugly under her arms. Her braid is coiled and pinned up on her head. Her small breasts struggle against the white cotton. "Soapy massage?" she asks, taking my hand and leading me back to the bath.

In the tub, hot mist, warm spray. Fingers float over me, on me. I tingle like a sleeping arm that just woke up. The egg game and then some.

The squick-squick of soapy breasts on my chest, belly, cock. Her hands, her mouth, a wandering finger between cheeks. I stop Katie before I'm a punchline in her Australian boom-boom joke.

On the bed in white towels our lips are a custom fit. Our tongues entwine like the plaits of her pony tail. I lick the space between her front teeth.

Ricki had a space between her teeth that she vowed never to fix. I always told her, "If it's good enough for Lauren Hutton . . ."

"Me like you," I say to Katie.

She laughs, holds a finger to my lips and says, "Shhh. Me take care of you."

Dr. Moody says I'm looking to be taken care of, to be the beloved, the one who takes none of the risks but has all the power. Whatever you say, Moody.

Katie lets her towel fall away to the bed. Around her waist is a pink belly chain. I give it a little tug.

"The good luck," she says.

I kiss the length of the chain, and then whisper between her thighs, "I take care of you." She wriggles. I put a finger inside her, and another, and then I trace my name. Her breathing quickens.

She pushes my hand away, catches her breath, and then asks: "Condom, no condom?"

I give the belly chain another tug, and then reach under my bed, into my stash, and hand her one of my condoms, American-made, not Asian-made, which Ned says break easily.

Later, she lies on me, wet belly to wet belly, and falls asleep. I wrap my arms around her and kiss the top of her head.

I don't think about the past or the future. In this perfect moment, I am connected. It's a mortise and tenon, Sensurround, broadband, intravenous oxytocin connection. I don't want to be anywhere else, with anyone else. And maybe this is enough. Maybe this relationship doesn't have to go anywhere or even any further. If I *were* to think about the future, I'd want to remember this moment, here, now, far from Boston.

After ten minutes, all ninety pounds of her gets heavy. Once it's time to sleep, I believe everyone should retreat to a neutral corner. I slide her off me. When I move away, she follows. When I slide her gently back to the other side of the bed, she groans, shoves me, and chases me back to my side. I fall asleep, content, and drug-free.

In the morning, while Katie showers, I lay out two twenties on her side of the bed. When she's done, I grab my watch and pants, and go into the bathroom. When I come out, the money is still there. Katie is naked and has her head out the window smoking a cigarette.

As she turns to face me, I notice she's wearing my sleep blindfold with one patch up. My little buccaneer.

"You funny girl," I say, walking toward her. She slowly takes off the blindfold, as if she's stripping. Then she holds it out the window.

"No!"

At her side, I look down: My blindfold is foundering in a giant puddle that is no doubt filled with infected mosquitoes. Slowly it sinks.

"Sorry, sorry." She breaks into a smile.

I do not smile.

A spiritual person might think: The universe is helping me shed the accoutrements and fears of an old life.

I think: How can you stay mad at a woman with an ass so small both cheeks fit in one hand?

"Breakfast?" I ask.

She nods and says, "What you do today?"

"Angkor Wat. How about if we meet tonight for dinner?" She nods again.

We dress, and leaving the room, I notice the money is gone.

In the restaurant, the patrons are mostly Western couples sitting and eating in silence. Katie and I order, and sit in silence.

When you're with a woman who barely speaks English, silence is expected and comfortable, a respite from struggling to communicate. Instead of talking, you smile, you look, you admire her bas-relief collarbones and wild lips.

Katie's cell phone rings. She checks the number. "Daddy," she says to me and then answers. "Moon bong, prawn long. Climb on, climb on."

I imagine meeting her family. I imagine supporting her family.

But what if that's not her father but her lunch date in two hours? What about tonight? What time does the meter start running?

I notice a mosquito bite on my arm, and then notice a slight headache and a backache. Flu-like symptoms: Malaria, dengue, guinea worms.

Our food arrives. Katie ends her call and picks at her rice and pork dish.

"Peoples look to me," she says.

"What?"

"Peoples look to me." She points to other diners and then back to herself. Everyone is wearing T-shirts, shorts, and flip-flops. Katie is still wearing her ride-'em cowboy, lady-of-the-evening outfit.

"You mean people are looking at you?"

"Peoples look to me."

She smiles, and leaves without even a "so long, partner."

Once she's gone, my headache eases, my back feels better. I eat my food and then start on hers.

I am nursing my second orange juice, when Katie reappears wearing a military outfit with fatigue pants and shirt, and Converse sneakers. Her ponytail has been replaited.

She looks at her half-empty plate and then at me. I spear a left-over sausage on my plate and feed it to her.

After breakfast, I walk her out of the hotel, kiss her, and climb into a tuk-tuk for the half-hour ride to Angkor Wat.

"I'll meet you later, tonight, back here at seven for dinner. OK?"

She frowns and talks in Khmer to the driver. Their conversation becomes animated and continues for several minutes. My head throbs.

I tap the driver on the back. "What's going on?

"She meet you here at seven."

The driver starts the engine. We leave Katie standing there. I wave. She smiles.

The tuk-tuk consists of a two-wheeled passenger cart hitched to the back of the driver's little motorcycle. The cart has two bench seats facing each other and an awning roof. There are no doors, or windows, or seat belts. My driver is maybe twenty years old and has agreed to take me to Angkor

Wat and a few other temples for seventeen dollars. He hands me a brochure describing the temples, and then gestures for me to sit. I notice that he's missing half his left pinky, severed clean.

On the road, he swivels around to face me and asks: "How much you pay for girl?"

"Huh?"

"I can get you younger, prettier who no smoke." He gives me the little OK sign. "She do ice cream."

"What?"

"Yum-yum." He makes a gesture licking an imaginary ice-cream cone.

I'm not sure how to respond. Is he insulting my taste, my girl? What did he and Katie talk about anyway? Did he lose that finger in a pimping deal gone wrong?

It gets me thinking: Should I have invited Katie? Did she change her clothes for me? Am I an idiot or just coming down with *P. falciparum*? Is she looting my room right now and throwing what she doesn't steal out the window?

The truth is I'm just as happy to have an afternoon to myself. I've been with Ned and Jorani constantly for the last week. And then Mary and now Katie. I haven't spent this much time with other people since I left Boston.

Since my last girlfriend.

Since Ricki.

While the driver and I sit in traffic, in dust, surrounded by the putt-putting spitfire of a thousand tiny motorcycles, I think about Ricki's last e-mail: She mentioned surgery. Maybe it's just vision correction or an errant gall bladder. What if there are complications? What if it's not a minor procedure, but something serious, like a brain tumor?

A fresh gust of dust, a break in the traffic, and we're on our way again. I sneeze into the Angkor Wat brochure and wonder: Why am I going sightseeing again? I hate sightseeing. Probably the same reason I keep dating. I keep hoping the next time will be different.

Angkor Wat is one of the world's largest religious structures, complete with a moat as wide as two football fields and outer walls two miles long. It was home to the Khmer Empire from the ninth to the fifteenth century, then it was ransacked and disappeared under jungle vegetation for more than 400 years. I must be here for some reason.

I enter the Wat, open to anything. I look around for a sign and find one: "Closed for renovation." The famous pine-cone domes are under reconstruction. Crap.

Inside one of the galleries, a long, flickering hallway. Echoes of a lost civilization. Ancient, dark, cavernous. I feel like I've been here before. I follow the scent of sandalwood and cloves down a high, narrow corridor. Stone floors, stone walls, a stone ceiling, more darkness. A few other tourists pass in a guided group. I come to an intersection of hallways. In the center, there's a large, seated Buddha, fatter than two Abes. An orange scarf is draped across three of his six arms.

A voice beckons.

"You buy incense, fifty cent?" A local man in flip-flops appears from behind me.

"No thanks," I say.

I'm expecting the hustler to give me the little OK sign, so I beat him to the punch line and make a giant hoop with my arms. "You want American girl, big-big?"

A uniformed man appears from an adjacent corridor. He has big black boots. "Sir, please remove your hat when entering our temples. Also, it is recommended that you buy the incense. It brings good luck."

Since "bad luck" probably means immediate arrest and a blindfolded stroll through a nearby minefield, I fork over 2,000 riel, about fifty cents, and move on.

The Wat's outer walls are supposed to be decorated with bas-reliefs, which I'm guessing are these carvings of half-clad nymphs and guardian angels in spiky, towering headdresses. I think of Katie, half-clad in her white towel.

On another wall, I contemplate a scene from Hindu mythology, the "Churning of the Ocean of Milk," which is supposed to depict good and evil, desire and suffering, consciousness and focus. All I see are carvings of a snake, a turtle, and a barefoot guy with limbs to spare. My head throbs. I'm suffering.

Then on to Angkor Thom, another major temple, more bas-reliefs, a belfry, and flying bats. I can't get out of there fast enough.

My driver and I cap our day at a smaller compound called Preah Khan. My back is now throbbing.

During our ride back to Siem Reap, I reflect on my experience at Angkor Wat:

• The place took 300 years to build, and I made it out in less than four hours with nothing to show but flu-like symptoms.

• Greek ruins, Khmer ruins. Once you've seen one pile of rubble, you've seen them all.

• The forty-dollar entry fee was equal to a night with Katie. I tap the driver on the shoulder. "Where can I buy some Hershey's chocolate bars?"

After a nap at the hotel, I wake with more aches: my neck, my elbows, my knees. It's seven fifteen. I drag myself to the lobby. Katie is sitting on a bench, cigarette in hand. She's wearing a black leather vest, black leather shorts, and black leather motorcycle boots. Stenciled around each eye, she has a half moon of purple flowers. I'm not sure if the stencils have any significance, but I assume she's dressed for a big night out. I consider her various outfits: Cowgirl, soldier, motorcycle moll.

"You look great," I say. "Ever heard of the Village People?"

She looks at me blankly. "You weird man." There's no smile. "Playboy man."

Behind her, a familiar fat figure and a familiar reedy figure are talking to an unfamiliar night guard. I don't recall inviting Ned and Jorani along for dinner.

Ned turns to me. "You're in the doghouse, pal. Something about you taking boom-boom girls to Angkor Wat and leaving Katie here."

"What?"

"Showing up late tonight because you're getting yum-yum in your room. You're an animal. I'm proud of you."

"Look, maybe I should have invited her to Angkor Wat. And yes the driver offered me girls but I told him 'no.'"

"The student has snatched the pebble from the master."

"Ned, wait a minute . . ."

"Convincing me won't do any good—I'm in the doghouse, too, for overindulging last night at Giddy Gordon's. Let's just all go for a nice dinner and you can smooth things out."

I feel my head: warm. I rub my stomach: queasy. I realize I left Katie's chocolates in the tuk-tuk three hours ago.

We take our Cambodian dates to a Thai restaurant. We look at our menus in silence. Ned and Jorani order Cokes, I order water, and Katie orders a beer with ice.

Jorani lays out some earrings on the table. Katie picks up a pair, fondles it, and puts it back. Jorani offers a second pair, in what appears to be the old two-for-one. No sale. This is the first time I've seen Jorani fail to close.

Katie's cell phone rings. She checks the number, and excuses herself from the table. I give Jorani four dollars for the earrings.

Jorani tells me that Katie works at a bar in Phnom Penh, is here on vacation, and plans to meet some friends later to go dancing.

"If you go out with them," Ned says, "be prepared to pick up the tab—for her and her friends."

"I'm feeling kind of crappy," I say. "Not really in the mood to play sugar daddy. I'll probably go back to the hotel after dinner."

"You're not taking those antimalarial pills, are you?" Ned asks.

Before I can answer, Katie returns. I ask Jorani to tell Katie that I'm not feeling well and to present some options:

• She can go to my hotel with me now.

• She can come by later after she's done partying with her friends.

• We can get together another night.

Katie listens and pouts. I motion for her to come with me, away from Ned and Jorani.

In the hallway: a Buddha statue, a poster promoting massage and free Internet, a sign promising jail for having sex with children.

I lean against the statue and say. "I like you." I give her the earrings. "Want to give me your cell phone number?"

"No gold or silver?" She snatches the earrings, turns, and stomps off to meet her friends.

After dinner, I head back to the hotel alone. My room smells like insecticide with a hint of vanilla shampoo and ARA cigarette smoke.

I take a double shot of Nyquil and read the potential side effects of the antimalarial pills: headache, nausea, fever, and hallucinations.

I open the windows to air out the place. Fuck the mosquitoes. I toss the pills into the puddle and watch the package sink and join my blindfold somewhere in the murk.

During a recent session, Moody asked, "Have you ever heard of attachment theory?" as he started scribbling on his legal pad.

"Is that about how you connect with your parents as a child is how you'll connect with your girlfriends as an adult?" I started scribbling in my own pocket notepad.

At this point in our therapy, we had begun practicing "extreme honesty," which meant we both said what was on our minds with minimal filtering.

"I feel that your scribbling is an attempt to mock me and get negative attention," he said.

I made another note, and then said: "*Your* scribbling makes me angry. I imagine that you're holding out on me, that you're being secretive and taking notes that you and your wife can laugh about tonight over Vouvray and vibrating butt plugs."

"That's very offensive, Randy."

"You're welcome."

After a short break, another five dollars, we had an enlightening discussion about the Three Negative Attachment Styles:

1) Needy

Desperate for any relationship, a life preserver, someone to keep them from going under.

They agree with the following:

"All I want is love. Love, love, love. Hugs and kisses all the time. Why can't I find someone to love me the way mama should have?"

Metaphor: The baby monkey whose mother has been replaced with a coat hanger covered in old dish towels.

2) Claustrophobic

Avoids relationships, claiming they don't need one.

They agree with the following:

"Life is unpredictable. People are unreliable. I am unpredictable and unreliable. If you don't depend on me and I don't depend on you, we'll get along fine."

Metaphor: a sperm whale fighting off an army of giant squids.

3) Ambivalent

Their connections tend to be intense, but short-lived. In relationships, they oscillate between needy and claustrophobic with an occasional pause in normalcy, which they find boring, or scary, or boring and scary.

They agree with the following:

"Life is suffering. Love is suffering. Suffering is pain. So to live and love requires prescription painkillers."

I told Moody there are worse things than ambivalence, such as insomnia and jogging injuries and dating a woman who loves pasta.

The overhead light in my room seems dimmer, the air cooler. A Nyquil nod overtakes me and I drift into a familiar, deep oblivion.

Back in Phnom Penh, packed for my flight to Melbourne, I say good-bye to Ned and Jorani outside the Tamarind.

Ned's tuk-tuk driver, Mr. Suk, pulls up to take me to the airport. "Thanks again for everything," I say to Ned and mean it.

"Next year in Battambang," Ned says, gripping my shoulder. He's no scammer or weenie. He's just a good guy.

I turn to Jorani. "Nice meeting you and thanks for being such a great hostess. I mean, for showing me around."

"You nice man," she says. "Katie no friendly."

Mr. Suk and I head to the airport. It's rush hour.

On the highway, a girl on the back of a motorcycle breast-feeds a child as her companion bobs and weaves through traffic.

I observe without snide commentary.

On the road shoulder, two men have dropped trousers and are peeing on the ground, russet-colored butts to the highway.

I keep waiting, but there's no chatter, no snarky interior monologue. This is a different kind of perfect moment.

When a sign appears for the airport, Mr. Suk turns to me: "Next year, you come, I find you nice girl." He points to the guidebook in my bag. "I know that book."

"You know Pittman?"

"No."

"Whatever."

He gives me the little OK sign and I give him one back. *I'm OK, you're OK, we're all OK.*

The Chronic Single's Handbook
Chapter Five
The three alternatives to marriage
1) Long-Term: Committed Relationship

- *Requirements: luck to find the right person.*
- *Rewards: clean laundry, matching dishes, a date on Saturday night, long-term appreciation.*
- *Risks: intimacy-induced asphyxiation, back-end loads, stretch marks, flatulence, hair loss, hair on back, hair in sink, eye rolling, palimony, asset reallocation.*

2) Intermediate-Term: Serial Monogamy

- *Requirements: steady supply of women, thick skin.*
- *Rewards: exciting sex, envy of attached friends, limited liability.*
- *Risks: high annual turnover rate, extreme volatility, loneliness between relationships.*

3) Short-term: Fee for Services

- *Requirements: cash reserves.*
- *Rewards: sexual diversification, envy of attached friends, no nagging, get to sleep alone after sex.*
- *Risks: capital depreciation, falling in love with a prostitute, STDs, and other hidden costs.*

CHAPTER EIGHT: AUSTRALIA

*Fate may come upon you unexpectedly, but you will always recognize
the ill wind that drifts from the canyon of distention.*
—W. PITTMAN

Civilization: Traffic lights, trash collection, freckles.

After dumping my bags at Melbourne's Wooluru Inn, a Best Western knockoff near the center of town, I amble down Swanston Street to the waterfront, the Yarra River, taking in the Aussie scene. A fly lands on my lip. I swat it away.

The tree-lined streets are wide, free of noodle carts, peeing kids, and whiney tuk-tuks. The only droning I hear is in my prefrontal lobe following a twelve-hour red-eye from Phnom Penh.

After four red-eyes, I'm now a man with a method. During a flight, I skip the sleeping pills, which don't seem to work at 40,000 feet, and instead drink the free beer and watch movies all night. In the morning, I feel like shit. So what?

Crossing Bourke Street, I spot the stone façade and copper dome of Melbourne's historic Flinders Street train station. Skyscrapers hover in the distance. Another fly. Another swat.

A woman in a suit exits the train station and waves. Do I know her? A tattooed girl on her cell phone waves too. Then a fat guy with a skateboard. Something tunnels in my nose, something skitters in my underwear. Flies are collecting on me as if I were a rotting carcass. I join everyone around me cursing, waving, and swatting.

I flee down Flinders Street and duck into the Melbourne Aquarium. Animal feeding time begins in five minutes. Then I notice the admission: twenty-five dollars. In Phnom Penh that's a night with a bar girl in size 00 jeans.

Outside again, the flies are feeding.

I've just traveled through Southeast Asia, a land of deadly mosquitoes, half-bald rats, and ruthless tuk-tuk drivers. A few Western bugs shouldn't faze me, but my T-shirt is now a vibrating vest of flies.

I make a dash for an Asian bistro across from the aquarium. In the dining room, tubular steel lights hang from a vaulted ceiling. The decor: steel and leather, stone and wood. The menu: fifteen dollars for a bowl of soup, not including a tip, something I haven't included in weeks. I'll take my chances with the flies.

Back on Flinders, I run bobbing and weaving by a movie theater: twelve dollars for a Mel Gibson flick. Jews don't pay retail for Mel Gibson movies.

Back at the Wooluru Inn, I confront the hotel clerk as if she were somehow to blame: "What's with the flies? I thought Australia was a civilized, first-world country."

She says nothing and hands me a tourist info card entitled, *"The Australian Bush Fly."*

Highlights:

• From October through January, bush flies are common in Melbourne.

• The insects feed on bodily fluids: tears, sweat, saliva, and mucous.

• Bush flies do not bite or sting. They lay their eggs in animal dung, not on humans.

• The Aussie Salute: A waving motion used by locals to repel the flies.

• Suggestion: Wear a hat with a mesh net that covers the face.

A sign behind the desk clerk advertises mesh-net hats with the Wooluru logo for thirty dollars. Jews don't pay retail for hats with logos.

My room is a $150-a-night suite with all the amenities: toilets with seats, signs with grammar, and all-you-can-drink potable water from the tap. I call room service and order a fifteen-dollar poached egg for dinner.

The next day, I wake at noon, drink a glass of water, and order another fifteen-dollar poached egg. After breakfast, I pace around the room and drink two more free glasses of water. I turn on the TV—all the shows and commercials are in English, what luxury—and then shut it off. Outside the window, pedestrians perform the Aussie Salute. For the hell of it, I thumb through the Melbourne Yellow Pages: "Automotive." "Car Hire." "Eating." "Escorts." *Hmmm.* "Real Blondes: Naughty, Cheeky, Wet & Wild." The price: $250 an hour. That's enough for ten naughty Khmer massages.

"Finance." "Fisheries." "Fitness Centres." *Hmmm.* The Bourke Street Health Club is around the corner. It's worth a go.

Out on the street, a woman with a quivering headdress of flies salutes me.

Racing to the gym, I notice a store front with a row of blondes inside chatting on the phone. One catches my eye, smiles, and then holds up an index finger to indicate she's almost done. Naughty, Cheeky, Wet & Wild.

I brush off and step inside.

She smiles, smoothes her skirt, and hands me a brochure featuring thongy women cavorting on a beach. I sit across from her in a cheery, yellow chair.

"How can I be of help?" Her twangy Aussie accent is somewhere between a British lilt and a Texas drawl. She points to my brochure, which advertises vacations in Singapore, Vietnam, and Thailand.

"I just came from Southeast Asia and was looking forward to a little civilization but I need to get away from these flies. Got anything with outdoor activities, like windsurfing, here in Australia? I'm on my own so a party scene, an easy place to meet people, would be good too."

She leans across her desk and touches my hand. "You know, it's nearing high season."

I shrink into my chair. "Got anything fun and, maybe, affordable?"

"How about surfing up north?" She points to a map above her. "We have budget packages to Ooloocoolow, Gamawawa, or Boohoowuwu. No flies there."

Baby talk from glossy lips. I look at the other towns on the map: Gympie North, Burpengary, Moorooka, Wooloowin, Yeerongpilly.

I touch her wrist. "I read that Yeow-Ouch-Ouch and Pottypoopoo are also nice this time of year."

"Beg yours?" She retracts her hand.

"Just kidding."

Her eyes are small, blue, and lifeless.

"Right," she says. "We have something in Keezerbeezer. You'll fly into Brisbane, hire a car, and stay at the Moringaranga Resort. At the beach, you can take surfing lessons. The whole package is only $2,950 for a week."

"What if I skip the car?"

She looks out the window and smiles at a passerby.

I pick at a cuticle. "What do you think a cab would cost?"

Her phone rings and she snatches the receiver out of its cradle.

"Yeah, Rosie, I'm about to finish up here."

She puts her hand on the mouthpiece and turns to me. "If you're looking to travel on the cheap, I don't think I can be of much help."

She gives me what appears to be an Aussie Salute.

Back at the hotel, I log onto travelscrooge, and find a hotel, the Royal Paradise, in Keezerbeezer. A one-week package, including flight and public transportation from the airport, costs $1,800, the same as two months in Phnom Penh or three months in Hoi An, cities where my long nose and white skin made me a celebrity, a handsome man. Here, I'm just another white guy too old to be wearing a backpack.

I turn to Pittman's book, which, to his credit, has been nearly 70 percent accurate, as he originally claimed. The chapter on Australia lists an array of Aussie gotchas: sharks the size of SUVs, crocodiles the size of sharks, six-foot birds, killer jellyfish, and a condition known as reverse-culture shock, the result of going from the exotic East back to the pasteurized West and finding that your life hasn't changed. But no mention of Keezerbeezer or flies. I make a note to send a card to Pittman about the flies.

Back on travelscrooge, I click on a Keezerbeezer video featuring thongy Aussie girls speaking twee English with a southern twang. I wash down an Ambien with a beer and charge the Keezerbeezer trip on my Visa.

Then I check my e-mail.

A note from Abe. Maybe he's getting divorced.

Burns:

Glad you're having fun in Tokyo. Same old shit here, but with a new twist: Amy wants to have a kid. In other developments:

You wouldn't believe the fucked-up thing that happened last week.
I'll tell you when you get back.

And one from Rachel. Maybe Arturo dumped her.
Hi Randall:
Abe said he was going to drop you a note. Heard you're
having a fabulous time in Kuala Lumpur. Arturo and I look for-
ward to hearing all about your trip when you get back in April!

And one from Uncle Heshie: Hopefully he's not in jail.
Hey Nephew,
See you at the airport on Dec. 15. All's well on the home
front. Nice pad.

Blog Entry: November 26
Melbourne, Australia
Hi All,
Happy Thanksgiving.
Sorry I've been out of touch. Here's a quick update:
• Spent two weeks taking in the sights of Cambodia: Phnom
Penh (the Paris of Southeast Asia) and Angkor Wat (the Athens
of Southeast Asia).
• Heading to Keezerbeezer, a quaint, Australian beach town
(the Edgartown of the Pacific) for surfing and relaxing. Keep
those cards and letters coming.
See you in a few,
—Burns

The flight to Brisbane takes about two hours. At the airport, I hop a train, and then a shuttle bus to Keezerbeezer for
a total of four hours door to door. No flies.

The Royal Paradise anchors a mall and has twenty floors
with a revolving restaurant on top. The amenities include

everything from conference rooms to babysitting to a water-front karaoke bar. My room has two queen beds, a furnished balcony, a wide-screen TV, a minibar, a microwave, and a welcome packet with a sleep blindfold. I'm done with hostels and Asian squalor.

I head for the hotel sauna to sweat out any red-eye residue. A guy wearing a towel, a wedding band, and terry-cloth slippers is slumped on the bench. He is sweating like a Russian mobster and pressing an open can of XXXX Bitter beer against his gray sideburns. I'm guessing he's about sixty. I take a seat opposite him.

A young woman opens the sauna door. She glances at the guy's paunch and then at my face. I haven't shaved in two days.

"Come on in, sweetheart," the guy says to her. "We're harmless."

She glances at the soft-sided cooler by the guy's feet. "Don't want to break up the party." The door slams behind her.

"Her loss," the guy says reaching into the cooler. "Tinny?" he asks me.

A sex-deprived, married guy, probably ditching the wife and kids for an hour—I'm definitely back in civilization.

He hands me a can of XXXX and then gives me the once-over: Keens with safety pins and board shorts with food stains.

"Traveling long?" he asks.

"Been on the road for a few months. Actually I guess I'm still on the road. Randy from Boston."

"Ron from Sydney. Where you coming from?"

"Thailand, Vietnam, Cambodia."

"Me and my mates used to holiday in Bangkok. Fell in love many times at Soi Cowboy. Nothing beats a good massage, eh?"

Should I confess to being a part of the club? I'm no longer in Asia. I'm back in the politically correct, straitlaced West. But Australians are supposed to be loose, rough and tumble, a country where men are still men and women are still naughty, cheeky, wet, and wild.

"Nothing beats Phnom Penh," I say.

"Boom-boom-boom!" He flashes me a tiny OK sign, finishes off his tinny, and pops open a fresh one. "You'll do all right here," he says. "Go up to Hennigan Avenue. When I was your age, used to leave the discos with a bird under each arm. No bar girls there, but you still have to buy them drinks. You married?"

"Nope."

"I'm turning forty-two tomorrow," he says. "Been married ten years. We got two ankle biters, both girls."

I take another sip and don't tell him my age.

"Just have to remember that any bird on holiday is looking for a good rooting. You single guys have it made."

I take a closer look at him: a graying tuft between pink teats, a graying fringe around a pink scalp—not exactly a stud. He could be full of crap. Then again, I'm not in Boston or Greece. Maybe Western women are different down under. Maybe I do have it made and just don't appreciate it.

Later that night, I change into my best rooting outfit, and ask the kid behind the concierge desk for directions to Hennigan Avenue.

He removes his earbuds: "Are you having me on? Sir, you don't want to go to Hennigan. It's all schoolies."

He explains that schoolies are high school kids that overrun Keezerbeezer after graduation, kind of like the bush flies in Melbourne or the college kids in Daytona Beach. The knowledgeable travel agent in Melbourne neglected to mention this.

"There's about 33,000 of them here for the week. But we've organized a special week of adult activities at the hotel."

"Adult activities?" I ask.

He hands me a list of events and a scorecard. "Schoolie-free activities. And for every activity you attend, you get points toward a fifty-dollar gift certificate."

"What can I get with the certificate?"

"A gift."

Activity #1: Happy Hour

The Bar Cow Cow is all polished stone, brushed steel, frosted glass. On the patio, people are clustered around a semicircular granite bar. The crowd is mostly guys, thirty and older. A few women are scattered about, and everyone is grouped off smoking, drinking, and laughing. I look around as if I'm waiting for someone, and then open a dinner menu.

Mulligatawny soup: sixteen dollars.

Pan-fried kangaroo: thirty-five dollars.

Wagyu rib fillet: seventy dollars.

I order an XXXX Bitter and stand at the bar. Next to me, a cheeky blonde adjusts a guy's collar. Australian for "spoken for."

Another couple arrives. He orders an XXXX Bitter. She flips through the drink menu.

"What's in the Creamy Cud?" she asks the bartender.

He rattles off seven ingredients.

"I don't really care for orange marmalade ice cream. Can I get another flavor?" she asks.

"How about vanilla bean?"

"Actually I don't care for ice cream. What's in the Rummy Ruminant?"

"Ice cream."

The guy who brought the woman looks at me and rolls his eyes.

"I saw that," she says to him.

He smiles, winks at me, and kisses the back of her head.

Once again, I'm the extra in someone else's romantic comedy. The bartender stamps my attendance card, I down the bitter beer and leave.

Activity #2: Sports

The next morning, I attend a ten A.M. group surfing class at the hotel beach. The skies are cloudless and fly-less. The waves are massive; when they crash the ground shakes.

My instructor is about five feet tall, smaller than a wave, and maybe sixteen years old. I'm the only one in the class. I ask about yesterday's attendance. He says there were more people and most were children.

"But there was one older lady," he says.

"How old?"

"Twenty-five."

An hour into my lesson, my sunglasses are broken, my hat is floating toward Vanuatu, and there's a burning sensation shooting down the back of my leg. The instructor stamps my attendance card. "Sorry about your sunnies, mate."

Back at the hotel, I chase three ibuprofen with a Vicodin and get into bed.

Activity #3: Pool Party

I wake at four P.M. and limp onto my balcony. The guy from the sauna is by the pool with what I'm assuming is his family. On the chair next to him, his pink wife is applying sunscreen to a pair of crimson little girls, while he is chatting up a young woman who looks similar to the one who declined his invitation in the sauna. A group of guys from last night's Cow Cow event enters the pool area. They look around, and then leave.

I put on my sleep blindfold and crawl back into bed.

Activity #4: Chocolate Tasting

At eight P.M., after showering, I head to the hotel sweet-shop. I find ribbons and bows, wrapped boxes and glass displays, one employee and me. I am followed by the same group of guys who come in, look around, and leave.

I don't particularly like chocolate but after sampling several pieces, I'm getting a nice buzz. Chocolate has theobromine, which is like caffeine, which I usually avoid because it keeps me up at night. A six-piece "Naughty Bits" gift box is on special for nine dollars. The selection includes chocolates topped with bacon as well as truffles filled with Jim Beam. *The James.* It sounds disgusting. In honor of Ned, I buy it. Back in my room, I suck down a Jim Beam truffle as an appetizer and eat a bacon-topped chocolate for dinner. I have another Jim Beam for dessert. My heart rate hits 110 beats per minute, the fat-burning rate on a treadmill.

Activity #5: Karaoke

Inside the Cow Cow, there are tables with candles and seats without people. While I'm sipping a XXXX at the bar, the MC calls out to me over the PA system: "Sir, if you get up and sing, you'll get double points for winning, there's no competition."

Why is everyone suddenly calling me "sir"?

I limp up to the microphone. A spotlight shines in my eyes. My hands tremble from the effects of theobromine. I squint.

"What's your song, mate?" the MC asks.

"How about something cheerful, like 'Eleanor Rigby'?"

Two more stamps on my score card, a heart rate of 130 beats per minute; my work here is done.

Back in my room, sleep eludes me. I review my food and drug intake for the day: Six ibuprofen, two Vicodin, six pieces of chocolate, bacon bits, beer, Jim Beam, more beer, and more Jim Beam. I wash down another Vicodin with a ten-dollar Heineken from the minibar.

While waiting for the pill to kick in, I turn on the TV and watch *Bushtucker: Australian for Grub.* According to the show, bushtucker is food originally eaten by the country's indigenous peoples before the arrival of Wagyu beef and mulligatawny soup. There's been a resurgent interest in the cuisine, which may include moths, ants, frogs, and of course, grubs. The narrator samples a live witchetty grub, which resembles a caterpillar. "Tastes a little like peanut butter," he says, licking his lips. I think of the smoky taste of Katie's mouth after she snacked on some black beetles.

Next I watch *Australia's Deadliest Jellyfish* and *Are You Smarter than a Schoolie?*

Two hours later, my eyeballs feel like they're going to roll back into my head. My hands are twitchy and my jaw is tired from grinding my teeth.

I stare deep into the medicine cabinet mirror: Gray stubble on my neck. Old. I take out a razor and remove the protective cover. When my mother was my age, she cheated on my stepfather. When her Uncle Morty reached my age, he hiked into the woods and handcuffed himself to a tree. His skeleton was found picked clean three years later. I look deeper still: Wide, anxious eyes. Hello, little baby monkey.

Chocolate and TV have always been a bad combination for me. The problems began as a child with after-school TV: *The Little Rascals, The Three Stooges, The Munsters.* While watching, I'd sip a glass of chocolate milk and nibble Count Chocula from the box. On a weekend, I could polish off a twenty-two-ounce bottle of Bosco and watch a dozen cartoons back-to-back.

My TV viewing soon became indiscriminate. I watched cross-country skiing, tarpon fishing, and cartoons starring girls. I neglected my gerbils and forgot to walk the dog. I watched alone and snuck a *TV Guide* in my lunch box.

I lied to my friends, my family, and to myself: I just needed a little something to help me relax after a long day of sniffing Magic Markers, eating crayons, and learning to spell curse words. But despite an electron hangover every morning, I never missed any school. As far as I was concerned, I didn't have a problem.

One day I fell off my bicycle and skinned my elbow. In the bathroom, I took a good look at myself: I was gaunt, disheveled, and had a picture-tube tan. Even at eleven years old, I knew I had to quit. But as soon as I felt the buzz of a TV screen or smelled chocolate syrup, I lost control.

By fifth grade, this was my typical Saturday:

8:30 A.M. Glass of milk with a shot of Bosco, bowl of Cocoa Puffs.

9:00–11:00 *Deputy Dawg, Help! . . . It's the Hair Bear Bunch!, Bewitched, Archie.*

11:01 Bathroom break, stepsister Harriet enters the den, ignores me, and leaves. Milk with Bosco, Cocoa Krispies with Bosco.

11:30–1:00 P.M. *Josie and the Pussycats, The Monkees, Lancelot Link: Secret Chimp.*

1:05 Stepdad: "Shut off that damn television and go outside!"

3:00 *Major League Baseball Game of the Week.*

4:00: Throw Nerf ball around den. Break lamp. Hide lamp.

5:00 *Wide World of Sports.*

5:10 Bosco with a shot of milk.

6:30 Dinner: liver with onions, Brussels sprouts, green jello mold; refuse to eat sprouts, no dessert.

7:30–10:00 *Mission: Impossible, My Three Sons, The Mary Tyler Moore Show*. Bosco straight from the bottle. Pee on carpet in Harriet's room.

10:05 Mom: "No, you can't watch *Mannix*, you have to go to bed." I argue. She threatens no TV for one week.

10:06 In bed, lights out.

2:00 A.M. In the kitchen: Bosco straight from the bottle, Count Chocula chaser; watch TV static for an hour.

Sunday: repeat, substituting animal shows for cartoons.

For twenty years, I have controlled my TV and chocolate habits by not keeping either in the house. Now my hotel room floor is strewn with chocolate foils and the TV drones in the background. At two A.M., I shut off everything and get into bed. I wake at 3:09 A.M., 4:15 A.M., and 6:33 A.M. from the same nightmare.

It's our annual family Chanukah dinner. Harriet is with a new husband and a new kid, Joey is with his foreign wife and eight-year-old daughter, Jan. I'm still single and sitting between my parents who are in their sixties. I'm in my sixties too. Everyone addresses me as "sir." Jan hands me a little wrapped box and says, "Uncle Randy, I don't want you to be alone anymore." Inside the box is a photo of her homely sixty-year-old teacher, Miss Phelps. There's a phone number with a note, "Call me, we'll party. Evelyn."

Back in my Royal Paradise bathroom, unable to sleep, I open my Tupperware container of medications and read the labels: hydrocortisone cream (do not ingest). Vicodin (do not take with alcohol), and Ambien (do not take with Vicodin). I read other labels, eventually get tired, and go to bed. I awake at eleven A.M. to a vacuum cleaner in the hallway banging against my door.

I slip off the blindfold. The room seems larger, emptier, more expensive. Out on the balcony, I survey the crowd at the pool: Not a single high-relief collarbone, or wingy shoulder blade, or heart-shaped calf. Everyone in the crowd is overweight.

I pop three ibuprofen, cover the TV with a towel, and call the concierge.

"Is there a health club nearby?"

"Sure. There's one right next to the Cow Cow."

I don my rooting outfit and head the opposite direction to Hennigan Avenue. I've had enough of the Cow Cow. As I walk, I think of schoolies and kids. Maybe that's the connection I've been missing in life—a child. I have money; I could adopt a little ankle-biter. Then when I'm old, I'll have someone to spend my savings and clean my pooper if Lenny won't. The little cookie scammer in Bangkok was kind of cute. Joey's daughter, Jan, is kind of cute.

Last Chanukah, Joey and I took Jan skiing for her first time.

At the rental shop: "I want pink boots," Jan said.

"The boots only come in blue," Joey said.

"They hurt."

"Ski boots are supposed to hurt," he said.

"I'm not wearing them."

"Jan, you have a choice: You can wear the boots and go skiing, or not wear the boots and we can sit in the lodge and drink beer all day."

"I'm a kid, I'm too little for beer and it tastes gross."

"No boots, no skiing.

Finally we got her outfitted and outside. After a half-hour wait on the lift line, we made it to the front. Little Jan was smiling and licking the mucous running from her nose. I patted her on the head. *Good girl.*

Then Joey said, "Jan, where are your mittens?"

Elapsed time: three hours.

Skiing: none

Two blocks from Hennigan Avenue, a shirtless schoolie in a ski hat skateboards toward me on the sidewalk. As he approaches, he raises his hand for a high five and smiles. "G'day, sir," he says. I nix the adoption idea and keep walking.

A few blocks farther, I spot a bookstore, head to the markdown table, and thumb through *The Man Who Made Lists: Love, Death, Madness, and the Creation of Roget's Thesaurus.* A keeper. I tuck it under my arm.

Next I'm wooed by *Score Like a Pro: How to Pick Up Beautiful Women.* Chapter One instructs fledgling hose-artists to build confidence by talking to strangers and offers a scoring system for tracking progress:

- Ask a stranger the time: one point
- Ask a woman the time: two points.
- Ask an attractive woman the time: three points.
- Ask follow-up questions: one point each.

Goal: Accumulate ten points a day for the first week.

Key to success: Hygiene. Take a shower, brush your teeth, and change your T-shirt.

Next to me, a young blonde is holding a book on Linux upside down.

"You having fun?" I ask.

"No English."

No problem. Three points.

I buy both the *Roget* and *Score Like a Pro* books for 50 percent off and head to the gym recommended by the concierge.

In the stretching area, I ask a woman doing a headstand. "Do you know what time it is?"

She says something unintelligible. Then I notice the facial mole: only two points.

I pass a woman doing lunges in a Yankees baseball hat. "Are you from New York?"

Smile, nod.

Another three.

"Do those lunges work your glutes?" I say.

She rolls her eyes.

Not my problem, one point.

Nine points in two hours. I hit the showers, change into a clean Red Sox T-shirt, and head to the Cow Cow to celebrate.

At the outside bar, a three-point waitress approaches.

"Can I get a XXXX?" I ask.

"Pot?" she asks.

"Had to quit, beer is fine."

"Very funny. OK, one pot of XXXX."

"Hey, your accent is normal," I say. "Where are you from?"

"Canada," she says.

"Me, too, eh?"

"Right. Last I heard, the Red Sox were American."

"Good one. Do you surf?" I ask.

"Every day."

"I bet you're a pretty good surfer," I say. "I'm still learning, but we should go sometime."

"Probably not a good idea. I'm kind of seeing someone."

"He's a lucky guy. If anything changes between now and the time you bring the pot, let me know." As I hear my own words, I'm impressed with myself.

The pot turns out to be a half-pint. Halfway through it, my theobromine agitation is overtaken by something more pleasant—oxytocin—strange because not only did I not touch the waitress, I got blown off. I finish my beer, leave the recommended Aussie tip of 10 percent, and hit the mall for a pair of overpriced sunglasses.

One-hundred dollars later, I'm back in my room. The maids have left chocolates on my pillow and removed the towel from the television. I can't help noticing the afternoon TV schedule: *Spiders and Snakes: Australia's Deadliest Critters* starts in five minutes.

I need a distraction, something that doesn't involve TV and chocolate. I open the *Roget* book, about a man who made lists to fend off anxiety and insanity. I grab a hotel pad and pen.

List #1: Positive things in my life
- My mortgage is small.
- My prostate is small.

List #2: Sex
- Age virginity lost: 17
- Years having sex: 28
- Number of sexual partners: 56
- Average new partners per year: 2
- Longest dry spell: 18 months (probably no worse than any married guy)

List #3: Love
- Number of times average person falls in love: 6
- Number of times I've fallen in love: 14
- My average frequency: once every 24 months
- Longest dry spell: 48 months

List #4: Relationships
- Longer than 3 months: 12
- Longer than a year: 4
- Longest: 3 years (Ricki, but it included 3-month-long breakups)
- Percentage of life in a relationship: 33
- Percentage of life depressed: 67
- Most disturbing trend: 7 girlfriends had men's names

List #5: Marriage
- Women who would have married me: 4
- Women I would have married: 4
- Women in both categories: none

Before I left, Dr. Moody offered some insights into why I was still single.

"You need to be aware of how your teasing comes across. Is it possible that some of these women, like Ricki, experienced it as something less than fun?"

"So what's your point?" I asked.

He reached for his notepad, scribbled something, and continued. "When a woman you like is calm, you worry that she's bored or that there's no spark."

I pulled out my pocket notepad and scribbled something.

He continued: "To get a rise out of them, to get their attention, you tease them."

I scribbled some more.

"OK," I said. "Maybe I am a childish, sadistic, rotten person. I know you don't believe in fate. But I do. Maybe it's my destiny to be single."

He scribbled. I scribbled.

"I understand your frustration. You just need to learn to get out of your own way. Don't give up yet. By the way," he

said, nodding at my notepad, "are you trying to get a rise out
of me?"

Abe offered some additional insights:

"Burns, you know what your problem is? You try to act
weird. I don't know if it's to get attention or what. Why don't
you just try acting normal for once?"

"Define normal."

"I'll tell you what normal isn't.

"A middle-aged guy who sleeps with fifty women and
finds something wrong with every one of them.

"A middle-aged guy who earns a six-figure salary and puts
heel taps on his flip-flops and drives a car held together with
Bondo.

"A middle-aged guy who spends all his time either dieting
or at the gym, like he's some kind of pro athlete or an underwear model, but is too scrawny to be either."

"So, what's your point?"

I skip dinner, slip on my sleep blindfold, and awake two
hours later to the sound of an envelope sliding under my
door: I've won a fifty-dollar gift certificate to the casino for
attending so many adult events. I celebrate with a minibar
Heinken and more of the *Score Like a Pro* book.

Chapter Two recommends developing an open-ended question that elicits more than a "yes" or "no" answer from a woman.

Key to Success: Focus on the mission and remember that
you have no control over outcomes. Envision success, see success. If you get stuck, observe your thoughts and feelings with
cool detachment and repeat today's affirmation: All is well in
my world.

The casino bar is down a set of stairs so wide it has
four lanes. The ceiling is covered with hanging crystals that

shimmer like glowworms. Two attractive blondes sit at the
bar. Both are dressed in business-casual, cocktail-party outfits
that show some leg, cleavage, and arm. Both have flowing, *I
Dream of Jeannie* hairdos.

I secure an open space near them at the bar and order a
beer. I envision success using my new open-ended, conversa-
tion-starting, pickup line:

Me: "Excuse me. I'm writing a book and need a woman's
opinion."

I picture them offering to help, breasts eager in their blouses.

Me: "I'm stuck on a section where the narrator is trying
to figure out whether women marry for love or security. What
do you think?"

I imagine how the women might respond:

"What's the name of the book?"

Me: "*The Chronic Single's Handbook.*"

Them: "What's it about?"

Me: "A chronically single guy who takes a trip around the
world looking to change his luck with love. It's a funny book
about loneliness."

What if they've been through bitter divorces?

What if they ask why I've never been married?

What if they ask if I've ever been to Phnom Penh?

Fuck it. I'll recycle my standard pickup line.

As I stand at the bar waiting for my beer, I become aware
of my hands. They feel exposed, like they should be doing
something, something manly or confident; they shouldn't just
hang by my side like dead carp.

I put them in my front pants' pockets, which *Score Like
a Pro* advises against because it's the sign of a beta male, the
guy with no confidence. I take my hands out of my pockets and cross them in front of me. But crossing your limbs

demonstrates unavailability. I cross them behind my back. Now I look like a waiter. Back in my pockets they go.

I look at the women again. They're both attractive. Too attractive. Not in my wheelhouse.

I'm not sure if it's a theobromine aftereffect or jet lag or reverse culture shock but I notice a feeling that I haven't had in weeks, like I'm shrinking, fading, becoming lighter, invisible, drifting, floating away like a lost balloon or a broken kite.

The women both glance at me and smile. They have lines around their mouths, gray roots, and one has a liver spot on her hand. All is well in my world.

As I open my mouth to ask if they're having fun, the casino lights start flashing and holiday music starts blasting. Jugglers, elves, and Santa-clad nymphs gambol down the four-lane stairway. I look at the women and roll my eyes.

"Where's your Christmas spirit?" one of them asks me.

Two points for her.

"When you get to be my age, you lose a little of it," I say.

"We are your age," the other one says. "I like your accent."

"It's a Melbourne accent." I turn to face them.

"Really? We're from Melbourne. How come we don't talk like Yanks?"

A guy with a large watch and gabardine pants comes over and puts his arm on the women's chairs, securing his flock from predators.

The women turn to face him.

He mentions something about some mutual friends.

He mentions his trip to Sydney.

They laugh.

Focus on the mission.

As he talks, he doesn't once acknowledge me.

I consider him with cool detachment.

What a putz. He's fat too.

I ask the bartender for my check.

The woman closest to me tugs my sleeve. "What's your name?"

"Randall."

"I'm Minkie."

We shake hands and she introduces me around.

The putz ignores me and talks to the other woman.

Minkie tells me that she's a travel agent. She has just returned from South Africa and has never heard of the Frisky Bonobo on Long Street. I probably won't impress her with my taste in accommodations, so I change the subject and tell her that I've been traveling for almost four months.

"I couldn't get away for that long," she says. "I'm divorced, two kids. You?"

"No wife, no kids, just some adorable moths that like to chew on my clothes. Do you want to see pictures?"

The putz leans in between the two women without looking at me.

"Ready to go upstairs?" he says.

I take out my keys, fiddle with them, and look around the room. I'm starting to drift away. Then there's a tug on my sleeve. "Want to come along?" Minkie asks me.

The four of us ascend the stairs.

The keys to success: Hygiene and focus.

At the entrance to the club, I tell the group that I'm going to the loo and will meet them inside. Out of habit in the bathroom, I check my tongue—all clear.

The doorman working the club is about my age and about twice my size. He scans my outfit and points to the Keen sandals.

"Sorry, mate, you need proper shoes to get in."

"Actually I'm visiting from the US and I'm supposed to meet some people in there. Any chance you might let me slide? I promise to be on my worst behavior."

"Sorry, mate. I'll get fired. You wouldn't want to see me without a job, would you?"

"But I'm supposed to meet these two birds. I could introduce you to one of them."

"I'm not sure my wife would like that."

The universe has spoken.

Back at the hotel, I check e-mail for my return-flight confirmation, which is in two days. There's a note from Ricki.

Hey Burns,

Just letting you know that I survived the surgery. Looks like you've survived your trip. Cambodia? Really? Didn't think you had it in you. Actually want to hear all about it. Call me when you're back in town this week. I'll be waiting.

—RRRRRR

The Chronic Single's Handbook
Chapter Six
What to Expect from Friends in Middle Age

Under Forty-Five Years Old:
- *Purpose of friends: Wingmen, counsel, placeholders for a girlfriend.*
- *Contact frequency: Daily.*
- *Amount of time you can tolerate them: Unlimited.*
- *Would you loan them money? "If I had any."*
- *Would you help them move? "No brainer."*
- *Shared interests: pussy, bench presses, tits, squats, chicken wings, funny beer commercials, getting hard at the wrong time, midgets, PMS, Rogaine, Chuck Palahniuk, sleeping late.*

Over Forty-Five Years Old:
- *Purpose of friends: Counsel, wingmen, business connections.*
- *Contact frequency: Monthly.*

- *Amount of time you can tolerate them: Three hours.*
- *Would you loan them money? "Depends on their credit score."*
- *Would you help this person move? "With my back, are you kidding me?"*
- *Shared interests: Menopause, rotator cuffs, kvetching, Achilles tendons, low-carb diets, whining, interest rates, getting soft at the wrong time, reading glasses, griping, ponderous biographies, sleeping pills.*

CHAPTER NINE: BOSTON REDUX

As the fool returns to his vomit, so the dog returns to his folly.
—R. Burns

Thirty hours after leaving Australia, I land in Boston, USA. Home. My pillow-top mattress. Ricki.

Ever since that last night in Keezerbeezer, I've been thinking about her nonstop. Grooved abs, wingy shoulder blades, intense, a little insane, maybe a lot insane, speaks English without an accent. It took twelve grand to figure out that my perfect woman, my outlier, was in Boston the whole time. No need to settle or die alone.

It's Friday at midnight and Logan looks like any of the fifteen airports I've seen in the last four months with a few exceptions: the falling snow, the Timberland boots, the winter coats the size of iron lungs. The terminal building seems smaller than I remember.

I shuffle into the arrival area, scan the sniffling masses, and imagine Ricki here, holding a cardboard sign with my name. Instead, a middle-aged guy on the periphery is waving at me. There's something familiar about him. The gray goatee, the groomed eyebrows, and the mink earmuffs. Uncle Heshie.

I wave back cautiously. The last time I saw Uncle Heshie was three years ago at a family function. I brought Ricki. He brought a woman named Natalie. Ricki wore a blue jean jacket, a peasant dress, and ears shot full of studs, loops, and feathers—the Cambridge-poet look. Natalie wore a red leather jacket, a miniskirt, and hooped earrings the size of a diaphragm—the Upper West Side bimbo look. They took an instant dislike to each other, and Heshie and I spent the party keeping our dates in separate corners.

"Hey, Buster Brown!" Uncle Heshie is shouting from five feet away. People turn to look. He clamps his arm around me and shakes my shoulder several times as if checking my range of motion. I can smell his leathery aftershave.

"You look great," he says. "Like you're finally filling out. How was the flight?"

"Painless. Watched some movies, drank some beer." Before I can ask what he means by "filling out," he reaches for my bag and I notice the bling on his wrist: the world's biggest watch. I think of Manrico, the middle-aged guys in Cambodia, and that putz with the two women in Australia. For the first time in my life, I feel embarrassed by my little, black Timex.

"I followed your blog," he says. "Looks like you had a crazy time."

"You don't know the half of it."

"Loved your pad." Heshie combs his goatee with manicured nails. "I can't believe how close you are to decent skiing. I was just at Killington with a friend. The trees were out of control."

My mind catches on the phrases "a friend" and "out of control." I try not to imagine what might have gone on in my apartment: Shower curtains covered in vegetable oil, gerbils covered in vegetable oil, and my recently painted ceiling covered in vegetable oil.

In the airport garage, Heshie opens the hatch to his black
Land Rover. "This backpack smells like rat piss. How did you
get it through customs?"

Thirty hours of in-flight movies weighs on me. I can't
come up with a response.

Twenty minutes later we pull up in front of my building.
Uncle Heshie drags my bag out of the back and hands it over.
"Randall, my boy, for your own good, I made a few upgrades
to your digs. As your uncle, it's my duty to see that you get
laid as much as possible, which means you got to get out of
Boston. The women in this town are beat; they dress like they
just came from an audition for *The Beverly Hillbillies*. Come
visit me in New York. I'll hook you up."

I don't bother explaining that he doesn't need to worry
about me, that I'm done with the singles' scene, and that I
already have a woman. Or at least, I will soon. He steps closer
and lays a fat, wet one on my cheek. "Good to have you back.
I won't come up. Gotta run. Here's the key."

It's not until the next morning, as I sink into my six-
inch pillow-top, that I begin to take inventory. Stacked on the
nightstand, my *Physicians' Desk Reference* and *Field Guide to
Intestinal Fauna* sit where I left them last fall. The wall opposite my bed is oddly blank: The Crane Beach painting is gone.

In the bathroom, there are a few additions:

• A textured Marimekko shower drape instead of my mil-
dewed, Three Stooges shower curtain.

• A fuzzy, turquoise toilet-seat cover and matching bathmat.

• A roll of plush toilet paper, the expensive stuff I never buy.
This will get me laid?

In my double-wide medicine cabinet, there's a bottle of
almond-scented massage oil and, next to my Vicodin, an
unfamiliar vial with a bow and a note: "Kiddo: Vicodin is for

pussies. Real men take Percocet." The label indicates that the prescription is refillable and came from a Heshie Moscowitz, MD. These might get me laid.

In the kitchen, more additions: My E. J. Korvette toaster oven has been replaced by a Viking convection microwave. On the refrigerator, my cork bulletin board has unfamiliar business cards for: home liquor delivery, Chinese takeout, a mobile dry cleaner, a Brazilian food truck, and Monique's Fitness—"We put the *purr* in personal training."

In the pantry: a wine rack with unopened bottles of pinot grigio, Green Chartreuse, and black sambuca. My collection of rubber bands, old grocery bags, and empty Poland Spring bottles, which I refill with tap water, is gone. The Crane Beach seascape is stuffed in my recycle bin. Ricki will approve.

In the refrigerator, a jar of pickled herring sports another bow and a note: "Welcome back to civilization. Use care when opening the freezer. Enjoy with a special lady." I slowly open it and frost drifts to the floor. Wedged between two frozen porterhouse steaks I didn't buy is a bottle of Grey Goose vodka the size of an Alaskan salmon. Ricki will definitely approve.

On my fortieth birthday, my mother pulled me aside: "If you don't stop being so picky, you'll end up like your Uncle Heshie," she said.

"You mean European vacations, European clothes, and European girlfriends half my age?"

"Randall, he has no family, no responsibilities, no one to take care of."

I look around my apartment now: thoughtful gifts, party supplies, and plush towels. This doesn't look like a place recently inhabited by an unhappy guy.

But I don't plan to end up like Heshie. Time to set up a date with Ricki. How about tonight? Or better yet, now, for brunch?

I call her home phone. Voice mail. I don't leave a message. Call her cell. More voice mail. I don't leave a message. Can't leave a message. What if she doesn't get it? What if she hasn't paid her phone bill? What if she had to pawn her phone? Fucking Verizon, fucking AT&T, fucking Apple. I call both her numbers again. Nothing.

She reads my blog and knows I got home last night. Where is she?

I'll go to her place, leave flowers, chocolates, or tequila, her favorite.

Maybe not. Flowers are kind of effeminate and expensive and presumptuous. She never ate chocolate. "Not good for the girlish figure," she always said. Tequila implies shots, too frat-like.

Maybe she's working. But on a Saturday? Knowing Ricki, she's sneaking in some freelance work and using the company's color printer. Always working the angles. That's my girl.

Or maybe she's at the gym. That's it. Her phone must be in her locker.

Or maybe she's in the hospital, complications from the recent surgery she wouldn't discuss over e-mail. What if she has a huge infected, disfiguring scar?

My computer dings; an e-mail from her.

Saw that you called. Getting my hair done. You free Thursday night? I owe you an apology.
—RRRRRR

Of course. She wants to look her best for me. Oxytocin flushes through my system.

We'll have drinks Thursday night. Then I'll invite her over for a Saturday night of Grey Goose and porterhouse steak. Maybe every Saturday after that will be our martini and steak night. And Sundays will be brunch and Patriots at the Minuteman. No, not the Minuteman. She hates the Minuteman.

And Abe. And Lenny. That's OK. Ricki and I will find another
club, our own club.

I pick up my phone, then put it down. I need to calm
down, can't appear desperate. I haven't seen her in two years.
I take several deep, slow breaths, and decide to wait an hour
before e-mailing her back.

I e-mail Abe who shoots back, "You home already?" He
agrees to arrange dinner and Monday-night football with the
gang at the Minuteman.

Things are looking up until I take a close look at my face
in the bathroom mirror. Heshie is right, I am filling out. I get
on the scale: 164 pounds, nine pounds more than I weighed
before the trip. Ricki likes skinny guys. I put myself to bed
with no dinner.

I awake at three A.M., stomach and thoughts churning.
I'm hungry. I'm fat. A month ago, I had sex with two Cambodian hookers. What if Ricki finds out?

I fetch a pad of paper left over from the Royal Paradise
hotel and address the weight issue:

Goal: Lose three pounds a week for three weeks.
Key to success:
• Remember: Eating is not entertainment.
Action Items:
• Breakfast: ½ cup of bran cereal, splash of soy milk.
• Lunch: raw garlic, raw onions, kale, canned sardines;
sprinkle with parmesan, douse with Tabasco sauce, finish with
more raw garlic. Ricki loves garlic.
• Snack: repeat breakfast.
• Dinner: repeat lunch.
• Go to bed hungry and nauseous.

Back in bed, I imagine sipping whisky-whisky with Ricki
on the back of a Greek ferry, where she brushes against me

and brushes against me again. I picture her emerging from my bathroom wearing only a white cotton towel.

What about the hookers?

Maybe it would turn her on. Or maybe it wouldn't. Eventually I find myself in my bathroom, in front of the double-wide.

Monday, twenty-four hours into the diet, I pull into the Minuteman parking lot feeling jet-lagged, queasy, and foggy from Percocet. Thursday can't come soon enough.

The bar looks dingier than I remember. And so does the crowd: down vests over chamois shirts, ski hats with pom-poms, running shoes with little toes, ears with buds, a floor covered with grimy backpacks.

For the first time in four months, I'm dressed like an adult: brown wide-wale corduroys, black wool pullover, cordovan shoes. No matter what I wear or what country I'm in, I'm out of sync. I'm not sure I care anymore.

The TVs are tuned to *Monday Night Football* and the still-undefeated Patriots are playing the hapless Jets. Some things are not meant to change. The club has the same oak bar, high stools, and pendant lights, but it seems smaller than I remember. This could be any yuppie pub in South Africa, Asia, or Australia.

Abe and Lenny are seated at the bar, watching the game. Abe is the first to notice me. "Look, it's the Jewish Marco Polo, the world's most interesting Heeb." He's wearing a fleece pullover in a soft hue of purple that only a wife would buy. He looks jowlier than ever.

Lenny glances down from the TV and points my way. "My hero, the world traveler. Just don't sit next to me. I don't want to catch anything." He's overdressed for a change: houndstooth sport coat, cuffed pants, and tasseled loafers without socks, even though it's thirty degrees outside. His eyes flit from me to an anorexic waitress.

I give Abe and Lenny a European kiss on each cheek.

"Where's Rachel? What's the score?" I ask.

"In the can. Zip-zip." Abe looks me up and down. "You look like you're still in one piece." He sounds disappointed. "Cop a squat and tell us about your adventures." He turns back to the overhead TV as Brady completes a ten-yard pass.

I take an open stool that's been reserved for me with Rachel's suit jacket. I motion for the bartender, and then look up at the TV. "Well, the high point of the trip was probably the bungee jumping in South Africa, pun intended." I expect a groan from Abe. No response.

"Welcome home!" Rachel says, as she sits down next to me. "We were all betting you'd come home with a wife. Where is she?" Rachel pats me on the back.

I grin but don't mention Ricki.

"You know how life can be," I say. "Sometimes the dog and his vomit go their separate ways. And then, sometimes they don't."

The bartender comes over, pad in hand. Abe, Lenny, and Rachel each order steak and fries, and a Guinness. I order a soda water with a chicken Caesar salad, dressing on the side.

"Burns, are you dieting again?" Abe looks down from the TV and pokes my stomach.

"Need to keep my boyish figure," I say.

"If you didn't bring anyone home, did you at least break a few hearts?" Lenny asks.

"Do you know the story about the fool and his folly? Anyway, I saw the temples of Angkor Wat. You know the ones that were covered by jungle for . . ."

I am drowned out by cheers as Brady completes a touchdown pass on the first drive. "It's going to be a short game," Abe shouts.

"So in Australia I was surfing this 200-foot wave when I was attacked by a hammer-headed platypus, and had to get a liver transplant."

"Poor *bubbe*," Abe says, glancing at his cell phone.

I offer a smile that could mean many things: "OK, so what's going on with you guys?"

They respond remaining glued to the TV.

Abe: "I'm going to be a life-support system for a baby and wife, and I'll probably never get laid again."

Lenny: "The whole dating scene is drying up and the prostitution ring was a bust, no pun intended. I'm going back on Match, going to start lying about my age. My mother's in the hospital for a change. I'm going to die alone."

Rachel: "Arturo and I . . ."

I immediately stop listening and look up at the TV.

"What are you going to do now that you're back?" Rachel asks.

"Not sure," I say. "I once read that life's journey is not about finding any one thing; it's about finding your place on a beach with kind eyes."

"Interesting philosophy," Rachel says.

"Did you get that from a bathroom wall in Angkor Wat?" asks Abe.

"It was inscribed on the toenail of the giant Reclining Buddha," I say, watching Lenny as he watches the anorexic waitress bend to pick up a fork.

"Anyone hear from Josh?" I ask.

"He's still with Ruby Rubenesque," Lenny says.

Abe cuts in. "You and Burns aren't happy unless a woman is wasting away on an IV drip."

Just like old times, I think, feeling a warm trickle of oxytocin.

"Karen wasn't that thin," I say.

"And neither was Calista Flockhart," Abe says.

Rachel asks: "By the way, did Ricki end up writing you?"

"As a matter of fact she wrote all the time." I pause for effect. "Unlike you schmucks."

Abe is the first to comment: "Didn't I write a couple of times? I read your blog almost every day. You're the writer, I'm not."

"I heard it offered lots of useful travel information," Rachel says.

"My home computer only gets TeenTwat.com," Lenny says.

Before I can analyze their responses for traces of malice or remorse, Lenny says: "You go all the way around the world, don't meet anyone, but your long-lost girlfriend comes back to haunt you?"

Abe says, "'Lost' is the operative word. I'd also add 'broken.'"

Rachel says, "I think it's kind of romantic. The hero's journey."

I decide not to mention that I am seeing Ricki in three days.

After the Patriots crush the Jets, Lenny stands up, dons his camel-hair topcoat, and turns to me. "Calista Flockhart is a porker," he says.

"A fat whale," I say.

He pats my shoulder. "Good to have you back, my brother."

Rachel kisses me on the cheek. "Welcome home, Randy. We missed you. Sorry I got to leave early. Have to get back to Arturo."

Once we're alone, Abe and I order dirty martinis.

"Cone of silence?" I ask.

"Cone activated. What's up?"

"I'm bullshit. Really, how come you didn't write? This was a huge event for me; this would be like me ignoring your wedding or your funeral."

"You're right. I'm sorry and I got no excuses. But you wouldn't believe the fucked-up thing that happened while you were gone."

He tells me about a mutual friend, Eli, whose wife of ten years caught him in bed with another guy. Since Eli's little coming-out event, none of our female friends will talk to him, and our male friends are afraid his gayness might rub off.

"I don't give a shit," Abe says. "I've known him for twenty years. He's staying with us till he figures out what to do. Amy can bitch all she wants."

Maybe the measure of loyalty is more than a few e-mails.

"That definitely qualifies as fucked-up," I say. "How is everyone else doing?"

"Soon after you left, the shit hit the turbine. Lenny's been having a tough time. His mother is his only close relative left and she's on her way out. And the miserable game is getting more miserable: Women can smell the desperation on him."

I sniff my wool pullover: It's either desperation, rat piss, or raw garlic.

Abe continues: "As for me, sometimes I think Amy and I are just one fight away from Match.com. But for better or worse, I'm going to stick it out. And now Rachel's got Arturo. We're all drifting apart. You said you were getting tired of Boston. Maybe you should make a move before you end up like Lenny."

I say nothing, but think: I already made a move.

After we finish our martinis, Abe puts on a pink ski hat and swats the pom-poms out of his face. "By the way, congrats on pulling off the trip. You made us all look like chicken shits. I mean that in a good way."

Out in the parking lot, I watch Abe zip off in his new Acura, "the Jap Jew-canoe." In six months, my Civic will be old enough to drink and buy cigarettes.

I sit on the hood; the sheet-metal winces and the cold seeps through my pants. A subfreezing breath flares in my nostrils. The air is dry, odorless, and clean. Winter in Boston. This is the time of year when smells hibernate, insomniacs sleep, and, according to DATES.XLS, I have the best luck with women. I feel my gloved thumb and forefinger settle into a little OK sign.

I haven't seen Ricki in two years, since our visit to Moody. I recall the fight that led to our brief foray into therapy.

It was a Sunday morning in bed. I was giving her a massage and working her glutes, when a cheddary, slaughterhouse odor slipped out.

"Ooops," she said. "Let me go wash up."

A toilet flush, a shower spray.

She hopped back in bed, "I'm ready, Doctor Feel Good."

From a fetal position I said, "The doctor isn't feeling so good."

"Because of, what, a little body odor?"

"I think I had some bad scrod for dinner last night."

"You know you've got some issues, bucko."

"I thought you liked me because of my issues."

"Not this one. You're the only guy I ever dated who never farts or poops."

"Babies and puppies poop. Cows and people shit."

"Thank you, Marlin Perkins. When do *you* take a shit? Do you wait till you go home? Is this why we never go away on vacation?"

At her place, I always evacuated everything that needed evacuating before my bedtime shower, the water running for maximum privacy.

"You're right," I say. "I never fart or shit. As far as I'm concerned, you don't either."

"What? You think little angels come down and carry my farts away?"

"Can we change the subject?"

"Why? It's a natural bodily function like eating or sex."

"Did you ever touch your poops when you were little?"

"What kind of weird question is that?"

"Never mind. How about if I fix you a nice bowl of bran, then leave, and you can blast out a nice shit the size of an anaconda, something worthy of *Mutual of Omaha's Wild Kingdom.*"

A week later, we saw Moody. A week after that, we were done.

Over the years, I've parsed the fight for keywords and subtext and identified the following: never vacation, inflexible, germaphobe.

But I've just returned from a sixteen-week trip, drank wine made of snake piss, and wiped my ass with my fingers. She said she's going to apologize. Major surgery can humble a person. Maybe she's finally out of debt. Maybe her new medication has mellowed her. People change.

As for me, I'll be less critical and stop with the ambivalence, teasing, and obsessing about her body.

Ricki could be my antidote to the Dark Place. I won't have to move to New York.

We'll grow old together, pick each other up after colonoscopies. I'll be her next of kin, her safe room, and she'll be mine. Instead of unreliable friends and family, Ricki and I will have each other. If she wants, we can get married. She'll move in, split the mortgage, save me 7K a year. We can even have separate bedrooms or separate apartments like celebrities. Life with Ricki will never be dull.

We meet for drinks at her favorite spot, the Pinko Lounge in Harvard Square. When I arrive, she's at the bar. Her dark hair is now shoulder length. She's wearing a butter-colored blazer, maybe to hide a few pounds. So what? At least it's not a black blazer.

I sneak up behind her, kiss her on the cheek, and sit down. "Hey," she says.

The space between her front teeth is gone. Instead of the usual shrapnel in each ear, she's wearing a large hoop the size of a diaphragm. For the first time, I notice her earlobes, tiny grapes. She seems softer, sharp edges smoothed.

I think of a story she used to tell about her brothers who would come home from football practice, yell "gas attack," pin nine-year-old Ricki to the shag carpet, and hold their sweaty jock straps over her face. I think of Harriet and Myrna. Something else we share.

Ricki checks me out: black dress shoes, black jeans, Bengal-striped shirt, silvery chest hair peeking out of my opened collar, the Guillaume of Paris look.

"So, you're looking decent enough," she says. "Maybe a little filled out. Don't people usually lose weight when they travel? How was the trip?"

"Decent enough. Saw some weird stuff. Ate some weird stuff."

She does a double-take on my left wrist. "That watch is kind of big."

"This old thing? Got it on a Bangkok street corner. It's a Pad Thai Philippe."

"Let me see that." She grabs my forearm, holds it close to her face. I feel her breath warm on my hand. "Patek Philippe," she says. "Must have cost five grand. You know what they say: Big watch, big . . ."

"Big safety-deposit box. My Uncle Heshie gave it to me."

"The Jappy New York doctor with the hooker girlfriend? Please give him my disregards."

Ricki squeezes my hand and laughs. I laugh with her and squeeze back.

Across the bar, a guy with gray-coiffed hair is sitting by himself. He's wearing an open-collared shirt with silvery chest hair peeking out. The bartender is chatting with him.

"You still doing graphic design and teaching pilates?" I ask Ricki.

"Yup, and I cleaned up my credit card debt and hired a financial planner. I'm a big girl now."

I feel a stirring where my money belt used to be. She moves a set of salt-and-pepper shakers around on the bar like chess pieces.

"So you made it around the world intact. Tell the truth: Were you offended by my e-mails?" Ricki asks.

"Well, your note about counterphobia was on the money. You know how I'm afraid of heights? In South Africa, I went bungee jumping off a bridge three times as high as the Empire State Building. One guy who jumped crapped in his trousers."

"I know, I read your blog. I believe I wrote that you are insane. Or if I didn't, let me confirm that now."

"Flatterer. I bet you say that to all the guys."

"Only the cute nut jobs."

I glance over at the gray-coiffed guy sitting alone. Tonight, I'm not that guy.

Ricki moves the salt-and-pepper shakers side by side.

"By the way, I was sorry to hear about Wiener the dachshund," I say. "And what about your surgery? Are you OK?"

She chooses this moment to take off her jacket.

"I think the surgery went well. What do you think?"

My eyes take a few seconds to adjust. The room seems dimmer and then brighter. My deprived stomach rumbles. I hear a loud clang; someone must have given the bartender an impressive tip.

"I went up two cup sizes," she says.

Her breasts are high and tight. Cleavage slices into her black T-shirt. I imagine unhooking her and being consumed airbag-style.

I'm not sure of the etiquette in this situation. Am I supposed to look? Comment? Squeeze the merchandise?

My *Score Like a Pro* book advises never to make a big deal of a woman's appearance.

"You look great," I say in a benign tone appropriate for complimenting a new hairstyle.

"I don't know. I think I should have gotten a smaller size. I feel like Betty Boop."

She adjusts the right one with two hands. "They still kind of hurt."

There is an awkward silence. We both drink. Then I say, "What did you want to apologize for?"

"What the hell are you talking about?" she says.

"Your e-mail said you wanted to apologize for something."

"You must have me confused with one of your sluts."

I know I should just let the comment pass, show I've changed, but I can't. I take out my phone to search for Ricki's message.

She sighs.

Just like old times.

The guy in the gray coif discusses the winter weather with the bartender in a voice loud enough for us to hear. Ricki leans over and cuts into their conversation: "All you people who whine about the cold should move out. This is fucking New England."

"So I hear," says the guy.

The bartender looks at Ricki, at me, says nothing, and hands us our check.

"Can you get this one, Burns? The financial planner put me on an austerity budget and I have to pee."

I glance at the gray-coiffed guy sitting by himself sipping a snifter with a few coffee beans adrift in it. He looks content. Heshie looked content. I recall one of Moody's droppings of wisdom: If you want to be content, stay single. If you don't want to be lonely, get married.

When Ricki returns, I look deep into her eyes for some clue as to how to proceed. I sense a disturbance, an electrical storm, and imagine her brain cells flashing and twitching and jumping like herring being chased by a large predator. I want to be that predator. My thoughts are interrupted when she stands up abruptly.

"Good to see you, Burns. Let's do this again."

Without thinking, I say: "Let's have dinner at my place Saturday night. I'll make a Cambodian dish, Moon Bong, Prawn Long."

"Only if you promise not to mix your food together like a four-year-old."

"It's a stir fry, already mixed."

We hug. I feel them against me intent, urgent. I don't think about the past or the future.

As we put on our coats to leave, I glance down at the bar: The salt-and-pepper shakers are gone.

For Saturday's dinner, I defrost one of Heshie's porterhouse steaks, cube and marinate it, and open the Grey Goose.

Ricki shows up thirty minutes late. She stomps the snow off her boots onto my newly refinished hardwood floor and hands me a box of chocolates. I flinch.

"For dessert," she says. "Relax, a little chocolate never killed anybody. Hey, did you see the weather report? Snow, heavy at times, blizzard conditions, a real nor'easter."

"And if you don't like winter, get the fuck out of New England," I say.

We high-five.

I take her shearling coat. Underneath she's wearing skinny jeans and a low-necked shirt with exposed lacy straps stretched to their wits' end. Her lips are wet with balm. She's smirking as if she has something to tell me. I imagine her hands on the back of my head steering my mouth to hers.

I make us each a huge martini, dip a pinky in my drink, and dab behind my ears. Ricki is busy looking around my apartment.

"Burns, you finally got rid of that seascape painting. Good move."

She laughs. I don't.

"Nice toilet-seat covers. You didn't get a sex change in Bangkok, did you?"

I let her comment drift by.

After dinner, a drink on the couch, where we first made love on our third date, after the escapade in the theater bathroom. There's a long silence, a good silence. We are content.

She moves her martini glass around the coffee table like a chess piece. I look into her eyes again. They're calm, no disturbances. Maybe she's finally forgiven me, ready to move on. I recall what she once said about wanting one guy, forever, ashes in the same urn.

Forever suddenly sounds like a long time. I imagine a sperm whale, a giant squid around its neck, being dragged to the sea floor. A breath lodges in my chest. My hands are not shaking but they feel like they could be.

Ricki reaches for a chocolate, her shirt rises, a swell of skin, a little pooch belly. She bites into something dark and cream-filled. *Not good for the girlish figure.*

There's a tingling behind my eyes, in my stomach, caffeine overload but I don't drink coffee. The sea floor is coming up fast.

I observe my feelings of ambivalence and claustrophobia and try to imagine them floating by like dead leaves, tampon applicators, and six-pack rings.

No such luck.

A prickly, crawling sensation begins on my arms, spreads to my legs, my feet, synapses firing nonstop.

"Are you OK?" Ricki is looking into my eyes.

"A little jet-lagged."

"Let me test drive the new toilet-seat cover," she says. "Maybe it's time to bust out an anaconda." She laughs. I try to laugh. While she's in the bathroom, I finish my martini and make another batch for us. My hands are now shaking.

A toilet flushes, a sink runs.

Back at the couch, I'm seated and she stands before me, my face is inches from the new breasts. I picture them pink, slick, and frisky, like newborn piglets. On her lips, a fresh coat of balm, a smirk, anticipation, invitation. I pull her to me and burrow nose-deep, earthy and woody, soft and warm. Her hands cup my ears. Then I feel a sharp yank.

"Burns! What the fuck are you doing?"

Lodged breaths and no words. My mind doubles over. I gasp for air.

"After all the bullshit you put me through, did you really think I'd sleep with you again, *ever*? Do you think I'm insane? Some kind of psycho masochist?"

I'm searching for a response when something detonates deep inside me. I bear down, grimace, but a silent garlic fart still manages to escape.

"Ooops," is all I can say.

A week later, I'm sitting in Moody's waiting room looking out the window. The snow is gone and the ground is gray and muddy. Bare trees scratch a low sky. My stomach is idling, a slow rumble. I'm tired, twitchy, and foggy from the diet or last night's Percocet.

Moody greets me with a handshake and I follow him down the hall to his office. I've been walking this same route for ten years. But today, a room is cordoned off, plastic sheets hang from the ceiling, and a crew of paint-spattered men paces, drinks coffee, and thinks big thoughts. I imagine a plaque: "This addition paid for by Randall Burns."

In his office, Moody sits. I sit. He pulls out my file.

"I saw Ricki for the first time in two years and she kicked me in the balls," I say.

"Literally?"

"Figuratively. She was the only friend who wrote me while I was gone. She said she started on antidepressants and wanted to apologize. She said she wanted to see me when I got home. Here I take a trip around the world looking for the woman of my dreams and by the time I get to Australia I think, wow, she's been in Boston the whole time. So when I get back, we meet for drinks, and were having a nice flirty time. Then she shows me her new boob job. I think: My welcome-back present? Two nights later, she comes over for dinner, low-cut everything, tits hanging out. We drink. We eat. And then I make a move. She claims she's shocked, says no fucking way in hell, like I'm the one who's insane. I thought she had changed. I thought I had changed. Maybe I am insane."

Moody reaches for his yellow pad

My thoughts come to a mental fork: I could reach for my little notepad and get into it with Moody, or I could keep talking and avoid a pissing match.

"Anyway I'm over it now and I'm thinking of calling Karen, the cheerful, stable one I dated awhile back. Remember her? Every week I'd come in wanting to break up with her and you'd say, 'Just give it another week.' She wasn't edgy, but she was OK. The sex was OK. She was nice enough."

I anticipate an encouraging Buddhist-like response about embracing life's possibilities and sitting with boredom and discomfort.

Moody stops scribbling and looks up at me. "You always find this type of woman dull and never connect with them. Why is this time going to be different?"

I lean forward in my seat and look him in the eye. "Doctor Moody, I just spent four months traveling the world, met some women, and had weird, short, depressing encounters with them. I realized all my relationships have been weird, short, and depressing. This trip has changed me. I'm ready for something different. To settle.

"I've had time to think. My intimacy issues? I get it. Life is about connecting with other people. Real connections, real relationships that deepen over time.

"My commitment issues? I can commit. I had the same job, same friends, and same car for fifteen years. That's longer than most marriages.

"My issues with women? Maybe I don't need a woman to be crazy and exciting all the time. I'm done with the fish theory and that stupid spreadsheet.

"For a chance at a real relationship, maybe with Karen, I'll change. I'll be on time. I'll buy her flowers. I'll call her every day. I'll remember her birthday, her friends' birthdays, her friends' names. I'll listen, really listen when she whines. I'll stay overnight after sex. I'll give her a corner of my closet.

"I'm tired of being chronically single. I'm sick of online dating. My friend Abe just got married and Rachel is on her way.

"Maybe *I'll* get married, do the whole fucking deal: six-figure wedding, six-figure honeymoon, six-figure divorce.

"Ha, ha. Just joking. But seriously, Doctor Moody, I'm going to need your help. There has to be some treatment that can help me settle for a boring, stable woman like Karen."

Moody taps my file with an index finger. "Randall, you're almost fifty years old. All the drugs and therapy in the world won't change who you're attracted to. These kooky, angry women get you going. We can't 'shrink' you into someone you're not."

I look out the window. Somewhere a lost balloon drifts.

"So are you saying I'm going to die alone?"

"Everyone dies alone. All I'm saying is relationships are difficult for you. Relationships are difficult, period. You have your health, you have friends, and your car still runs. Maybe you should get on with your life and quit waiting around for the right woman."

"So my life is going to be one long romantic drought with some hookers and rocky, three-month relationships thrown in?"

"Maybe."

"Would that be OK?"

"That would be OK."

The Chronic Single's Handbook
Chapter Seven
Obtaining Your Minimum Daily Requirements of Oxytocin

The medical staff at The Chronic Single's Handbook *has found that individuals who do not receive adequate oxytocin risk prolonged visits to the Dark Place.*

For a chronic single, the recommended dose of oxytocin is five units a day, about half the amount required by the general population. Note: During good times, excess oxytocin can be stored like fat for later use.

Oxytocin Benefits from Common Activities: (for a 155-pound man)

- *Flirting with personal trainer with the sparkly navel: 1 unit*
- *Watching thirty minutes of sports with a stranger at a bar: 2 units*
- *Drinks with an old friend: 3 units*
- *Drinks with the personal trainer with the sparkly navel: 4 units • Sex with a long-time partner: 5 units**
- *Naughty massage: 6 units***
- *Sex with the personal trainer with the sparkly navel: 7 units*

*Generally, anyone in a relationship has access to an endless supply of oxytocin. However, as a relationship ages and rots, the human body produces stress hormones that negate any health benefits of oxytocin. Also, following a disagreement, a significant other may choose to withhold oxytocin for several months. (See footnote** below.)

**In times of prolonged oxytocin deprivation, it is wise to consider the advice of former NFL lineman Conrad Dobler: "If it flies, floats, or fucks, rent it."

CHAPTER TEN: BOSTON POSTERIOR

The morning sun streams through my bay window and illuminates a Marimekko shower drape and a double-wide medicine cabinet that was once populated with rows of golden vials.

It's been a year since I got laid off, four months since getting flattened by Ricki, and three weeks since Moody and I had an amicable split. He kept the Ambien and I kept the $125 an hour. I never did call Karen.

After breakfast, I walk around Boston. The local scents have come out of hibernation: brisk and mossy, the greens of pine, grass, and dill. Up ahead, a line of people are waiting to enter the Museum of Science. I still don't care for crowds or sightseeing or museums filled with divorced mothers and sticky kids, but today, admission is free.

Inside, the museum smells cool and metallic like an empty refrigerator. The halls are packed with strollers, women wearing flannel shirts and peasant dresses, and men in dungarees and big boots—*The Beverly Hillbillies*.

I'm wearing gabardine trousers, a rep tie, and my big watch.

At an exhibit called "Creatures of the Sea," I contemplate the blob fish, the spiny pufferfish, and the fangtooth fish.

At my side, a small voice: "Mister. What does the stingray do?"

It's a child about five or six. A middle-aged guy talking to a young boy who is not his son is not a smart idea.

"Mister, what does the stingray do?"

I look around for the matching adult and can't find one.

"Well, little buddy, the stingray is very friendly," I say. "He floats around the bottom of the sea like a space ship. But don't pet him on the tail—it's like a switchblade."

"Mister, what's your name?"

"The name is Perkins, Marlin Perkins."

A woman with short hair and no makeup runs over, claims the child, and apologizes. I feel a trickle of oxytocin from this small interaction. My first unit of the day.

I drift over to an exhibit called "Asian Mammals," a row of large, stuffed critters in different poses. The smells: leathery and dusty, like a cobbler's shop.

I grasp a gooey railing and read the wall plaque:

"Bengal Tigers generally live alone except for brief interludes during mating season."

"Bali Cattle: After mating, bulls lead solitary lives or may wander the countryside with other bulls."

The chronic singles of the animal world. Do they worry about dying alone?

I detect a smell that doesn't belong: warm, creamy, vanilla. To my left, a woman's voice. "Look kid, I don't know anything about tigers. Go ask your mother before one of them gobbles you up."

The woman is tall, blonde, and wearing heels, a fitted skirt, and lipstick. An exposed bra strap shines like a ribbon. Tiny lines around her mouth, about my age.

She lifts her purse and a tube of Purell falls to the floor. I pick it up and hand it back to her. Her fingers are long, her nails are lacquered. When our eyes meet, I sense a disturbance, an electrical storm. I imagine us Rollerblading, sharing a porterhouse, a martini, an urn.

Wait a minute: I give up on women, accept my fate as chronically single, and now I meet an outlier, a wand, who doesn't like kids, at the Museum of Frigging Science?

Fat chance.

During my final visit with Moody, he handed me a thick manila envelope with my name on it and wished me well. "Randall, remember that intimacy is not the only path to happiness. Many famous artists and scholars never married, some had few if any romantic partners: Beethoven, Kant, Isaac Newton, Beatrix Potter, the list goes on. Today, one out of seven Americans between thirty-five and fifty-four has never been married. There are 112 million single people in this country."

"Is that supposed to make me feel better?"

"I know you find lists and stats soothing. I dug some up for you."

"So I'm going to die alone but have lots of company."

"You want what you want."

"What does that mean?"

"The heart is a lonely hunter."

"Wasn't that a novel by Carson McCullers?"

"You know what I mean, Randall."

After the session, I decided to take a hiatus from the experts, the Moodys and Pittmans of the world. Maybe they *are* right about 70 percent of the time. But flipping a coin, I'd be right 50 percent of the time and save on copays, pills, and exotic trips that lead nowhere.

The blonde at the railing is disinfecting her hands and reading about the Bali cattle. She glances at me and then glances again.

"Having fun?" I ask.

ACKNOWLEDGMENTS

This novel took seven years to write and involved four top-to-bottom rewrites with input from friends, relatives, and people whom I barely knew who offered to help, just because.

I'd like to thank my beta readers who provided encouragement and invaluable input on the various drafts: BFFF Susan Avery; cousin, author, and inspiration Susan Tejada; friend and former boss Bill Snyder; Northwestern alum and après-ski expert Dave Wallace; friend and French expert Rosemary Jaffe; author and counsel Marlene Fanta Shyer; brother for more-than-a-college-term Jeff Kaufman; fellow schemer and ranter Sam Nejame; cousin, writer, and the first Jewish safari guide in the history of the world Mathew Dry; playwright Debbie Wiess; writer, writing instructor, and performer Daniel Gewertz; and novelist and all-around great influence Erica Ferencik.

During the last seven years, I belonged to numerous writing groups. The longest-lasting one called NTK was kept afloat by writer friends Joan FitzGerald, Susan Phillips, and Tim Stone.

A big thanks to actor and playwright Michael Mack, author and publisher Jeffrey Zygmont, the GrubStreet writing center in Boston, and the folks at The Permanent Press: copy editor Barbara Anderson, as well as copublishers Chris Knopf and Martin and Judith Shepard who took a chance on a whiney guy from Boston.

I'd also like to thank my parents, Tom and Judy Ross, whose encouragement helped me stick with this project through all its ups and downs, twists and turns, and disappointments and successes.

Finally, I'd like to thank my indispensable editor and writing coach, Carey Adams at anyforkintheroad.com, for her assistance transforming this manuscript from 150 pages of blog scratch into a publishable novel.